Kicking Bird knew he had witnessed something precious, something that had provided a solution to one of the puzzles surrounding the white man . . . the puzzle of what to call him.

A man should have a real name, he thought as he rode to meet Lieutenant Dunbar, particularly when it is a white who acts like this one.

He remembered the old names, but none of them really fit. Now he felt certain that this was the right one. It suited the white soldier's personality. People would remember him by this. And Kicking Bird himself, with two witnesses to back him up, had been present at the time the Great Spirit revealed it.

He said it to himself several times as he came down the slope. The sound of it was as good as the name itself.

Dances With Wolves.

DANCES WITH WOLVES

Michael Blake

FAWCETT GOLD MEDAL • NEW YORK

A Fawcett Gold Medal Book
Published by Ballantine Books
Copyright © 1988 by Michael Blake

Library of Congress Catalog Card Number: 88-91114

ISBN 0-449-13448-2

Manufactured in the United States of America

First Edition: October 1988
Fifth Printing: November 1990

In the end, inspiration is everything.

This is for Exene Cervenka

CHAPTER I

one

Lieutenant Dunbar wasn't really swallowed. But that was the first word that stuck in his head.

Everything was immense.

The great, cloudless sky. The rolling ocean of grass. Nothing else, no matter where he put his eyes. No road. No trace of ruts for the big wagon to follow. Just sheer, empty space.

He was adrift. It made his heart jump in a strange and profound way.

As he sat on the flat, open seat, letting his body roll along with the prairie, Lieutenant Dunbar's thoughts focused on his jumping heart. He was thrilled. And yet, his blood wasn't racing. His blood was quiet. The confusion of this kept his mind working in a delightful way. Words turned constantly in his head as he tried to conjure sentences or phrases that would describe what he felt. It was hard to pinpoint.

On their third day out the voice in his head spoke the words "This is religious," and that sentence seemed the rightest yet. But Lieutenant Dunbar had never been a religious man, so even though the sentence seemed right, he didn't quite know what to make of it.

1

If he hadn't been so carried away, Lieutenant Dunbar probably would have come up with the explanation, but in his reverie, he jumped right over it.

Lieutenant Dunbar had fallen in love. He had fallen in love with this wild, beautiful country and everything it contained. It was the kind of love people dream of having with other people: selfless and free of doubt, reverent and everlasting. His spirit had received a promotion and his heart was jumping. Perhaps this was why the sharply handsome cavalry lieutenant had thought of religion.

From the corner of his eye he saw Timmons duck his head to one side and spit for the thousandth time into the waist-high buffalo grass. As it so often did, the spittle came out in an uneven stream that caused the wagon driver to swipe at his mouth. Dunbar didn't say anything, but Timmons's incessant spitting made him recoil inwardly.

It was a harmless act, but it irritated him nonetheless, like forever having to watch someone pick his nose.

They'd been sitting side by side all morning. But only because the wind was right. Though they were but a couple of feet apart, the stiff, little breeze was right, and Lieutenant Dunbar could not smell Timmons. In his less than thirty years he'd smelled plenty of death, and nothing was so bad as that. But death was always being hauled off or buried or sidestepped, and none of these things could be done with Timmons. When the air currents shifted, the stench of him covered Lieutenant Dunbar like a foul, unseen cloud.

So when the breeze was wrong, the lieutenant would slide off the seat and climb onto the mountain of provisions piled in the wagon's bed. Sometimes he would ride up there for hours. Sometimes he would jump down into the tall grass, untie Cisco, and scout ahead a mile or two.

He looked back at Cisco now, plodding along behind the wagon, his nose buried contentedly in his feed bag, his buckskin coat gleaming in the sunshine. Dunbar smiled at the sight of his horse and wished briefly that horses could live as long as men. With luck, Cisco would be around for ten or twelve more years. Other horses would follow, but this was a once-in-a-lifetime animal. There would be no replacing him once he was gone.

As Lieutenant Dunbar watched, the smallish buckskin suddenly lifted his amber eyes over the lip of his feed bag as if to see where the lieutenant was and, satisfied with a glance, went back to nibbling at his grain.

Dunbar squared himself on the seat and slid a hand inside his tunic, drawing out a folded piece of paper. He was worried about this sheet of army paper because his orders were written down here. He had run his dark, pupilless eyes across this paper half a dozen times since he left Fort Hays, but no amount of study could make him feel any better.

His name was misspelled twice. The liquor-breathed major who had signed the paper had clumsily dragged a sleeve over the ink before it dried, and the official signature was badly smeared. The order had not been dated, so Lieutenant Dunbar had written it in himself once they were on the trail. But he had written with a pencil, and the lead clashed with the major's pen scratchings and the standard printing on the form.

Lieutenant Dunbar sighed at the official paper. It didn't look like an army order. It looked like trash.

Looking at the order reminded him of how it came to be, and that troubled him even more. That weird interview with the liquor-breathed major.

In his eagerness to be posted he'd gone straight from the train depot to headquarters. The major was the first and only person he'd spoken to between the time he'd arrived and the time later that afternoon when he'd clambered up on the wagon to take his seat next to the stinking Timmons.

The major's bloodshot eyes had held him for a long time. When he finally spoke, the tone was baldly sarcastic.

"Indian fighter, huh?"

Lieutenant Dunbar had never seen an Indian, much less fought one.

"Well, not at this moment, sir. I suppose I could be. I can fight."

"A fighter, huh?"

Lieutenant Dunbar had not replied to this. They stared silently at one another for what seemed a long time before the major began to write. He wrote furiously, ignorant of the sweat cascading down his temples. Dunbar could see more oily drops sitting in formation on top of the nearly bald head. Greasy strips of the major's remaining hair were plastered along his skull. It was a style that reminded Lieutenant Dunbar of something unhealthy.

The major paused in his scribbling only once. He coughed up a wad of phlegm and spat it into an ugly pail at the side of the desk. At that moment Lieutenant Dunbar wished the encounter to be over. Everything about this man made him think of sickness.

Lieutenant Dunbar had it pegged better than he knew, because this major had, for some time, clung to sanity by the slenderest thread, and the thread had finally snapped ten minutes before Lieutenant Dunbar walked into the office. The major had sat calmly at his desk, hands clasped neatly in front of him, and forgotten his entire life. It had been a powerless life, fueled by the pitiful handouts that come to those who serve obediently but make no mark. But all the years of being passed over, all the years of lonely bachelorhood, all the years of struggle with the bottle, had vanished as if by magic. The bitter grind of Major Fambrough's existence had been supplanted by an imminent and lovely event. He would be crowned king of Fort Hays some time before supper.

The major finished writing and handed the paper up.

"I'm posting you at Fort Sedgewick; you report directly to Captain Cargill."

Lieutenant Dunbar stared down at the messy form.

"Yes, sir. How will I be getting there, sir?"

"You don't think I know?" the major said sharply.

"No, sir, not at all. It's just that I don't know."

The major leaned back in his chair, shoved both hands down the front of his pants, and smiled smugly.

"I'm in a generous mood and I will grant your boon. A wagon loaded with goods of the realm leaves shortly. Find the peasant who calls himself Timmons and ride with him." Now he pointed at the sheet of paper in Lieutenant Dunbar's hand. "My seal will guarantee your safe conduct through one hundred and fifty miles of heathen territory."

From the beginning of his career Lieutenant Dunbar had known not to question the eccentricities of field-grade officers. He had saluted smartly, said, "Yes, sir," and turned on his heel. He had located Timmons, dashed back to the train to pick up Cisco, and had been riding out of Fort Hays within half an hour.

And now, as he stared at the orders after a hundred miles on the trail, he thought, I suppose everything will work out.

He felt the wagon slowing. Timmons was watching something in the buffalo grass close by as they came to a halt.

"Look yonder."

A splash of white was lying in the grass not twenty feet from the wagon, and both men climbed down to investigate.

It was a human skeleton, the bones bleached bright white, the skull staring up at the sky.

Lieutenant Dunbar knelt next to the bones. Grass was growing through the rib cage. And arrows, a score or more, sticking out like pins on a cushion. Dunbar pulled one out of the earth and rolled it around in his hands.

As he ran his fingers along the shaft, Timmons cackled over his shoulder.

"Somebody back east is wonderin', 'Why don't he write?' "

two

That evening it rained buckets. But the downpour came in shifts as summer storms are wont to do, somehow seeming not so damp as other times of the year, and the two travelers slept snugly under the tarp-draped wagon.

The fourth day passed much the same as the others, without event. And the fifth and the sixth. Lieutenant Dunbar was disappointed about the lack of buffalo. He had not seen a single animal. Timmons said the big herds sometimes disappeared altogether. He also said not to worry about it because they'd be thick as locusts when they did show up.

They'd not seen a single Indian either, and Timmons had no explanation for this. He did say that if he ever saw another Indian, it would be too soon, and that they were much better off not being hounded by thieves and beggars.

But by the seventh day Dunbar was only half listening to Timmons.

As they ate up the last miles he was thinking more and more about arriving at his post.

three

Captain Cargill felt around inside his mouth, his eyes staring up as he concentrated. A light of realization, followed quickly by a frown.

Another one's loose, he thought. Goddammit.

In a woebegone way the captain looked first at one wall, then another in his dank sod quarters. There was absolutely nothing to see. It was like a cell.

Quarters, he thought sarcastically. Goddamn quarters.

Everyone had been using that term for more than a month, even the captain. He used it unashamedly, right in front of his men. And they in front of him. But it wasn't an inside thing, a lighthearted jest among comrades. It was a true curse.

And it was a bad time.

Captain Cargill let his hand fall away from his mouth. He sat alone in the gloom of his goddamn quarters and listened. It was quiet outside, and the quiet broke Cargill's heart. Under normal circumstances the air outside would be filled with the sounds of men going about their duties. But there had been no duties for many days. Even busywork had fallen by the wayside. And there was nothing the captain could do about it. That's what hurt him.

As he listened to the terrible silence of the place he knew that he could wait no longer. Today he would have to take the action he had been dreading. Even if it meant disgrace. Or the ruin of his career. Or worse.

He shoved the "or worse" out of his mind and rose heavily to his feet. Making for the door, he fumbled for a moment with a loose button on his tunic. The button fell away from its thread and bounced across the floor. He didn't bother to pick it up. There was nothing to sew it back on with.

As he stepped into the bright sunshine, Captain Cargill allowed himself to imagine one last time that a wagon from Fort Hays would be standing there in the yard.

But there was no wagon. Just this dismal place, this sore on the land that didn't deserve a name.

Fort Sedgewick.

Captain Cargill looked hung over as he stood in the doorway of his sod cell. He was hatless and washed-out, and he was taking stock one last time.

There were no horses in the flimsy corral that not so long ago was home to fifty. In two and a half months the horses were stolen, replaced, and stolen again. The Comanches had helped themselves to every one.

His eyes drifted to the supply house just across the way. Aside from his own goddamn quarters, it was the only other standing structure at Fort Sedgewick. It had been a bad job from the start. No one knew how to build with sod, and two weeks after it went up, a good part of the roof had caved in. One of the walls was sagging so badly that it seemed impossible for it to stand at all. Surely it would collapse soon.

It doesn't matter, Captain Cargill thought, stifling a yawn.

The supply house was empty. It had been empty now for the better part of a month. They had been living on what was left of the hard crackers and what they could shoot on the prairie, mostly rabbits and guinea fowl. He had wished so hard for the buffalo to come back. Even now his taste buds sat up at the thought of a hump steak. Cargill pursed his lips and fought back a sudden tearing in his eyes.

There was nothing to eat.

He walked fifty yards across open, bare ground to the edge of the bluff on which Fort Sedgewick was built and stared down at the quiet stream winding noiselessly a hundred feet below. A coating of miscellaneous trash lined its banks, and even without benefit of an updraft, the rank odor of human waste wafted into the captain's nostrils. Human waste mixed with whatever else was rotting down there.

The captain's gaze swept down the gentle incline of the bluff just as two men emerged from one of the twenty or so sleeping holes carved out of the slope like pockmarks. The filthy pair stood blinking in the bright sunshine. They stared sullenly up at the captain but made no sign of acknowledgment. And neither did Cargill. The soldiers ducked back into their hole as if the sight of their commander had forced them back in, leaving the captain standing alone on top of the bluff.

He thought of the little deputation his men had sent to the sod hut eight days ago. Their appeal had been reasonable. In fact, it had been necessary. But the captain had decided against a ruling. He still hoped for a wagon. He had felt it was his duty to hope for a wagon.

In the eight days since, no one had spoken to him, not a single word. Except for the afternoon hunting trips, the men had stayed close by their holes, not communicating, rarely being seen.

Captain Cargill started back for his goddamn quarters, but he halted halfway there. He stood in the middle of the yard staring at the tops of his peeling boots. After a few moments of reflection, he muttered, "Now," and marched back the way he had come. There was more spring in his step as he gained the edge of the bluff.

Three times he called down for Corporal Guest before there was movement in front of one of the holes. A set of bony shoulders draped in a sleeveless jacket appeared, and then a dreary face looked back up at the bank. The soldier was suddenly paralyzed with a coughing fit, and Cargill waited for it to die down before he spoke.

"Assemble the men in front of my goddamn quarters in five minutes. Everybody, even those unfit for duty."

The soldier tipped his fingers dully against the side of his head and disappeared back into the hole.

Twenty minutes later the men of Fort Sedgewick, who looked more like a band of hideously abused prisoners than they did soldiers, had assembled on the flat, open space in front of Cargill's awful hut.

There were eighteen of them. Eighteen out of an original fifty-eight. Thirty-three men had gone over the hill, chancing whatever waited for them on the prairie. Cargill had sent a mounted patrol of seven men after the biggest batch of deserters. Maybe they were dead or maybe they had deserted too. They had never come back.

Now just eighteen wretched men.

Captain Cargill cleared his throat.

"I'm proud of you all for staying," he began.

The little assembly of zombies said nothing.

"Gather up your weapons and anything else you care to take out of here. As soon as you're ready we will march back to Fort Hays."

The eighteen were moving before he finished the sentence,

stampeding like drunkards for their sleeping holes below the bluff, as if afraid the captain might change his mind if they didn't hurry.

It was all over in less than fifteen minutes. Captain Cargill and his ghostly command staggered quickly onto the prairie and charted an easterly route for the 150 miles back to Hays.

The stillness around the failed army monument was complete when they were gone. Within five minutes a solitary wolf appeared on the bank across the stream from Fort Sedgewick and paused to sniff the breeze blowing toward him. Deciding this dead place was better left alone, he trotted on.

And so the abandonment of the army's most remote outpost, the spearhead of a grand scheme to drive civilization deep into the heart of the frontier, became complete. The army would regard it as merely a setback, a postponement of expansion that might have to wait until the Civil War had run its course, until the proper resources could be marshaled to supply a whole string of forts. They would come back to it, of course, but for now the recorded history of Fort Sedgewick had come to a dismal halt. The lost chapter in Fort Sedgewick's history, and the only one that could ever pretend to glory, was all set to begin.

four

Day broke eagerly for Lieutenant Dunbar. He was already thinking about Fort Sedgewick as he blinked himself awake, gazing half-focused at the wooden slats of the wagon a couple of feet above his head. He was wondering about Captain Cargill and the men and the lay of the place and what his first patrol would be like and a thousand other things that ran excitedly through his head.

This was the day he would finally reach his post, thus realizing a long-standing dream of serving on the frontier.

He tossed aside his bedding and rolled out from underneath the wagon. Shivering in the early light, he pulled on his boots and stomped around impatiently.

"Timmons," he whispered, bending under the wagon.

The smelly driver was sleeping deeply. The lieutenant nudged him with the toe of a boot.

"Timmons."

"Yeah, what?" the driver blubbered, sitting up in alarm.

"Let's get going."

five

Captain Cargill's column had made progress, just under ten miles by early afternoon.

A certain progress of the spirit had been made as well. The men were singing, proud songs from buoyed hearts, as they straggled across the prairie. The sounds of this lifted Captain Cargill's spirits as much as anyone's. The singing gave him great resolve. The army could put him in front of a firing squad if it wanted, and he would still smoke his last cigarette with a smile. He'd made the right decision. No one could dissuade him of that.

And as he tramped across the open grassland, he felt a long-lost satisfaction rushing back to him. The satisfaction of command. He was thinking like a commander again. He wished for a real march, one with a mounted column of troops.

I'd have flankers out right now, he mused. I'd have them out a solid mile to the north and south.

He actually looked to the south as the thought of flankers passed through his mind.

Then Cargill turned away, never knowing that if flankers

had been probing a mile south at that very moment, they would have found something.

They would have discovered two travelers who had paused in their trek to poke around a burned-out wreck of a wagon lying in a shallow gully. One would carry a foul odor about him, and the other, a severely handsome young man, would be in uniform.

But there were no flankers, so none of this was discovered.

Captain Cargill's column marched resolutely on, singing their way east toward Fort Hays.

And after their brief pause, the young lieutenant and the teamster were back on their wagon, pressing west for Fort Sedgewick.

CHAPTER II

one

On the second day out Captain Cargill's men shot a fat buffalo cow from a small herd of about a dozen and laid over a few hours to feast Indian-style on the delicious meat. The men insisted on roasting a slab of hump for their captain, and the commander's eyes welled with joy as he sank in his remaining teeth and let the heavenly meat melt in his mouth.

The luck of the column held, and around noon on the fourth day out they bumped into a large army surveying party. The major in charge could see the full story of their ordeal in the condition of Cargill's men, and his sympathy was instant.

With the loan of half a dozen horses and a wagon for the sick, Captain Cargill's column made excellent time, arriving at Fort Hays four days later.

two

It happens sometimes that those things we fear the most turn out to harm us the least, and so it was for Captain Cargill. He was not arrested for abandoning Fort Sedgewick, far from it. His men, who a few days before were dangerously close to overthrowing him, told the story of their privations at Fort Sedgewick, and not a single soldier failed to single out Captain Cargill as a leader in whom they had complete confidence. To a man they testified that, without Captain Cargill, none of them would have made it through.

The army of the frontier, its resources and morale frayed to the point of breaking, listened to all this testimony with joy.

Two steps were taken immediately. The post commandant relayed the full story of Fort Sedgewick's demise to General Tide at regional headquarters in St. Louis, ending his report with the recommendation that Fort Sedgewick be permanently abandoned, at least until further notice. General Tide was inclined to agree wholeheartedly, and within days Fort Sedgewick ceased to be connected with the United States government. It became a nonplace.

The second step concerned Captain Cargill. He was elevated to full hero status, receiving in rapid succession the Medal of Valor and a promotion to major. A "victory dinner" was organized in his behalf at the officers' mess.

It was at this dinner, over drinks after the meal, that Cargill heard from a friend the curious little story that had fueled most of the talk around the post just prior to his triumphant arrival.

Old Major Fambrough, a midlevel administrator with a lackluster record, had gone off his rocker. He had stood one afternoon in the middle of the parade ground, jabbering incoherently about his kingdom and asking over and over for his crown. The poor fellow had been shipped east just a few days ago.

As the captain listened to the details of this weird event, he, of course, had no idea that Major Fambrough's sad departure had also carried away all trace of Lieutenant Dunbar. Officially, the young officer existed only in the addled recesses of Major Fambrough's cracked brain.

Cargill also learned that, ironically, a wagonload of provisions had finally been dispatched by the same unfortunate major, a wagon bound for Fort Sedgewick. They must have passed each other on the march back. Captain Cargill and his acquaintance had a good laugh as they imagined the driver pulling up to that awful place and wondering what on earth had happened. They went so far as to speculate humorlessly about what the driver would do and decided that if he was smart, he would continue west, selling off the provisions at various trading posts along the way. Cargill staggered half-drunk to his quarters in the wee hours, and his head hit the pillow with the wonderful thought that Fort Sedgewick was now only a memory.

So it came to be that only one person on earth was left with any notion as to the whereabouts or even the existence of Lieutenant Dunbar.

And that person was a poorly groomed bachelor civilian who mattered very little to anyone.

Timmons.

CHAPTER III

one

The only sign of life was the ragged piece of canvas flapping gently in the doorway of the collapsed supply house. The late afternoon breeze was up, but the only thing that moved was the shred of canvas.

Had it not been for the lettering, crudely gouged in the beam over Captain Cargill's late residence, Lieutenant Dunbar could not have believed this was the place. But it was spelled out clearly.

"Fort Sedgewick."

The men sat silently on the wagon seat, staring about at the skimpy ruin that had turned out to be their final destination.

At last Lieutenant Dunbar hopped down and stepped cautiously through Cargill's doorway. Seconds later he emerged and glanced at Timmons, who was still sitting on the wagon.

"Not what you'd call a goin' concern," Timmons shouted down.

But the lieutenant didn't answer. He walked to the supply house, pulled the canvas flap aside, and leaned in. There was nothing to see, and in a moment he was walking back to the wagon.

Timmons stared down at him and started to shake his head.

"May as well unload," the lieutenant said matter-of-factly.

"What for, Lieutenant?"

"Because we've arrived."

Timmons squirmed on the seat. "There ain't nothin' here," he croaked.

Lieutenant Dunbar glanced around at his post.

"Not at the moment, no."

A silence passed between them, a silence that carried the tension of a standoff. Dunbar's arms hung at his sides while Timmons fingered the team's reins. He spat over the side of the wagon.

"Everybody's run off . . . or got kilt." He was glaring hard at the lieutenant, as if he wasn't going to have any more of this nonsense. "We might jus' as well turn 'round and get started back."

But Lieutenant Dunbar had no intention of going back. What had happened to Fort Sedgewick was something for finding out. Perhaps everyone had run off and perhaps they were all dead. Perhaps there were survivors, only an hour away, struggling to reach the fort.

And there was a deeper reason for his staying, something beyond his sharp sense of duty. There are times when a person wants something so badly that price or condition cease to be obstacles. Lieutenant Dunbar had wanted the frontier most of all. And now he was here. What Fort Sedgewick looked like or what its circumstances were didn't matter to him. His heart was set.

So his eyes never wavered as he spoke, his voice flat and dispassionate.

"This is my post and those are the post's provisions."

They stared each other down again. A smile broke on Timmons's mouth. He laughed.

"Are you crazy, boy?"

Timmons said this knowing that the lieutenant was a pup, that he had probably never been in combat, that he had never been west, and that he had not lived long enough to know anything. "Are you crazy, boy?" The words had come as though from the mouth of a fed-up father.

He was wrong.

Lieutenant Dunbar was not a pup. He was gentle and dutiful, and at times he was sweet. But he was not a pup.

He had seen combat nearly all his life. And he had been successful in combat because he possessed a rare trait. Dunbar had an inborn sense, a kind of sixth sense, that told him when to be tough. And when this critical moment was upon him, something intangible kicked into his psyche and Lieutenant Dunbar became a mindless, lethal machine that couldn't be turned off. Not until it had accomplished its objective. When push came to shove, the lieutenant pushed first. And those that shoved back regretted doing so.

The words "Are you crazy, boy?" had tripped the mechanism of the machine, and Timmons's smile began a slow fade as he watched Lieutenant Dunbar's eyes turn black. A moment later Timmons saw the lieutenant's right hand lift, slowly and deliberately. He saw the heel of Dunbar's hand light softly on the handle of the big Navy revolver he wore on his hip. He saw the lieutenant's index finger slip smoothly through the trigger guard.

"Get your ass off that wagon and help me unload."

The tone of these words had a profound effect on Timmons. The tone told him that death had suddenly appeared on the scene. His own death.

Timmons didn't bat an eye. Nor did he make a reply. Almost in a single motion he tied the reins to the brake, leaped down from his seat, walked briskly to the rear of the wagon, threw open the tailgate, and lifted out the first item of portage he could put his hands on.

two

They crammed as much as they could into the half-caved-in supply house and stacked the rest in Cargill's former quarters.

CHAPTER IV

one

Saying the moon would be up and that he wanted to make time, Timmons pulled out at twilight.

Lieutenant Dunbar sat on the ground, made himself a smoke, and watched the wagon grow smaller in the distance. The sun left about the same time the wagon disappeared, and he sat in the dark a long time, glad for the company of silence. After an hour he started to stiffen, so he got up and plodded to Captain Cargill's hut.

Suddenly tired, he flopped fully clothed on the little bed he'd made amidst the supplies and laid his head down.

His ears were very big that night. Sleep was hard in coming. Every little noise in the darkness asked for an explanation that Dunbar could not provide. There was a strangeness in this place at night that he hadn't felt during the day.

Just as he would begin to slip off, the snap of a twig or a tiny, far-off splash in the stream would bring him wide-awake again. This went on for a long time, and gradually it wore Lieutenant Dunbar down. He was tired and he was as restless as he was tired, and this combination opened the door wide to an unwelcome visitor. In through the door of Lieutenant

Dunbar's sleepless sleep marched doubt. Doubt challenged him hard that first night. It whispered awful things into his ear. He had been a fool. He was wrong about everything. He was worthless. He might as well be dead. Doubt that night brought him to the verge of tears. Lieutenant Dunbar fought back, quieting himself with kind thoughts. He fought far into the morning, and in the wee hours close to dawn, he finally kicked doubt out and fell asleep.

two

They had stopped.

There were six of them.

They were Pawnee, the most terrible of all the tribes. Roached hair and early wrinkles and a collective set of mind something like the machine Lieutenant Dunbar could occasionally become. But there was nothing occasional about the way the Pawnee saw things. They saw with unsophisticated but ruthlessly efficient eyes, eyes that, once fixed on an object, decided in a twinkling whether it should live or die. And if it was determined that the object should cease to live, the Pawnee saw to its death with psychotic precision. When it came to dealing death, the Pawnee were automatic, and all of the Plains Indians feared them as they did no one else.

What had caused these six Pawnee to stop was something they had seen. And now they sat atop their scrawny horses, looking down on a series of rolling gullies. A tiny wisp of smoke was curling into the early morning air about half a mile away.

From their vantage point on a low rise they could see the smoke clearly. But they could not see the source. The source was hidden in the last of the gullies. And because they could not see all that they wanted, the men had begun to talk it over, chattering in low, guttural tones about the smoke and what it might be. Had they felt stronger, they might have ridden down at once, but they had already been away from home for a long time, and the time away had been a disaster.

They had begun with a small party of eleven men, making the trek south to steal from the horse-rich Comanches. After riding for almost a week they had been surprised at a river crossing by a large force of Kiowas. It was a lucky thing that they escaped with only one man dead and one wounded.

The wounded man held on for a week with a badly punctured lung, and the burden of him slowed the party greatly. When at last he died and the nine marauding Pawnee could resume their search unencumbered, they had nothing but bad luck. The Comanche bands were always a step or two ahead of the hapless Pawnee, and for two more weeks they found nothing but cold trails.

Finally they located a large encampment with many fine horses and rejoiced in the lifting of the bad cloud that had followed them for so long. But what the Pawnee didn't know was that their luck hadn't changed at all. In fact, it was only the worst kind of luck that had brought them to this village, for this band of Comanches had been hit hard only a few days before by a strong party of Utes, who had killed several good warriors and made off with thirty horses.

The whole Comanche band was on the alert, and they were in a vengeful mood as well. The Pawnee were discovered the moment they began to creep into the village, and with half of the camp breathing down their necks, they fled, stumbling through the alien darkness on their worn-out ponies. It was only in retreat that luck finally found them. All of them should have died that night. In the end, however, they lost only three more warriors.

So now these six disheartened men, sitting on this lonely rise, their ribbed-out ponies too tired to move underneath them, wondered what to do about a single feathery stream of smoke half a mile away.

To debate the merits of whether to make an attack was

very Indian. But to debate a single wisp of smoke for half an hour was a much different matter, and it showed just how far the confidence of these Pawnee had sunk. The six were split, one cell for withdrawing, the other for investigating. As they dallied back and forth, only one man, the fiercest among them, remained steadfast from the first. He wanted to swoop down on the smoke immediately, and as the jawboning dragged on, he grew more and more sullen.

After thirty minutes he drew away from his brethren and started silently down the slope. The other five came along-side, inquiring as to what his action might be.

The sullen warrior replied caustically that they were not Pawnee and that he could no longer ride with women. He said they should stick their tails between their legs and go home. He said they were not Pawnee, and he said that he would rather die than haggle with men who were not men.

He rode toward the smoke.

The others followed.

three

As much as he disliked Indians, Timmons knew virtually nothing of their ways. The territory had been relatively safe for a long time. But he was only one man with no real way to defend himself, and he should have known enough to make a smokeless fire.

But that morning he had rolled out of his stinking blankets with a powerful hunger. The idea of bacon and coffee had been the only thing on his mind and he had hastily built a nice little fire with green wood.

It was Timmons's fire that had attracted the hurting little band of Pawnee.

He was squatting at the fire, his fingers wrapped around the skillet handle, drinking in the bacon fumes, when the arrow hit him. It drove deep into his right buttock, and the force of it knocked him clear across the fire. He heard the whoops before he saw anyone, and the cries sent him into a panic. He crow-hopped into the gully and, without breaking stride, clambered up the incline, a brightly feathered Pawnee arrow jutting from his ass.

Seeing that it was just one man, the Pawnee took their time. While the others looted the wagon, the fierce warrior who had shamed them into action galloped lazily after Timmons.

He caught the teamster just as he was about to clear the slope leading out of the gully. Here Timmons suddenly stumbled to one knee, and when he rose he turned his head to the sound of hoofbeats.

But he never saw the horse or its rider. For a split second he saw the stone war club. Then it slammed into the side of his skull with such force that Timmons's head literally popped open.

four

The Pawnee rifled through the supplies, taking as much as they could carry. They unhitched the nice team of army horses, burned the wagon, and rode past Timmons's mutilated body without so much as a parting glance. They had taken all they wanted from it. The teamster's scalp flopped near the tip of his killer's lance.

The body lay all day in the tall grass, waiting for the wolves to discover it at nightfall. But the passing of Timmons carried more significance than the snuffing of a single life. With his death an unusual circle of circumstances had come full.

The circle had closed around Lieutenant John J. Dunbar. No man could be more alone.

CHAPTER V

one

He, too, made a fire that morning, but his was going much earlier than Timmons's. In fact, the lieutenant was halfway through his first cup of coffee an hour before the driver was killed.

Two camp chairs had been included in the manifest. He spread one of these in front of Cargill's sod hut and sat for a long time, an army blanket draped over his shoulders, a big standard-issue cup cradled in his hands, watching the first full day at Fort Sedgewick unfold before his eyes. His thoughts fell quickly on action, and when they did, doubt marched in again.

With a startling suddenness, the lieutenant felt overwhelmed. He realized that he had no idea where to begin, what his function should be, or even how to regard himself. He had no duties, no program to follow, and no status.

As the sun rose steadily behind him, Dunbar found himself stuck in the chilly shade of the hut, so he refilled his cup and moved the camp chair into the direct sunlight of the yard.

He was just sitting down when he saw the wolf. It was standing on the bluff opposite the fort, just across the river.

The lieutenant's first instinct was to frighten it off with a round or two, but the longer he watched his visitor, the less sense this idea made. Even at a distance he could tell that the animal was merely curious. And in some hidden way that never quite bubbled to the surface of his thoughts, he was glad for this little bit of company.

Cisco snorted over in the corral, and the lieutenant jerked to attention. He had forgotten all about his horse. On his way to the supply house he glanced over his shoulder and saw that his early morning visitor had turned tail and was disappearing below the horizon beyond the bluff.

two

It came to him at the corral as he was pouring Cisco's grain into a shallow pan. It was a simple solution and it kicked doubt out once more.

For the time being he would invent his duties.

Dunbar made a quick inspection of Cargill's hut, the supply house, the corral, and the river. Then he set to work, starting first with the garbage choking the banks of the little stream.

Though not fastidious by nature, he found the dumping ground a complete disgrace. Bottles and trash were strewn everywhere. Broken bits of gear and shreds of uniform material lay encrusted in the banks. Worst of all were the carcasses, in varying stages of decay, which had been dumped mindlessly along the river. Most of them were small game, rabbits and guinea fowl. There was a whole antelope and part of another.

Surveying this squalor gave Dunbar his first real clue as to what might have happened at Fort Sedgewick. Obviously it had become a place in which no one took pride. And then, without knowing, he hit close to the truth.

Maybe it was food, he thought. Maybe they were starving.

He worked straight through noon, stripped down to his long undershirt, a seedy pair of pants, and a set of old boots, sifting methodically through the garbage about the river.

There were more carcasses sunk in the stream itself, and his stomach churned queasily as he dragged the oozing animal bodies from the fetid mud of the shallow water.

He piled everything on a sheet of canvas, and when there was enough for a load, he tied the canvas up like a sack. Then, with Cisco providing the muscle, they lugged the awful cargo to the top of the bluff.

By midafternoon the stream was clear, and though he wasn't certain, the lieutenant could swear it was running faster. He made a smoke and rested awhile, watching the river flow past. Freed of its filthy parasites, it looked like a real stream again, and the lieutenant felt a little swelling of pride in what he had done.

As he came to his feet he could feel his back tighten. Unaccustomed as he was to this sort of work, he found the soreness not unpleasant. It meant he had accomplished something.

After policing up the last, tiny scraps of refuse, he climbed to the top of the bluff and confronted the pile of scum that rose nearly to his shoulder. He poured a gallon of fuel oil on the heap and set it ablaze.

For a time he watched the great column of greasy, black smoke boil into the empty sky. But all at once his heart sunk as he realized what he had done. He should never have started the fire. Out here a blaze of this size was like setting off a flare on a moonless night. It was like pointing a huge, flaming arrow of invitation at Fort Sedgewick.

Someone was bound to be drawn in by the column of smoke, and the someone would most likely be Indians.

three

Lieutenant Dunbar sat in front of the hut until dusk, constantly scanning the horizon in every direction.

No one came.

He was relieved. But as he sat through the afternoon, a Springfield rifle and his big Navy at the ready, his sense of isolation deepened. At one point the word *marooned* slipped into his mind. It made him shudder. He knew it was the right word. And he knew he might have to be alone for some time to come. In a deep and secret way he wanted to be alone, but being marooned had none of the euphoria he had felt on the trip out with Timmons.

This was sobering.

He ate a skimpy dinner and filled out his first day's report. Lieutenant Dunbar was a good writer, which made him less averse to paperwork than most soldiers. And he was eager to keep a scrupulous record of his stay at Fort Sedgewick, particularly in light of his bizarre circumstances.

> *April 12, 1863*
>
> *I have found Fort Sedgewick to be completely unmanned. The place appears to have been rotting for some time. If there was a contingent here shortly before I came, it, too, must have been rotting.*
>
> *I don't know what to do.*
>
> *Fort Sedgewick is my post, but there is no one to report to. Communication can only take place if I leave, and I don't want to abandon my post.*
>
> *Supplies are abundant.*
>
> *Have assigned myself cleanup duty. Will attempt to strengthen supply house, but don't know if one man can do job.*
>
> *Everything is quiet here on the frontier.*
>
> *Lt. John J. Dunbar, U.S.A.*

On the verge of sleep that night he had the awning idea. An awning for the hut. A long sunshade extending from the entrance. A place to sit or work on days when the heat inside quarters became unbearable. An addition to the fort.

And a window, cut out of the sod. A window would make a big difference. Could shrink the corral and use the extra posts for other construction. Maybe something could be done with the supply house after all.

Dunbar was asleep before he'd cataloged all the possibilities for busying himself. It was a deep sleep and he dreamed vividly.

He was in a Pennsylvania field hospital. Doctors had gathered at the foot of his bed, a half dozen of them in long, white aprons soaked with the blood of other ''cases.''

They were discussing whether to take his foot off at the ankle or at the knee. The discussion gave way to an argument, the argument turned ugly, and as the lieutenant watched, horrified, they began to fight.

They were bashing each other with the severed limbs of previous amputations. And as they swirled about the hospital, swinging their grotesque clubs, patients who had lost limbs leaped or crawled from their pallets, desperately sorting through the debris of the battling doctors for their own arms and legs.

In the middle of the melee he escaped, galloping crazily through the main doors on his half-blown-away foot.

He hobbled into a brilliant green meadow that was strewn with Union and Confederate corpses. Like dominoes in reverse, the corpses sat up as he ran past and aimed pistols at him.

Finding a gun in his hand, Lieutenant Dunbar shot each of the corpses before they could squeeze off a round. He fired rapidly and each of his bullets found a head. And each head blew apart on impact. They looked like a long line of melons, each of them exploding in turn from perches on the shoulders of dead men.

Lieutenant Dunbar could see himself at a distance, a wild figure in a bloody hospital gown, dashing through a gauntlet of corpses, heads flying into space as he went.

Suddenly there were no more corpses and no more firing.

But there was someone behind him calling in a beautiful voice.

"Sweetheart . . . sweetheart."

Dunbar looked over his shoulder.

Running behind him was a woman, a handsome woman with high cheeks and thick sandy hair and eyes so alive with passion that he could feel his heart beating stronger. She was dressed only in men's pants and she ran with a blood-drenched foot in her outstretched hand, as if in offering.

The lieutenant glanced down at his own wounded foot and found it gone. He was running on a white stump of bone.

He came awake, sitting upright in shock, groping wildly for his foot at the end of the bed. It was there.

His blankets were damp with sweat. He fumbled under the bed for his kit and hastily rolled a smoke. Then he kicked off the clammy blankets, propped himself on the pillow, and puffed away, waiting for it to get light.

He knew exactly what had inspired the dream. The basic elements had actually taken place. Dunbar let his mind wander back to those events.

He had been wounded in the foot. By shrapnel. He had spent time in a field hospital, there had been talk of taking off his foot, and not being able to bear the thought of this, Lieutenant Dunbar had escaped. In the middle of the night, with the terrible groans of wounded men echoing through the ward, he'd slipped out of bed and stolen the makings of a dressing. He'd powdered the foot with antiseptic, wrapped it heavily with gauze, and somehow jammed it into his boot.

Then he had snuck out a side door, stolen a horse, and, having no place else to go, rejoined his unit at dawn with a cock-and-bull story about a flesh wound to the toe.

Now he smiled to himself and thought, What could I have been thinking of?

After two days the pain was so great that the lieutenant wanted nothing more than to die. When the opportunity presented itself, he took it.

Two opposing units had sniped at each other across three hundred yards of denuded field for the better part of an afternoon. They were hidden behind low stone walls bordering opposite ends of the field, each unsure of the other's strength, each unsure about mounting a charge.

Lieutenant Dunbar's unit had launched an observation balloon, but the rebels had promptly shot it down.

It had remained a standoff, and when tensions reached their climax in the late afternoon, Lieutenant Dunbar reached his own personal breaking point. His thoughts focused unwaveringly on ending his life.

He volunteered to ride out and draw enemy fire.

The colonel in charge of the regiment was unsuited for war. He had a weak stomach and a dull mind.

Normally he would never have permitted such a thing, but on this afternoon he was under extreme pressure. The poor man was at a complete loss, and for some unexplained reason, thoughts of a large bowl of peach ice cream kept intruding into his mind.

To make matters worse, General Tipton and his aides had just recently taken up an observation position on a high hill to the west. His performance was being watched, yet he was powerless to perform.

The topper was this young lieutenant with the bloodless face, talking to him in clenched tones about drawing fire. His wild, pupilless eyes scared the colonel.

The inept commander consented to the plan.

With his own mount coughing badly, Dunbar was allowed to take his pick of the stock. He took a new horse, a small, strong buckskin named Cisco, and managed to get himself into the saddle without crying out from pain while the whole outfit watched.

As he walked the buckskin toward the low stone wall, a few pings of rifle fire came across the field, but otherwise it was dead silent and Lieutenant Dunbar wondered if the silence was real or if it always became this way in the moments before a man died.

He kicked Cisco sharply in the ribs, jumped the wall, and tore across the bare field, bearing straight down on the center of the rock wall that hid the enemy. For a moment the rebels were too shocked to shoot, and the lieutenant covered the first hundred yards in a soundless vacuum.

Then they opened up. Bullets filled the air around him like spray from a spigot. The lieutenant didn't bother to fire back. He sat straight up so as to make a better target and kicked Cisco again. The little horse flattened his ears and flew at the wall. All the while Dunbar waited for one of the bullets to find him.

But none did, and when he was close enough to see the eyes of the enemy, he and Cisco veered left, running north in a straight line, fifty yards out from the wall. Cisco was digging so hard that dirt jumped from his back hooves like the wake from a fast boat. The lieutenant maintained his upright posture, and this proved irresistible to the Confederates. They rose like targets in a shooting gallery, pouring out rifle fire in sheets as the solitary horseman dashed past.

They couldn't hit him.

Lieutenant Dunbar heard the firing die. The line of riflemen had run out. As he pulled up he felt something burning in his upper arm and discovered that he'd been nicked in the bicep. The prickle of heat brought him briefly back to his senses. He looked down the line he had just passed and saw that the Confederates were milling about behind the wall in a state of disbelief.

His ears were suddenly working again and he could hear shouts of encouragement coming from his own line far across the field. Then he was aware once more of his foot, throbbing like some hideous pump deep in his boot.

He wheeled Cisco into an about-face, and as the little buckskin surged against the bit, Lieutenant Dunbar heard a thunderous cheer. He looked across the field. His brothers in arms were rising en masse behind the wall.

He laid his heels against Cisco's side and they charged ahead, racing back the way they had come, this time to probe the other Confederate flank. The men he had already passed were caught with their pants down and he could see them frantically reloading as he sped by.

But ahead of him, down along the unprobed flank, he could see riflemen coming to their feet, the guns settling in the crooks of their shoulders.

Determined not to fail himself, the lieutenant suddenly and impulsively let the reins drop and lifted both his arms high into the air. He might have looked like a circus rider, but what he felt was final. He had raised his arms in a final gesture of farewell to this life. To someone watching, it might have been misconstrued. It might have looked like a gesture of triumph.

Of course Lieutenant Dunbar had not meant it as a signal to anyone else. He had only wanted to die. But his Union comrades already had their hearts in their throats, and when they saw the lieutenant's arms fly up, it was more than they could bear.

They streamed over the wall, a spontaneous tide of fighting men, roaring with an abandon that curdled the blood of the Confederate troops.

The men in the beechnut uniforms broke and ran as one, scrambling in a twisted mess toward the stand of trees behind them.

By the time Lieutenant Dunbar pulled Cisco up, the blue-coated Union troops were already over the wall, chasing the terrified rebels into the woods.

His head suddenly lightened.

The world around him went into a spin.

The colonel and his aides were converging from one direction, General Tipton and his people from another. They'd both seen him fall, toppling unconscious from the saddle, and each man quickened his pace as the lieutenant went down. Running to the spot in the empty field where Cisco stood quietly next to the shapeless form lying at his feet, the colonel and General Tipton shared the same feelings, feelings that were rare in high-ranking officers, particularly in wartime.

They each shared a deep and genuine concern for a single individual.

Of the two, General Tipton was the more overwhelmed. In twenty-seven years of soldiering he had witnessed many acts of bravery, but nothing came close to the display he had witnessed that afternoon.

When Dunbar came to, the general was kneeling at his side with the fervency of a father at the side of a fallen son.

And when he found that this brave lieutenant had ridden onto the field already wounded, the general lowered his head as if in prayer and did something he had not done since childhood. Tears tumbled into his graying beard.

Lieutenant Dunbar was not in shape to talk much, but he did manage a single request. He said it several times.

"Don't take my foot off."

General Tipton heard and recorded that request as if it were a commandment from God. Lieutenant Dunbar was taken from the field in the general's own ambulance, carried to the general's regimental headquarters, and, once there, was placed under the direct supervision of the general's personal physician.

There was a short scene when they arrived. General Tipton ordered his physician to save the young man's foot, but after a quick examination, the physician replied that there was a strong possibility he would have to amputate.

General Tipton took the doctor aside then and told him,

"If you don't save that boy's foot, I will have you cashiered for incompetence. I will have you cashiered if it's the last thing I do."

Lieutenant Dunbar's recovery became an obsession with the general. He made time each day to look in on the young lieutenant and, at the same time, look over the shoulder of the doctor, who never stopped sweating in the two weeks it took to save Lieutenant Dunbar's foot.

The general said little to the patient in that time. He only expressed fatherly concern. But when the foot was finally out of danger, he ducked into the tent one afternoon, pulled a chair close to the bed, and began to talk dispassionately about something that had formed in his mind.

Dunbar listened dumbfounded as the general laid out his idea. He wanted the war to be over for Lieutenant Dunbar because his actions on the field, actions that the general was still thinking about, were enough for one man in one war.

And he wanted the lieutenant to ask him for something because, and here the general lowered his voice, "We are all in your debt. I am in your debt."

The lieutenant allowed himself a thin smile and said, "Well . . . I have my foot, sir."

General Tipton didn't return the smile.

"What do you want?" he said.

Dunbar closed his eyes and thought.

At last he said, "I have always wanted to be posted on the frontier."

"Where?"

"Anywhere . . . just on the frontier."

The general rose from his chair. "All right," he said, and started out of the tent.

"Sir?"

The general stopped short, and when he looked back at the bed, it was with an affection that was disarming.

"I would like to keep the horse. . . . Can I do that?"

"Of course you can."

Lieutenant Dunbar had pondered the interview with the general for the rest of the afternoon. He had been excited about the sudden, new prospects for his life. But he had also felt a twinge of guilt when he thought of the affection he had seen in the general's face. He had not told anyone that he was only trying to commit suicide. But it seemed far too late now. That afternoon he decided he would never tell.

And now, lying in the clammy blankets, Dunbar made up his third smoke in half an hour and mused about the mysterious workings of fate that had finally brought him to Fort Sedgewick.

The room was growing lighter, and so was the lieutenant's mood. He steered his thoughts away from the past and into the present. With the zeal of a man content with his place, he began to think about today's phase of the cleanup campaign.

CHAPTER VI

one

Like a youngster who would rather skip the vegetables and get right to the pie, Lieutenant Dunbar passed over the difficult job of shoring up the supply house in favor of the more pleasant possibilities of constructing the awning.

Digging through the provisions, he found a set of field tents that would supply the canvas, but no amount of searching would produce a suitable instrument with which to stitch, and he wished he hadn't been so quick in burning the carcasses.

He scoured the banks downriver for a good part of the morning before he found a small skeleton that yielded several strong slivers of bone that could be used for sewing.

Back at the supply house he found a thin length of rope that unraveled into the thread size he had imagined. Leather would have been more durable, but in making all his improvements, Lieutenant Dunbar liked the idea of assigning a temporary aspect to the work. Holding down the fort, he thought, chuckling to himself. Holding down the fort until it came fully to life again with the arrival of fresh troops.

37

Though careful to avoid expectations, he was sure that, sooner or later, someone would come.

The sewing was brutal. For the remainder of the second day he stitched doggedly at the canvas, making good progress. But by the time he knocked off late that afternoon, his hands were so sore and swollen that he had difficulty preparing his evening coffee.

In the morning his fingers were like stone, far too stiff to work the needle. He was tempted to try anyway, for he was close to finishing. But he didn't.

Instead, he turned his attention to the corral. After careful study, he cannibalized four of the tallest and sturdiest posts. They had not been sunk deep, and it didn't take much time to pull them out.

Cisco wasn't going to go anywhere, and the lieutenant toyed briefly with the idea of leaving the corral open. In the end, however, he decided a noncorral would violate the spirit of the cleanup campaign, so he took another hour to rearrange the fencing.

Then he spread the canvas in front of the sleeping hut and sank the posts deep, packing them tight as he could with the heavy soil.

The day had turned warm, and when he was finished with the posts, the lieutenant found himself traipsing into the shade of the sod hut. He sat on the edge of the bed and leaned back against the wall. His eyes were getting heavy. He lay down on the pallet to rest a moment and promptly fell into a deep, delicious sleep.

two

He woke flushed with the sensuous afterglow of having surrendered completely, in this case to a nap. Stretching out languidly, he dropped his hand over the side of the bed and, like a dreamy child, let his fingertips play lightly over the dirt floor.

He felt wonderful, lying there with nothing to do, and it occurred to him then that, in addition to inventing his own duties, he could also set his own pace. For the time being, anyway. He decided that, in the same way he had surrendered to the nap, he would give himself more leeway with other pleasures as well. Wouldn't hurt to cut myself a little slack, he thought.

Shadows were creeping across the hut's doorway, and curious about how long he had slept, Dunbar slid a hand inside his trousers and pulled out the simple, old pocket watch that had been his father's. When he brought it to his face he saw that it had stopped. For a moment he considered trying to set an approximate time, but instead he placed the old, worn timepiece on his stomach and lapsed into a meditation.

What did time matter to him now? What did it ever matter? Well, perhaps it was necessary in the movement of things, men and materials, for instance. For cooking things correctly. For schools and weddings and church services and going to work.

But what did it matter out here?

Lieutenant Dunbar rolled himself a smoke and hung the heirloom on a convenient hook a couple of feet above the bed. He stared at the numbers on the watch's face as he smoked, thinking how much more efficient it would be to work when a person felt like it, to eat when a person was hungry, to sleep when a person was sleepy.

He took a long drag on the cigarette and, throwing his arms contentedly behind his head, blew out a stream of blue smoke.

How good it will be to live without time for a while, he thought.

Suddenly there was the sound of heavy footfalls just outside. They started and stopped and started again. A moving shadow passed over the entrance to the hut and a moment later Cisco's big head swung through the doorway. His ears were pricked and his eyes were wide with wonder. He looked like a child invading the sanctity of his parents' bedroom on a Sunday morning.

Lieutenant Dunbar laughed out loud. The buckskin let his ears fall and gave his head a long, casual shake, as if pretending this little embarrassment hadn't happened. His eyes roamed the room with a detached air. Then he looked pointedly at the lieutenant and stamped his hoof in the way horses do when they want to shake off the flies.

Dunbar knew he wanted something.

A ride probably.

He'd been standing around for two days.

three

Lieutenant Dunbar was not a fancy rider. He'd never been schooled in the subtleties of horsemanship. His frame, deceptively strong despite being slim, had not known organized athletics.

But there was something about horses. He had loved them from boyhood; perhaps that was the reason. But the reason doesn't really matter. What matters is that something extraordinary happened when Dunbar swung onto the back of a horse, especially if it was a gifted horse like Cisco.

Communication took place between horses and Lieutenant Dunbar. He had the knack of deciphering the language of a horse. And once that was mastered, the sky was the limit. He had mastered Cisco's dialect almost at once, and there was little they couldn't do. When they rode it was with the grace of a dance team.

And the purer the better. Dunbar had always preferred a bare back to a saddle, but the army, of course, permitted no such thing. People got hurt, and it was out of the question for long campaigns.

So when the lieutenant stepped inside the shadowy supply house, his hand went automatically for the saddle in the corner.

He checked himself. The only army here was him, and Lieutenant Dunbar knew he would not get hurt.

He reached instead for Cisco's bridle and left the saddle behind.

They weren't twenty yards from the corral when he saw the wolf again. It was staring from the spot it had occupied the day before, on the edge of the bluff just across the river.

The wolf had begun to move, but when he saw Cisco come to a halt, he froze, stepped deliberately back into his original position, and resumed staring at the lieutenant.

Dunbar stared back with more interest than he had the day before. It was the same wolf, all right, two white socks on the front paws. He was big and sturdy, but something about him gave Dunbar the impression he was past his prime. His coat was scruffy, and the lieutenant thought he could see a jagged line along the muzzle, most likely an old scar. There was an alertness about him that signified age. He seemed to watch everything without moving a muscle. Wisdom was the word that came to the lieutenant's mind. Wisdom was the bonus of surviving many years, and the tawny old fellow with the watchful eyes had survived more than his share.

Funny he's come back again, Lieutenant Dunbar thought.

He pushed forward slightly and Cisco stepped ahead. As he did, Dunbar's eye picked up movement and he glanced across the river.

The wolf was moving, too.

In fact, he was keeping pace. This went on for a hundred yards before the lieutenant asked Cisco to stop again.

The wolf stopped, too.

On impulse, the lieutenant wheeled Cisco a quarter turn and faced across the chasm. Now he was staring straight into the wolf's eyes, and the lieutenant felt certain he could read something there. Something like longing.

He was beginning to think about what the longing might be when the wolf yawned and turned away. He kicked himself into a trot and disappeared.

four

April 13, 1863

Though well supplied, I have decided to ration my goods. The missing garrison or a replacement should be here anytime. I cannot imagine it will be too much longer now.

In any event, I'm striving to consume stores in the way I would if I were part of the post rather than the whole affair. It will be hard with the coffee, but I shall try my best.

Have begun the awning. If my hands, which are in poor condition just now, should be up to snuff in the morning, I might have it up by tomorrow P.M.

Made a short patrol this P.M. Discovered nothing.

There is a wolf who seems intent on the goings-on here. He does not seem inclined to be a nuisance, however, and, aside from my horse, is the only visitor I have had. He has appeared each afternoon for the past two days. If he comes calling tomorrow, I will name him Two Socks. He has milky-white socks on both front paws.

Lt. John J. Dunbar, U.S.A.

CHAPTER VII

one

The next few days went smoothly.

Lieutenant Dunbar's hands came back and the awning went up. Twenty minutes after he had raised it, when he was relaxing beneath the sprawling shade, bent over a barrel, rolling a smoke, the breeze kicked up and the awning collapsed.

Feeling ridiculous, he pawed his way out from under, studied the failure for a few minutes, and hit on the idea of guide wires as a solution. He used rope for wire, and before the sun went down, Dunbar was back in the shade, with his eyes closed, puffing on another handmade cigarette while he listened to the pleasant sound of canvas flapping gently overhead.

Using a bayonet, he sawed out a wide window in the sod hut and draped a scrap of canvas over it.

He worked long and hard on the supply house, but except for clearing away a large part of the sagging wall, he made little progress. A gaping hole was the final result. The original sod crumbled each time he tried to build it up, so Lieutenant Dunbar covered the hole with yet another sheet of canvas and washed his hands of the rest. From the start the supply house had been a losing business.

Lying on his bunk in the late afternoons, Dunbar returned over and over to the problem of the supply house, but as the days passed, he thought of it less. The weather had been beautiful, with none of the violence of spring. The temperatures couldn't be more perfect, the air was feathery, and the breeze, which made the canvas window curtain billow above his head on these late afternoons, was sweet.

The day's little problems seemed easier to solve as time went by, and when his work was finished the lieutenant would lie back on the bunk with his cigarette and marvel at the peace he felt. Invariably his eyes would grow heavy, and he fell into the habit of napping for half an hour before supper.

Two Socks became a habit, too. He appeared at his customary spot on the bluff each afternoon, and after two or three days, Lieutenant Dunbar began to take his silent visitor's comings and goings for granted. Occasionally he would notice the wolf trotting into view, but more often than not, the lieutenant would glance up from some little task and there he would be, sitting on his haunches, staring across the river with that curious but unmistakable look of longing.

One evening, while Two Socks was watching, he laid a fist-sized chunk of bacon rind on his own side of the river. The morning after, there was no trace of the bacon, and though he had no proof, Dunbar felt certain that Two Socks had taken it.

two

Lieutenant Dunbar missed some things. He missed the company of people. He missed the pleasure of a stiff drink. Most of all, he missed women, or rather a woman. Sex hardly entered his mind. But sharing did. The more settled he became in the free and easy pattern of life at Fort Sedgewick, the more he wanted to share it with someone, and when the lieutenant thought of this missing element, he would drop his chin and stare morosely at nothing.

Fortunately, these lapses of spirit passed away quickly. What he might have lacked was pale in light of what he had. His mind was free. There was no work and there was no play. Everything was one. It didn't matter whether he was hauling water up from the stream or tying into a hearty dinner. Everything was the same, and he found it not at all boring. He thought of himself as a single current in a deep river. He was separate and he was whole, all at the same time. It was a wonderful feeling.

He loved the daily reconnaissance rides on Cisco's bare back. Each day they rode out in a different direction, sometimes as far as five or six miles from the fort. He saw no buffalo and no Indians. But this disappointment was not great. The prairie was glorious, ablaze with wildflowers and overrun with game. The buffalo grass was the best, alive as an ocean, waving in the wind for as far as his eyes could see. It was a sight he knew he would never grow tired of.

On the afternoon before the day Lieutenant Dunbar did his laundry, he and Cisco had ridden less than a mile from the post when, by chance, he looked over his shoulder and there was Two Socks, coming along in his easy trot a couple of hundred yards back.

Lieutenant Dunbar pulled up and the wolf slowed.

But he didn't stop.

He veered wide, picking up his trot again. When he was abreast of them the old wolf halted in the high grass, fifty yards to the lieutenant's left, and settled on his haunches, waiting as if for a signal to begin again.

They rode deeper into the prairie and Two Socks went with them. Dunbar's curiosity led him to perform a series of stops and starts along the way. Two Socks, his yellow eyes always vigilant, followed suit each time.

Even when Dunbar changed course, zigzagging here and there, he kept up, always maintaining his fifty yards of distance.

When he put Cisco into an easy canter, the lieutenant was astounded to see Two Socks ease into a lope of his own.

When they stopped, he looked out at his faithful follower and tried to conjure up an explanation. Surely this animal had known man somewhere along the line. Perhaps he was half-dog. But when the lieutenant's eyes swept the wilderness all about him, running unbroken toward every horizon, he could not imagine Two Socks as anything but a wolf.

"Okay," the lieutenant called out.

Two Socks picked up his ears.

"Let's go."

The three of them covered another mile before startling a small herd of antelope. The lieutenant watched the white-rumped pronghorns bound over the prairie until they were almost out of sight.

When he turned to check Two Socks's reaction, he could no longer see him.

The wolf was gone.

Clouds were building in the west, towering thunderheads filled with lightning. As he and Cisco started back, Dunbar kept an eye on the storm front. It was moving toward them, and the prospect of rain made the lieutenant's face look sour.

He really had to do his laundry.

The blankets had started to smell like dirty socks.

CHAPTER VIII

one

Lieutenant Dunbar was right in step with the time-honored tradition of predicting weather.

He was wrong.

The spectacular storm slipped through during the night without loosing a single drop of rain on Fort Sedgewick, and the day that broke the next morning was the purest pastel blue, air that was like something for drinking, and merciful sun that toasted everything it touched without searing a single blade of grass.

Over coffee, the lieutenant reread his official reports of days past and concluded he had done a pretty fair job of putting down facts. He debated the subjective items for a time. More than once he took up his pen to cross out a line, but in the end he changed nothing.

He was pouring a second cup when he noticed the curious cloud far to the west. It was brown, a dusky brown cloud, lying low and flat at the base of the sky.

It was too hazy to be a cloud. It looked like smoke from a fire. The lightning from the night before must have struck something. Perhaps the prairie had been set afire. He made a mental note to keep an eye on the smoky cloud and to make his afternoon ride in that direction if it persisted. He had heard that prairie fires could be huge and fast-moving.

two

They had come in the day before, close to twilight, and unlike Lieutenant Dunbar, they had been rained on.

But their spirits were not dampened in the least. The last leg of the long trek from a winter camp far to the south was finished. That, and the coming of spring, made for the happiest of times. Their ponies were growing fatter and stronger with each succeeding day, the march had toned everyone after months of relative inactivity, and preparations would begin at once for the summer hunts. That made them happier still, happy in the pit of each and every belly. The buffalo were coming. Feasting was right around the corner.

And because this had been a summer camp for generations, a strong spirit of homecoming lightened the hearts of everyone, all 172 men, women, and children.

The winter had been mild and the band had come through it in excellent shape. Today, on the first morning home, it was a camp of smiles. Youngsters frolicked in the pony herd, warriors swapped stories, and the women mowed through the chores of breakfast with more gaiety than usual.

They were Comanche.

The smoke cloud Lieutenant Dunbar thought was a prairie fire had risen from their cooking fires.

They were camped on the same stream, eight miles west of Fort Sedgewick.

three

Dunbar grabbed up everything he could find that needed washing and stuffed it in a rucksack. Then he draped the foul blankets over his shoulders, searched out a chunk of soap, and headed down the river.

As he squatted by the stream, pulling laundry out of the sack, he thought, Sure would like to wash what I got on.

But there would be nothing left to wear while everything dried.

There was the overcoat.

But how stupid, he said to himself. With a little laugh he said out loud, "It's just me and the prairie."

It was a good feeling to be naked. He even laid his officer's hat aside in the spirit of the thing.

When he bent toward the water with an armful of clothes, he saw a reflection of himself in the glassy surface, the first he'd seen in more than two weeks. It gave him pause.

His hair was longer. His face looked leaner, even with the beard that had sprouted. He'd definitely lost some weight. But the lieutenant thought he looked good. His eyes were as keen as he'd ever seen them, and as though he were acknowledging his affection for someone, he smiled boyishly at the reflection.

The longer he looked at the beard, the less he liked it. He ran back for his razor.

The lieutenant didn't think about his skin while he shaved. His skin had always been the same. White men come in many shades. Some are white as snow.

Lieutenant Dunbar was white enough to put your eyes out.

four

Kicking Bird had left camp before dawn. He knew his leaving would not be questioned. He never had to answer for his movements, and rarely for his actions. Not unless they were poorly taken actions. Poorly taken actions could lead to catastrophe. But though he was new, though he had been a fullfledged medicine man for only a year, none of his actions had led to catastrophe.

In fact, he had performed well. Twice he had worked minor miracles. He felt good about the miracles, but he felt just as good about the bread and butter of his job, seeing to the dayto-day welfare of the band. He performed myriad administrative duties, attended to squabbles of wide-ranging import, practiced a fair amount of medicine, and sat in on the endless councils that took place daily. All this in addition to providing for two wives and four children. And all of it done with one ear and one eye cocked to the Great Spirit; always listening, always watching for the slightest sound or sign.

Kicking Bird shouldered his many duties honorably, and everyone knew it. They knew it because they knew the man. Kicking Bird did not have a self-serving bone in his body, and wherever he rode, he rode with the weight of great respect.

Some of the other early risers might have wondered where he was going on that first morning, but they never dreamed of asking.

Kicking Bird was not on a special mission. He had ridden onto the prairie to clear his head. He disliked the big movements: winter to summer, summer to winter. The tremendous clang of it all distracted him. It distracted the ear and eye he tried to keep cocked at the Great Spirit, and on this first morning after the long march, he knew the din of setting up camp would be more than he could manage.

So he had taken his best pony, a broad-backed chestnut, and ridden off toward the river, following it several miles until he came to a knobby rise he had known since boyhood.

There he waited for the prairie to reveal itself, and when it did, Kicking Bird was pleased. It had never looked so good to him. All the signs were right for an abundant summer. There would be enemies, of course, but the band was very strong now. Kicking Bird couldn't suppress a smile. He was sure it would be a prosperous season.

After an hour his exhilaration had not diminished. Kicking Bird said to himself, I will make a walk in this beautiful country, and he kicked his pony into the still-rising sun.

five

He had sunk both blankets into the water before he remembered that laundry must be pounded. There wasn't a single rock in sight.

Clutching the dripping blankets and the rest of the clothes against his chest, Lieutenant Dunbar, the laundry novice, wandered downstream, stepping lightly in his bare feet.

A quarter mile later he found an outcropping that made for a nice bench. He worked up a good lather and, as a novice will do, rubbed the soap rather tentatively into one of the blankets.

By and by he got the hang of it. With each article the routine of soaping, beating, and rinsing became more assured, and toward the end Dunbar was flying through his work with the single-mindedness, if not the precision, of a seasoned laundress.

In only two weeks out here he had cultivated a new appreciation for detail and, knowing the first pieces had been botched, he redid them.

A scrubby oak was growing partway up the slope and he hung his laundry there. It was a good spot, full of sun and not too breezy. Still, it would take a while for everything to dry, and he'd forgotten his tobacco fixings.

The naked lieutenant decided not to wait.

He started back for the fort.

six

Kicking Bird had heard disconcerting stories about their numbers. On more than one occasion he had heard people say they were as plentiful as birds, and this gave the shaman an uneasy feeling in the back of his mind.

And yet, on the basis of what he had actually seen, the hair mouths inspired only pity.

They seemed to be a sad race.

Those poor soldiers at the fort, so rich in goods, so poor in everything else. They shot their guns poorly, they rode their big, slow horses poorly. They were supposed to be the white man's warriors, but they weren't alert. And they frightened so easily. Taking their horses had been laughable, like plucking berries from a bush.

They were a great mystery to Kicking Bird, these white people. He could not think of them without getting his mind baffled.

The soldiers at the fort, for instance. They lived without families. And they lived without their greatest chiefs. With the Great Spirit in evidence everywhere, for all to see, they worshipped things written down on paper. And they were so dirty. They didn't even keep themselves clean.

Kicking Bird could not imagine how these hair mouths could sustain themselves for even a year. And yet they were said to flourish. He did not understand it.

He had begun this line of thinking when he thought of the fort, when he thought of going near it. He expected them to be gone, but he thought he would see anyway. And now, as he sat on his pony, looking across the prairie, he could see at first glance that the place had been improved. The white man's fort was clean. A great hide was rolling in the wind. A little horse, a good-looking one, was standing in the corral. There was no movement. Not even a sound. The place should have been dead. But someone had kept it alive.

Kicking Bird urged his pony to a walk.

He had to have a closer look.

seven

Lieutenant Dunbar dallied as he made his way back along the stream. There was so much to see.

In a strangely ironic way he felt much less conspicuous without his clothes. Perhaps that was so. Every tiny plant, every buzzing insect, seemed to attract his attention. Everything was remarkably alive.

A red-tailed hawk with a ground squirrel dangling from its talons flew right in front of him, not a dozen feet overhead.

Halfway back he paused in the shade of a cottonwood to watch a badger dig out his burrow a few feet above the waterline. Every now and then the badger would glance back at the naked lieutenant, but he kept right on digging.

Close to the fort Dunbar stopped to watch the entanglement of two lovers. A pair of black water snakes were twisting ecstatically in the shallows of the stream, and like all lovers, they were oblivious, even when the lieutenant's shadow fell across the water.

He trudged up the slope enraptured, feeling as strong as anything out here, feeling like a true citizen of the prairie.

As his head cleared the rise, he saw the chestnut pony.

In the same instant he saw the silhouette, creeping in the shade under the awning. A split second later the figure stepped into the sun and Dunbar ducked down, settling into a cleft just below the bluff's lip.

He squatted on jellied legs, his ears as big as dishes, listening with a concentration that made hearing seem the only sense he possessed.

His mind raced. Fantastic images danced across the lieutenant's closed eyes. Fringed pants. Beaded moccasins. A hatchet with hair hanging from it. A breastplate of gleaming bone. The heavy, shining hair spilling halfway down his back. The black, deep-set eyes. The great nose. Skin the color of clay. The feather bobbing in the breeze at the back of his head.

He knew it was an Indian, but he had never expected anything so wild, and the shock of it had stunned him as surely as a blow to the head.

Dunbar stayed crouched below the bluff, his buttocks grazing the ground, beads of cold sweat coating his forehead. He could not grasp what he had seen. He was afraid to look again.

He heard a horse nicker and, sucking up his courage, peeked slowly over the bluff.

The Indian was in the corral. He was walking up to Cisco, a looped length of rope in his hand.

When Lieutenant Dunbar saw this, his paralysis evaporated. He stopped thinking altogether, leaped to his feet, and scrambled over the top of the bluff. He shouted out, his bellow cracking the stillness like a shot.

"You there!"

eight

Kicking Bird jumped straight into the air.

When he whirled to meet the voice that had startled him out of his skin, the Comanche medicine man came face-to-face with the strangest sight he had ever seen.

A naked man. A naked man marching straight across the yard with his fists balled, with his jaw set, and with skin so white that it hurt the eyes.

Kicking Bird stumbled backward in horror, righted himself, and instead of jumping the corral fence, he tore right through it. He raced across the yard, vaulted onto his pony, and galloped off as if the devil were on his tail.

Not once did he look back.

CHAPTER IX

one

April 27, 1863

Have made first contact with a wild Indian.

One came to the fort and tried to steal my horse. When I appeared he became frightened and ran off. Do not know how many more might be in the vicinity but am assuming that where there is one there are sure to be more.

Am taking steps to prepare for another visitation. I cannot make an adequate defense but will try to make a big impression when they come again.

I'm still alone, however, and unless troops arrive soon, all may be lost.

The man I encountered was a magnificent-looking fellow.

Lt. John J. Dunbar, U.S.A.

Dunbar spent the next two days taking steps, many of them geared toward creating an impression of strength and stability. It might have seemed lunatic, one man trying to prepare for the onslaught of countless enemies, but the lieutenant possessed a certain strength of character that allowed for working hard when he had very little. It was a good trait and it helped make him a good soldier.

He went about his preparations as if he were just another man at the post. His first order of business was to cache the provisions. He sorted through the entire inventory, separating only the most essential items. The rest he buried with great care in holes around the fort.

He stashed the tools, lamp oil, several kegs of nails, and other miscellaneous building materials in one of the old sleeping holes. Then he covered it with a piece of canvas tarp, spread several yards of dirt over the site, and after hours of meticulous landscaping, the cache looked like a natural part of the slope.

He carried two boxes of rifles and a half-dozen small barrels of gunpowder and shot onto the grassland. There he spaded up more than twenty pieces of prairie, each about a foot square, each with the sod and grass clinging to one another. At the same spot he dug a deep hole, roughly six by six, and buried the ordnance. By the end of the afternoon he had replaced the sections of sod and grass, tamping them down so carefully that not even the most practiced eye could have detected a disturbance. He marked the place with a bleached buffalo rib, which he drove into the ground at an angle a few yards in front of the secret spot.

In the supply house he found a pair of U.S. flags, and using two of the corral posts as poles, he flew them, one from the roof of the supply house, the other from the roof of his quarters.

The afternoon rides were pared down to short, circular patrols that he made around the fort, always keeping his post within sight.

Two Socks appeared as usual on the bluff, but Dunbar was too busy to pay him much attention.

He took to wearing a full uniform at all times, keeping his

high-topped riding boots shining, his hat free of dust, and his face shaved. He went nowhere, not even to the stream, without a rifle, a pistol, and a beltful of ammunition.

After two days of fevered activity he felt he was as ready as he could get.

> *April 29, 1863*
> *My presence here must have been reported by now.*
> *Have made all the preparations I can think of.*
> *Waiting.*
>
> *Lt. John J. Dunbar, U.S.A.*

two

But Lieutenant Dunbar's presence at Fort Sedgewick had not been reported.

Kicking Bird had kept The Man Who Shines Like Snow locked away in his thoughts. For two days the medicine man stayed to himself, deeply disturbed by what he had seen, struggling mightily for the meaning of what he first believed to be a nightmarish hallucination.

After much reflection, however, he admitted to himself that what he had seen was real.

In some ways this conclusion created more problems. The man was real. He had life. He was over there. Kicking Bird further concluded that The Man Who Shines Like Snow must be linked in some way to the fate of the band. Otherwise the Great Spirit would not have bothered to present the vision of him.

He had taken it upon himself to divine the meaning of this, but try as he might, he could not. The whole situation troubled him like nothing he had ever experienced.

His wives knew there was some kind of trouble as soon as

he returned from the fateful ride to Fort Sedgewick. They could see a distinct change in the expression of his eyes. But outside of taking extra care with their husband, the women said nothing as they went about their work.

three

There was a handful of men who, like Kicking Bird, carried great influence in the band. None was more influential than Ten Bears. He was the most venerated, and at sixty years, his toughness, his wisdom, and the remarkably steady hand with which he guided the band were exceeded only by his uncanny ability to know which way the winds of fortune, no matter how small or large, were going to shift next.

Ten Bears could see at first glance that something had happened to Kicking Bird, whom he looked on as an important staff member. But he, too, said nothing. It was his custom, and it served him well, to wait and watch.

But by the end of the second day it seemed apparent to Ten Bears that something serious might have happened, and late in the afternoon he paid a casual visit to Kicking Bird's home.

For twenty minutes they smoked the medicine man's tobacco in silence before slipping into bits and pieces of chit-chat concerning unimportant matters.

At just the right moment Ten Bears drove the conversation deeper with a general question. He asked how Kicking Bird felt, from a spiritual point of view, about prospects for the summer.

Without going into detail, the medicine man told him the signs were good. A priest who cares not to elaborate about his work was a dead giveaway to Ten Bears. He was certain something had been held back.

Then, with the skill of a master diplomat, Ten Bears asked about potentially negative signs.

The two men's eyes met. Ten Bears had trapped him in the most gentle way.

"There is one," said Kicking Bird.

As soon as he said that, Kicking Bird felt a sudden release, as though his hands had been unbound, and it all spilled out: the ride, the fort, the beautiful buckskin horse, and The Man Who Shines Like Snow.

When he finished, Ten Bears relit the pipe and puffed thoughtfully before laying it between them.

"Did he look like a god?" he asked.

"No. He looked like a man," replied Kicking Bird. "He walked like a man, sounded like a man. His form was as a man's. Even his sex was as a man's."

"I have never heard of a white man without clothes," said Ten Bears, and his expression turned suspicious. "His skin actually reflected the sun?"

"It stung the eyes."

The men fell into silence once again.

Ten Bears got to his feet.

"I will think about this now."

four

Ten Bears shooed everyone out of his lodge and sat by himself for more than an hour, thinking about what Kicking Bird had told him.

It was hard thinking.

He had only seen white men on a few occasions, and like Kicking Bird, he could not fathom their behavior. Because of their reputed numbers they would have to be watched and somehow controlled, but until now, they had been nothing beyond a persistent nuisance to the mind.

Ten Bears never liked thinking about them.

How could any race be so mixed-up? he thought.

But he was drifting from the point, and inwardly Ten Bears chastised himself for his messy thinking. What did he really know about the white people? He knew next to nothing. . . . That, he had to admit.

This strange being at the fort. Perhaps it was a spirit. Perhaps it was a different type of white man. It was possible, Ten Bears conceded, that the being Kicking Bird had seen was the first of a whole new race of people.

The old headman sighed to himself as his brain filled to overflowing. There was already so much to do, with the summer hunting. And now this.

He could not come to a conclusion.

Ten Bears decided to call a council.

five

The meeting convened before sunset, but it lasted long into the evening, long enough to draw the collective attention of the village, especially the young men, who gathered in little groups to speculate about what their elders might be discussing.

After an hour's worth of preliminaries they got down to business. Kicking Bird related his story. When he was finished Ten Bears solicited the opinions of his fellows.

They were many, and they were wide-ranging.

Wind In His Hair was the youngest among them, an impulsive but seasoned fighter. He thought they should send a party immediately, a party to ride down and shoot arrows into the white man. If he was a god, the arrows would have no effect. If he was mortal, they would have one less hair mouth to worry about. Wind In His Hair would be happy to lead the party.

His suggestion was rejected by the others. If this person was a god, it would not be a good idea to shoot arrows into him. And killing a white man had to be handled with a certain delicacy. A dead white man might produce many more live ones.

Horn Bull was known to be conservative. No one would dare to question his bravery, but it was true that he usually opted for discretion in most matters. He made a simple suggestion. Send a delegation to parlay with The Man Who Shines Like Snow.

Wind In His Hair waited until Horn Bull had finished this rather long declaration. Then he leaped on the idea with a vengeance. The gist of his speech pounded home a point that no one cared to dispute. Comanches did not send respected warriors to ask the business of a single puny, trespassing white man.

No one said much after this, and when they began again, the talk shifted to other topics, such as preparations for the hunt and the possibility of sending war parties to various tribes. For another hour the men sifted through scraps of rumor and hard information that might have some bearing on the band's welfare.

When at last they returned to the touchy question of what to do about the white man, Ten Bears's eyes were drooping and his head began to nod. There was no point in going any further tonight. The old man was already snoring lightly as they left his lodge.

The matter remained unresolved.

But that did not mean action was not going to be taken.

Any small, close-knit group is hard-pressed to keep secrets, and later that night Horn Bull's fourteen-year-old son heard his father mumble the essence of the council's discussion to a visiting uncle. He heard about the fort and the Man Who Shines Like Snow. And he heard about the beautiful buckskin horse, the stout little mount Kicking Bird had described as the equal of ten ponies. It fired his imagination.

Horn Bull's son could not sleep with this knowledge in his head, and late that night he crept out of the lodge to tell his two best friends what he knew, to tell of the grand opportunity he had chanced upon.

As he expected, Frog Back and Smiles A Lot balked at first. There was only one horse. How could one horse be split three ways? That was not much. And the possibility of a white god prowling around down there. That was a lot to think about.

But Horn Bull's son was ready for them. He'd thought it all out. The white god, that was the best part. Didn't they all want to take the warpath? And when the time came, wouldn't they have to accompany veteran warriors? And wasn't it likely that they would see little direct action? Wasn't it likely that they would have little chance to distinguish themselves?

But to ride against a white god. Three boys against a god. That would be something. People might make up songs about that. If they pulled it off, the chances were good that all three would soon be leading war parties instead of just following along.

And the horse. Well, Horn Bull's son would own the horse, but the other two could ride it. They could race it if they wanted.

Now, who can say this is not a great plan?

Their hearts were already thumping as they stole across the river and cut three good mounts out of the pony herd. On foot, they led the horses away from the village, then circled it in a wide arc.

When they were finally clear, the boys kicked their ponies into a gallop, and singing songs to keep their hearts strong, they rode along the darkened prairie, staying close by the stream that would take them directly to Fort Sedgewick.

six

For two nights Lieutenant Dunbar was all soldier, sleeping with one ear open.

But the teenagers who came did not come like pranksters out for a thrill. They were Comanche boys and they were engaged in the most serious action of their young lives.

Lieutenant Dunbar never heard them come in.

The galloping hooves and the boys' whooping woke him, but they were only sounds, melting into the vastness of the prairie night, by the time he stumbled through the door of the hut.

seven

The boys rode hard. Everything had gone perfectly. Taking the horse had been easy, and best of all, they had not even seen the white god.

But they were taking no chances. Gods could do many fantastic things, particularly when angered. The boys didn't stop for any backslapping. They rode full-out, determined not to slow until they'd reached the safety of the village.

They weren't two miles from the fort, however, when Cisco decided to exercise his will. And it was not his will to go with these boys.

They were at a full run when the buckskin wheeled sharply away. Horn Bull's son was pulled off his pony as if he'd been low-bridged by a tree limb.

Frog Back and Smiles A Lot tried to give chase, but Cisco kept running, the long lead line trailing behind him. He had true speed, and when the speed gave out, his stamina took over.

The Indian ponies wouldn't have caught him if they'd been fresh.

eight

Dunbar had just gotten a pot of coffee going and was sitting morosely by his fire when Cisco trotted casually into the flickering light.

The lieutenant was more relieved than he was surprised. Having his horse stolen had made him mad as a hornet. But Cisco had been stolen before, twice to be exact, and like a faithful dog, he had always found a way to come back.

Lieutenant Dunbar gathered in the Comanche lead line, checked his horse for cuts, and, with the sky turning pink in the east, led the little buckskin down the slope for a drink.

While he sat by the stream, Dunbar watched the surface. The river's little fish were beginning to bite at the hordes of invisible insects lighting on top of the water, and the lieutenant suddenly felt as helpless as a mayfly.

The Indians could have killed him as easily as they had stolen his horse.

The idea of dying bothered him. I could be dead by this afternoon, he thought.

What bothered him even more was the prospect of dying like an insect.

He decided then and there that, if he was going to die, it would not be in bed.

He knew that something was in motion, something that made him vulnerable in a way that sent a chill up his spine. He might be a citizen of the prairie, but that didn't mean he was accepted. He was the new kid in school. Their eyes would be on him.

His spine was still tingling as he led Cisco back up the slope.

nine

Horn Bull's son had broken his arm.

He was given over to Kicking Bird as soon as the bedraggled trio of would-be warriors entered the village.

The boys had begun to worry from the moment Horn Bull's son found that his arm would not work. If no one had gotten hurt, they might have been able to keep their botched raid a secret. But immediately there had been questions, and the boys, though they might be given to sprucing up the facts, were Comanche. And Comanches had great difficulty lying. Even Comanche boys.

While Kicking Bird worked on his arm, and with his father and Ten Bears listening, Horn Bull's son told the truth of what had happened.

It was not unusual for a stolen horse to break away from its captors and return home, but because they might be dealing with a spirit, the matter of the horse took on a great importance and the older men questioned the injured boy closely.

When he told them the horse had not spooked, that he had broken away deliberately, the faces of his elders grew noticeably longer.

Another council was called.

This time everyone knew what it was about, for the story of the boys' misadventure quickly became the talk of the camp. Some of the more impressionable people in the village suffered brief bouts of the jitters when they learned that a strange white god might be lurking in the neighborhood, but mostly everyone went about their business with the feeling that Ten Bears's council would figure something out.

Still, everyone was anxious.

Only one among them was truly terrified.

CHAPTER X

one

She'd been terrified the summer before, when it was discovered that white soldiers had come into the country. The band had never met the hair mouths, except for killing several on isolated occasions. She had hoped they would never meet them.

When the white soldiers' horses were stolen late last summer, she had panicked and run off. She was sure the white soldiers would come to the village. But they didn't.

Still, she was on pins and needles until it was determined that, without their horses, the white soldiers were practically helpless. Then she had been able to relax a little. But it wasn't until they broke camp and were on the winter trail that the awful cloud of fear that followed her all summer finally lifted.

Now summer was on them again, and all along the trail from the winter camp she had prayed fiercely for the hair mouths to be gone. Her prayers had not been answered, and once again her days were troubled, hour by hour.

Her name was Stands With A Fist.

She alone, among all the Comanches, knew that the white man was not a god. The story of Kicking Bird's encounter did puzzle her, however. A single naked white man? Out here? In the Comanche homeland? It didn't make sense. But no matter. Without knowing precisely why, she knew he was not a god. Something old told her so.

She heard the story that morning, on her way to the once-a-month lodge, the one set aside for menstruating women. She'd been thinking of her husband. Normally she did not like going to the lodge because she would miss his company. He was wonderful, a brave, handsome, and altogether exceptional man. A model husband. She had never been struck by him, and though both their babies had died (one in childbirth, the other a few weeks later), he had stubbornly refused to take another wife.

People had urged him to take another wife. Even Stands With A Fist had suggested it. But he said simply, "You are plenty," and she had never spoken of it again. In her secret heart she was proud that he was happy with her alone.

She missed him terribly now. Before they broke winter camp he'd taken a large party against the Utes. Nearly a month had passed with no word of him or the other warriors. But because she was already cut off from him, going to the once-a-month lodge had not seemed as hard as usual. As she made ready to leave that morning, the young Comanche woman was comforted by the notion that a close friend or two would be sequestered with her, women with whom the time would pass easily.

But on her way to the lodge she heard of Kicking Bird's odd story. Then she heard the story of the foolish raid. Stands With A Fist's morning had exploded in her face. Once more a great dread had settled on her square, straight shoulders like an iron blanket, and she entered the once-a-month lodge badly shaken.

But she was very strong. Her beautiful light brown eyes, eyes that shone with intelligence, revealed nothing as she sewed and chatted through the morning with her friends.

They knew the danger. The whole band knew. But it served no one to talk about it. So no one did.

All afternoon her tough, tiny frame moved about the lodge, showing nothing of the heavy blanket hanging over it.

Stands With A Fist was twenty-six years old.

For almost twelve of those years she had been a Comanche. Before that she had been white.

Before that she had been . . . what was it?

She only thought of the name on the rare occasions when she could not avoid thinking about the whites. Then, for some inexplicable reason, it would pop up in front of her eyes.

Oh, yes, she thought in Comanche, I remember it. Before, I was Christine.

Then she would think of before, and it was always the same. It was like passing through an old, misty curtain and the two worlds became one, the old mingling with the new. Stands With A Fist was Christine and Christine was Stands With A Fist.

Her complexion had darkened over the years, and the whole of her appearance had a distinctly wild cast about it. But despite two full-term pregnancies, her figure was like that of a white woman. And her hair, which refused to grow beyond her shoulders and refused to stay straight, still held a pronounced cherry tint. And, of course, there were the two light brown eyes.

Stands With A Fist's great fear was well founded. She could never hope to escape it. To a white eye there would always be something strange about the woman in the once-a-month lodge. Something not altogether Indian. And to the knowing eyes of her own people there was something not altogether Indian, even after all this time.

It was a terrible, heavy burden, but Stands With A Fist never spoke of it, much less complained. She carried it silently and with great bravery through every day of her Indian life, and she carried it for one monumental reason.

Stands With A Fist wanted to stay where she was.

She was very happy.

CHAPTER XI

one

Ten Bears's council ended without resolution, but this was not an uncommon occurrence.

More often than not, a critical council ended indecisively, thus signaling the start of a whole new phase of the band's political life.

It was at these times that, should they choose to do so, people took independent action.

two

Wind In His Hair had lobbied hard for a second plan. Ride down and take the horse without harming the white man. But instead of boys, send men this time. The council rejected his second idea, but Wind In His Hair was not angry with anyone.

He had listened openly to all opinions and offered his solution. The solution had not been adopted, but the arguments against it had not convinced Wind In His Hair that his plan was poor.

He was a respected warrior, and like any respected warrior, he retained a supreme right.

He could do as he pleased.

If the council had been adamant, or if he put his plan into action and it went badly, there was a possibility he would be thrown out of the band.

Wind In His Hair had already considered this. The council had not been adamant; it had been befuddled. And as to himself . . . well . . . Wind In His Hair had never done badly.

So once the council had ended, he strode down one of the camp's more populous avenues, looking in on several friends as he went, saying the same thing at each lodge.

"I'm going down to steal that horse. Want to come?"

Each friend answered his question with one of their own.

"When?"

And Wind In His Hair had the same answer for everyone.

"Now."

three

It was a little party. Five men.

They rode out of the village and onto the prairie at a studied pace. They took it easy. But that didn't mean they were jovial.

They rode grimly, like blank-faced men going to the funeral of a distant relative.

Wind In His Hair had told them what to do when they went for the ponies.

"We'll take the horse. Watch him on the way back. Ride all around him. If there is a white man, don't shoot him, not unless he shoots at you. If he tries to talk, don't talk back. We'll take the horse and see what happens.''

Wind In His Hair wouldn't have admitted it to anyone, but he felt a wave of relief when they were in sight of the fort.

There was a horse in the corral, a good-looking one.

But there was no white man.

four

The white man had turned in well before noon. He slept for several hours. Around midafternoon he woke, pleased that his new idea was working.

Lieutenant Dunbar had decided to sleep during the day and stay up with a fire all night. The ones who stole Cisco had come at dawn, and the stories he'd heard always singled out dawn as the preferred hour of attack. This way he would be awake when they came.

He felt a little groggy after his long nap. And he'd perspired a lot. His body felt sticky. This was as good a time as any to get in a bath.

That's why he was hunkered down in the stream with a head full of suds and water up to his shoulders when he heard the five horsemen thundering along the bluff.

He thrashed out of the stream and went instinctively for his pants. He fumbled with the trousers before throwing them aside in favor of the big Navy revolver. Then he scurried up the slope on all fours.

five

They all got a look at him as they rode out with Cisco.

He was standing on the edge of the bluff. Water was dripping down his body. His head was covered with something white. There was a gun in his hand. All this was seen in glances thrown over shoulders. But no more than that. They were all remembering Wind In His Hair's instructions. With one warrior holding Cisco and the rest bunched around, they tore out of the fort in tight formation.

Wind In His Hair hung back.

The white man hadn't moved. He was standing still and straight on the edge of the bluff, his gun hand hanging by his side.

Wind In His Hair could have cared less about the white man. But he cared greatly about what the white man represented. It was every warrior's most constant enemy. The white man represented fear. It was one thing to withdraw from the field of battle after a hard fight, but to let fear fly in his face and do nothing . . . Wind In His Hair knew he could not let this happen.

He took his frantic pony in hand, swung him around, and galloped down on the lieutenant.

six

In his wild scramble up the bluff Lieutenant Dunbar was everything a soldier should be. He was rushing to meet the enemy. There were no other thoughts in his head.

But all that left him the moment he surmounted the bluff.

He had geared himself for criminals, a gang of lawbreakers, burglars who needed punishing.

What he found instead was a pageant, a pageant of action so breathtaking that, like a kid at his first big parade, the lieutenant was powerless to do anything but stand there and watch it go by.

The furious rush of the ponies as they pounded past. Their shining coats, the feathers flying from their bridles and manes and tails, the decorations on their rumps. And the men on their backs, riding with the abandon of children on make-believe toys. Their rich, dark skins, the lines of sinewy muscle standing out clearly. The gleaming, braided hair, the bows and lances and rifles, the paint running in bold lines down their faces and arms.

And everything in such magnificent harmony. Together, the men and horses looked like the great blade of a plow rushing across the landscape, its furrow barely scratching the surface.

It was of a color and speed and wonder he had never imagined. It was the celebrated glory of war captured in a single living mural, and Dunbar stood transfixed, not so much a man as he was a pair of eyes.

He was in a deep fog, and it had just begun to dissipate when Dunbar realized one of them was coming back.

Like a sleeper in a dream, he struggled to come awake. His brain was trying to send commands, but the communication kept breaking down. He could not move a muscle.

The rider was coming fast, stampeding toward him on a collision course. Lieutenant Dunbar did not think of being run over. He did not think of dying. He had lost all capacity for thought. He stood unmoving, focused trancelike on the pony's dilated nostrils.

seven

When Wind In His Hair was within thirty feet of the lieutenant, he pulled up so sharply that, for a moment, his horse literally sat on the ground. With a great spring upward, the excited pony gained his feet and began at once to dance and pitch and whirl. Wind In His Hair held him close all the while, barely aware of the gyrations going on underneath him.

He was glaring at the naked, motionless white man. The figure was absolutely still. Wind In His Hair could not see him blinking. He could see the bright white chest heaving slowly up and down, however. The man was alive.

He seemed not to be afraid. Wind In His Hair appreciated the white man's lack of fear, but at the same time, it made him nervous. The man should be afraid. How could he not be? Wind In His Hair felt his own fear creeping back. It was making his skin tingle.

He raised his rifle over his head and roared out three emphatic sentences.

"I am Wind In His Hair!"

"Do you see that I am not afraid of you?"

"Do you see?"

The white man did not answer, and Wind In His Hair suddenly felt satisfied. He had come straight to the face of this would-be enemy. He had challenged the naked white man, and the white man had done nothing. It was enough.

He spun his pony around, gave him his head, and dashed off to rejoin his friends.

eight

Lieutenant Dunbar watched dazedly as the warrior rode away. The words were still echoing in his head. The sound of the words, anyway, like the barking of a dog. Though he had no idea what they meant, the sounds had seemed a pronouncement, as if the warrior was telling him something.

Gradually he began to come out of it. The first thing he

felt was the revolver in his hand. It was extraordinarily heavy. He let it drop.

Then he sank slowly to his knees and rolled back on his buttocks. He sat for a long time, drained as he had never been before, weak as a newborn puppy.

For a time he thought he might never move again, but at last he got to his feet and wobbled to the hut. It was only with a supreme effort that he managed to roll a cigarette. But he was too weak to smoke it, and the lieutenant fell asleep after two or three puffs.

nine

The second escape had a different wrinkle or two, but in general, things went the way they had before.

About two miles out the five Comanches settled their horses into an easy lope. There were riders to the rear and on either side, so Cisco took the only route left to him.

He went forward.

The men had just begun to exchange a few words when the buckskin leaped as if he'd been stung on the rump, and shot ahead.

The man holding the lead line was pulled straight over the head of his pony. For a few fleeting seconds Wind In His Hair had a chance for the lead line bouncing along the ground behind Cisco, but he was an instant too late. It slipped through his fingers.

After that all that remained was the chase. It was not so merry for the Comanches. The man who had been pulled off had no chance at all, and the remaining four pursuers had no luck.

One man lost his horse when it stepped into a prairie dog hole and snapped a foreleg. Cisco was quick as a cat that afternoon, and two more riders were thrown trying to make their ponies imitate his lightning zigs and zags.

That left only Wind In His Hair. He kept pace for several hundred yards, but when his own horse finally began to play out, they still had closed no ground, and he decided it wasn't worth running his favorite pony to death for something he couldn't catch.

While the pony caught his breath, Wind In His Hair watched the buckskin long enough to see that he was heading in the general direction of the fort, and his frustration was tempered with the notion that perhaps Kicking Bird was right. It might be a magic horse, something belonging to a magic person.

He met the others on his way back. It was obvious that Wind In His Hair had failed, and no one inquired as to the details.

No one said a word.

They made the long ride home in silence.

CHAPTER XII

one

Wind In His Hair and the men returned to find their village in mourning.

The party that had been out so long against the Utes had come home at last.

And the news was not good.

They'd stolen only six horses, not enough to cover their own losses. They were empty-handed after all that time on the trail.

With them were four badly injured men, of which only one would survive. But the real tragedy was counted in the six men who had been killed, six very fine warriors. And worse yet, there were only four blanket-shrouded corpses on the travois.

They had not been able to recover two of the dead, and sadly, the names of these men would never be spoken again.

One of them was Stands With A Fist's husband.

two

Because she was in the once-a-month lodge, word had to be passed from outside by two of her husband's friends.

She seemed to take the news impassively at first, sitting still as a statue on the floor of the lodge, her hands entwined on her lap, her head bowed slightly. She sat like that most of the afternoon, letting grief eat its way slowly through her heart while the other women went about their business.

They watched her, however, partly because they all knew how close Stands With A Fist and her husband had been. But she was a white woman, and that, more than anything else, was cause for watching. None of them knew how a white mind would work in this kind of crisis. So they watched with a mixture of caring and curiosity.

It was well they did.

Stands With A Fist was so deeply devastated that she didn't make a peep all afternoon. She didn't shed a single tear. She just sat. All the while her mind was running dangerously fast. She thought of her loss, of her husband, and finally of herself.

She played back the events of her life with him, all of it appearing in fractured but vivid detail. Over and over, one particular time came back to her . . . the one and only time she had cried.

It was on a night not long after the death of their second child. She had held out, trying everything she knew to keep from caving in to the misery. She was still holding out when the tears came. She tried to stop them by burying her face in the sleeping robe. They had already had the talk about another wife, and he had already said the words, "You are plenty." But it was not enough to stem the grief of the second baby's passing, grief she knew he shared, and she had buried her wet face in the robe. But she could not stop, and the tears led to sobbing.

When it was over she lifted her head and found him sitting

quietly at the edge of the fire, poking at it aimlessly, his unfocused eyes looking through the flames.

When their eyes met she said, "I am nothing."

He made no reply at first. But he looked straight into her soul with an expression so peaceful that she could not resist its calming effect. Then she had seen the faintest of smiles steal across his mouth as he said the words again.

"You are plenty."

She remembered it so well: his deliberate rise from the fire, his little motion that said, "Move over," his easy slide under the robe, his arms gathering her in so softly.

And she remembered the unconsciousness of the love they made, so free of movement and words and energy. It was like being borne aloft to float endlessly in some unseen, heavenly stream. It was their longest night. When they would reach the edge of sleep they would somehow begin again. And again. And again. Two people of one flesh.

Even the coming of the sun did not stop them. For the first and only times in their lives, neither left the lodge that morning.

When sleep finally did find them, it was simultaneous, and Stands With A Fist remembered drifting off with the feeling that the burden of being two people was suddenly so light that it ceased to matter. She remembered feeling no longer Indian or white. She felt herself as a single being, one person, undivided.

Stands With A Fist blinked herself back to the present of the once-a-month lodge.

She was no longer a wife, a Comanche, or even a woman. She was nothing now. What was she waiting for?

A hide scraper was lying on the hard-packed floor only a few feet away. She saw her hand around it. She saw it plunge deep into her breast, all the way to the hilt.

Stands With A Fist waited for the moment when everyone's attention was elsewhere. She rocked back and forth a few times, then lurched forward, covering the few feet across the floor on all fours.

Her hand went to it cleanly, and in a flash, the blade was in front of her face. She lifted it higher, screamed, and drove down with both hands, as if clasping some dear object to her heart.

In the middle of the split second it took the scraper to complete its flight, the first woman arrived. Though she missed the hands that held the knife there was enough of a collision to deflect its downward flight. The blade traveled sideways leaving a tiny track on the bodice of Stands With A Fist's dress as it passed over the left breast, ripped through the doeskin sleeve, and plowed into the fleshy part of her arm just above the elbow.

She fought like a demon, and the women had a tough time prying the scraper out of her hand. Once it was free, all the fight went out of the little white woman. She collapsed into the sisterly arms of her friends, and like the flood that comes when a stubborn valve is tripped, she began to sob convulsively.

They half carried, half dragged the tiny ball of shaking and tears to bed. While one friend cradled her like a baby, two others stopped the bleeding and patched up her arm.

She cried for so long that the women had to take turns holding her. At last her breathing started to grow less intense and the sobs faded to a steady whimpering. Then, without opening her tear-swollen eyes, she spoke repeating the same words over and over, chanting them softly to no one but herself.

"I am nothing. I am nothing. I am nothing."

In the early evening they filled a hollowed-out horn with a thin broth and fed it to her. She began with hesitant sips, but the more she drank, the more she needed. She drained the last of it with a long gulp and lay back on the bedding, her eyes wide as they stared past her friends to the ceiling.

"I am nothing," she said again. But now the tone of her pronouncement was measured with serenity, and the other women knew she had passed through the most dangerous stage of her grief.

With kind words of encouragement, murmured sweetly,

they stroked her tangled hair and tucked the edges of a blanket around her small shoulders.

three

At about the same time exhaustion carried Stands With A Fist into a deep, dreamless sleep, Lieutenant Dunbar woke to the sound of hooves, stamping in the doorway of his sod hut.

Not knowing the sound, and hazy from his long sleep, the lieutenant lay quiet, blinking himself back awake while his hand fumbled along the floor for the Navy revolver. Before he could find it, he recognized the sound. It was Cisco, come back again.

Still on guard, Dunbar slipped noiselessly off the bunk, and creeping past his horse in a crouch, he went outside.

It was dark but early yet. The evening star was alone in the sky. The lieutenant listened and watched. No one was about.

Cisco had followed him into the yard, and when Lieutenant Dunbar absently laid a hand on his neck, he found the hair stiff with dried sweat. He grinned then and said out loud:

"I guess you gave them a hard time, didn't you? Let's get you a drink."

Leading Cisco down to the stream, he was amazed at how strong he felt. His paralysis at the sight of the afternoon raid, though he recalled it vividly, seemed something far away. Not dim, but far away, like history. It was a baptism, he concluded, a baptism that had catapulted him from imagination to reality. The warrior who had ridden up and barked at him had been real. The men who took Cisco had been real. He knew them now.

As Cisco fiddled with the water, splashing it with his lips, Lieutenant Dunbar let his mind run further along this vein of thought and struck pay dirt.

Waiting, he thought, That's what I've been doing.

He shook his head, laughing inwardly to himself. I've been waiting. He chucked a stone into the water. Waiting for what? For someone to find me? For Indians to take my horse? To see a buffalo?

He couldn't believe himself. He'd never walked on eggs, and yet that was what he'd been doing these last weeks. Walking on eggs, waiting for something to happen.

I better put a stop to this right now, he said to himself.

Before he could think any further, his eyes caught something. Color was reflecting off the water on the other side of the stream.

Lieutenant Dunbar glanced up the slope behind him.

An enormous harvest moon was beginning to rise.

On pure impulse, he swung onto Cisco's back and rode to the top of the bluff.

It was a magnificent sight, this great moon, bright as an egg yolk, filling the night sky as if it were a whole new world come to call just on him.

He hopped off Cisco, made himself a smoke, and watched spellbound as the moon climbed quickly overhead, its gradations of topography clear as a map.

As it rose, the prairie grew brighter and brighter. He had known only darkness on previous nights, and this flood of illumination was something like an ocean suddenly drained of its water.

He had to go into it.

They rode at a walk for half an hour, and Dunbar enjoyed every minute of it. When he finally turned back, he was charged with confidence.

Now he was glad for all that had happened. He wasn't going to mope anymore about soldiers who refused to arrive. He was not going to change his sleeping habits. He was not going to patrol in scared little circles, and he was not going to pass any more nights with one ear and one eye open.

He wasn't going to wait any longer. He was going to force the issue.

Tomorrow morning he was going to ride out and find the Indians.

And what if they ate him up?

Well, if they ate him up, the devil could have the leftovers.

But there would be no more waiting.

four

When she opened her eyes at dawn, the first thing she saw was another pair of eyes. Then she realized there were several sets of eyes staring down at her. It all came rushing back, and Stands With A Fist felt a sudden wave of embarrassment at all this attention. She'd made the attempt in such an undignified, un-Comanche-like way.

She wanted to hide her face.

They asked her how she felt and if she wanted to eat, and Stands With A Fist said yes, she felt better, and yes, it would be good to eat.

While she ate she watched the women go about their little bits of business, and this, along with the sleep and the food, had a restorative effect. Life was moving ahead, and seeing this made her feel more like a person again.

But when she felt around for her heart, she could tell by the stabbing that it was broken. It would have to be healed if she was to continue in this life, and that could be best accomplished with a reasoned and thorough mourning.

She must mourn for her husband.

To do that properly she must leave the lodge.

It was still early when she made ready to go. They braided her tangled hair and sent two youngsters off on errands: one to fetch her best dress, the other to cut one of her husband's ponies from the herd.

No one discouraged her when Stands With A Fist ran a belt through the scabbard of her finest knife and fastened it at her waist. They had prevented something irrational the day before, but she was calmer now, and if Stands With A Fist still wanted to take her life, then so be it. Many women had done so in years past.

They trailed behind her as she walked out of the lodge, so beautiful and strange and sad. One of them gave her a leg up onto the pony. Then the pony and the woman walked away, heading out of the basin that held the camp and onto the open prairie.

No one cried after her, no one wept, and no one waved good-bye. They only watched her go. But each of her friends was hoping she would not be too hard on herself and that she would come back.

All of them were fond of Stands With A Fist.

five

Lieutenant Dunbar was hurrying through his preparations. He'd already slept past sunrise and he'd wanted to be up at dawn. So he hurried through his coffee, puffing away on his first cigarette while his mind tried to order everything as efficiently as possible.

He jumped on the dirty work first, starting with the flag on the supply house. It was newer than the one flying from his own quarters, so he climbed the crumbling sod wall and pulled it down.

He split a corral pole, shoved it into the side of his boot, and, after careful measurement, lopped a few inches off the top. Then he attached the flag. It didn't look bad.

He worked for more than an hour on Cisco, trimming up the fetlocks around each hoof, combing out his mane and tail, and greasing the heavy black hair of both with bacon fat.

Most of the time was spent on his coat. Lieutenant Dunbar rubbed it out and brushed it down a half-dozen times until, at last, he stepped back and saw that there was no point in doing more. The buckskin was shining like something on the glossy page of a picture book.

He tied his horse up short, to keep him from lying down in the dust, and hustled back to the sod hut. There, he pulled out his dress uniform and went over every inch with a fine brush, snatching off stray hairs and flicking away the smallest balls of lint. He polished all the buttons. If he'd had paint, he might have touched up the epaulets and yellow stripes running down the outside of each trouser leg. He made do with the brush and a little spittle. When he was done the uniform looked more than passable.

He spit-shined his new knee-length riding boots and set them next to the uniform he'd laid out on the bed.

When it was finally time to work on himself, he picked up a rough towel and his shaving kit and hotfooted it down to the stream. He jumped in, soaped himself down, rinsed, and jumped back out, the whole operation taking less than five minutes. Taking care not to nick himself, the lieutenant shaved twice. When he could run a hand over his jaw and neck without hitting a whisker, he scampered back up the bluff and got dressed.

six

Cisco bent his neck and stared quizzically at the figure coming toward him, paying special attention to the bright red sash fluttering at the man's waist. Even if the sash had not been there, it's likely the horse's eyes would have remained fixed. No one had seen Lieutenant Dunbar in quite this form before. Cisco certainly hadn't, and he knew his master as well as anyone.

The lieutenant always dressed to get by, putting little emphasis on the glitter of parades or inspections or meetings with generals.

But if the finest army minds had put their heads together in order to produce the ultimate junior officer, they would have fallen far short of what Lieutenant Dunbar had wrought on this crystal-clear May morning.

Right down to the big Navy revolver swinging gently at his hip, he was every young girl's dream of the man in uniform. The vision he presented was so full of dash and sparkle that no feminine heart could have failed to skip a beat at the sight of him. The most cynical head would have been compelled to turn, and the tightest lips would have found themselves forming the words:

"Who is that?"

After slipping the bit into Cisco's mouth, he grabbed a hunk of mane and swung effortlessly onto the buckskin's glossy back. They trotted over to the supply house, where the lieutenant leaned down and picked up the guidon and flag leaning against the wall. He slid the staff into his left boot, grasped the standard with his left hand, and guided Cisco toward the open prairie.

When he'd gone a hundred yards Dunbar stopped and looked back, knowing there was a possibility he would never see this place again. He glanced at the sun and saw that it was no later than midmorning. He would have plenty of time to find them. Off to the west he could see the flat, smoky cloud that had appeared three mornings in a row. That would have to be them.

The lieutenant looked down at the toes of his boots. They were reflecting the sunlight. A little sigh of doubt came out of him, and for a split second he wished for a stiff shot of whiskey. Then he clucked to Cisco, and the little horse rolled into a lope that carried them west. The breeze was up and Old Glory was popping as he rode out to meet . . . to meet he knew not what.

But he was going.

seven

Without being planned at all, Stands With a Fist's mourning was highly ritualistic.

She had no intention of dying now. What she wanted was to clean out the warehouse of grief inside her. She wanted the most thorough cleansing possible, and so she took her time.

Quiet and methodical, she rode for almost an hour before she happened upon a spot that suited her, a place where the gods were likely to congregate.

To one who lived on the prairie it would pass for a hill. To anyone else it would have been nothing more than a bump on the land, like a small swell on a broad, flat sea. There was a single tree at its crest, a knobby old oak that somehow clung to life despite being mangled through the years by passersby. In every direction it was the only tree she could see.

It was a very lonely place. It seemed just right. She climbed to the top, slid off her pony, walked a few feet down the backside of the slope, and sat cross-legged on the ground.

The breeze was bouncing her braids around, so she reached up, undid them both, and let her cherry-colored hair fly in the wind. Then she closed her eyes, began to rock quietly back and forth, and concentrated on the terrible thing that had happened in her life, concentrated on it to the exclusion of all else.

Not many minutes later, the words to a song took shape in her head. She opened her mouth and verses tumbled out, as sure and strong as something she had diligently rehearsed.

Her singing was high. Sometimes her voice cracked. But she sang with her whole heart, with a beauty far surpassing something sweet to the ear.

The first was a simple song, celebrating his virtues as a warrior and a husband. Toward the end of it, a couplet came to her. It went:

> "He was a great man,
> He was great to me."

She paused before she sang these lines. Lifting her closed eyes to the sky, Stands With A Fist pulled her knife from its scabbard and deliberately sliced a two-inch cut on her forearm. She dropped her head and peeked at the cut. The blood was coming well. She resumed her singing, holding the knife fast in one hand.

She slashed herself several more times in the next hour. The incisions were shallow, but they produced a lot of blood, and this pleased Stands With A Fist. As her head grew lighter, her concentration grew stronger.

The singing was good. It told the whole story of their lives in a way that talking to someone wouldn't. Without going into detail, she left out nothing.

At last, when she'd made up a beautiful verse imploring the Great Spirit to give him an honored place in the world beyond the sun, a sudden surge of emotion hit her. There was little she hadn't covered. She was finishing, and that meant good-bye.

Tears flooded her eyes as she hiked up the doeskin dress to slash one of her thighs. She drew the blade across her leg hastily and gave a little gasp. The cut was very deep this time. She must have hit a major vein or artery, because when Stands With A Fist looked down, she could see the red gushing out with every beat of her heart.

She could try to stop the bleeding or she could go on singing.

Stands With A Fist chose the latter. She sat with her feet stretched out, letting her blood soak into the ground as she lifted her head high and wailed the words:

> "It will be good to die.
> It will be good to go with him.
> I will be going after."

eight

Because the breeze was blowing into her face, she never heard the rider's approach.

He'd noticed the slope from far out and decided that, since he'd seen nothing yet, it would be a good place to take a sighting. If he still couldn't see anything when he got there, he might climb that old tree.

Lieutenant Dunbar was halfway up the rise when the wind brought a strange, sad sound to his ears. Going with caution, he cleared the slope's crest and saw a person sitting a few feet down the hill, just in front of him. The person's back was turned. He couldn't say for sure whether it was a man or a woman. But it was definitely an Indian.

A singing Indian.

He was sitting still on Cisco's back when the person turned to face him.

nine

She couldn't have said what it was, but Stands With A Fist suddenly knew there was something standing behind her, and she turned to see.

She only caught a glimpse of the face below the hat before a surprise gust of wind whipped the colored flag around the man's head.

But the glimpse was enough. It told her he was a white soldier.

She didn't jump or run. There was something spellbinding about the image of the solitary horse soldier. The great colored flag and the shining pony and the sun blinking off the ornaments on his clothes. And now the face again as the flag unfurled: a hard, young face with shining eyes. Stands With

A Fist blinked several times, unsure if she was seeing a vision or a person. Nothing had moved but the flag.

Then the soldier shifted his seat on the horse. He was real. She rolled to her knees and started to draw away down the slope. She didn't make a sound, nor did she rush. Stands With A Fist had woken from one nightmare to find herself in another, one that was real. She moved slowly because she was too horrified to run.

ten

Dunbar was shocked when he saw her face. He didn't say the words, not even in his head, but if he had, the lieutenant would have said something like, "What kind of woman is this?"

The sharp little face, the tangled cherry hair, and the intelligent eyes, wild enough to love or hate with equal intensity, had thrown him completely. It didn't occur to him then that she might not be an Indian. Only one thing was on his mind at the moment.

He had never seen a woman who looked so original.

Before he could move or speak, she rolled to her knees, and he saw that she was covered with blood.

"Oh my God," he gasped.

It wasn't until she'd backed all the way down the slope that he raised his hand and called out softly.

"Wait."

At the sound of the word, Stands With A Fist broke into a stumbling run. Lieutenant Dunbar trotted after her, pleading for her to stop. When he had closed to within a few yards, Stands With A Fist glanced back, lost her footing, and went down in the high grass.

When he got to her she was crawling, and every time he tried to reach down he had to pull away, as if afraid to touch a wounded animal. When he finally took her around the shoulders, she flipped onto her back and clawed out at his face.

"You're hurt," he said, batting away her hands. "You're hurt."

For a few seconds she fought hard, but the steam went out of her fast and he had her by the wrists in no time. With the last of her strength she bucked and kicked under him. And when she did, something bizarre happened.

In the delirium of her struggle an old English word, one she hadn't spoken for many years, came to her. It slipped out of her mouth before she could stop it.

"Don't," she said.

It gave them both pause. Lieutenant Dunbar couldn't believe he'd heard it, and Stands With A Fist couldn't believe she'd said it.

She threw her head back and let her body sag against the ground. It was too much for her. She moaned a few Comanche words and passed out.

eleven

The woman in the grass continued to breathe. Most of her wounds were superficial, but the one on her thigh was dangerous. Blood was still seeping steadily from it, and the lieutenant kicked himself for having thrown away the red sash a mile or two back. It would have made a perfect tourniquet.

He'd been ready to throw away more. The longer he'd ridden and the less he'd seen, the more ridiculous his plan had seemed. He'd thrown the sash away as something useless, silly really, and was ready to fold up the flag (which also seemed silly) and return to Fort Sedgewick when he saw the rise and the solitary tree.

His belt was new and too stiff, so with the woman's knife, he cut a strip out of the flag and tied it high on her thigh. The flow of blood diminished right away, but he still needed a compress. He stripped off his uniform, wriggled out of his long johns, and cut the underwear in half. Then he wadded up the top and pressed it against the deep gash.

For ten terrible minutes Lieutenant Dunbar knelt next to her, naked in the grass, both hands pushing hard against the compress. Once during that time he thought she may have died. He placed a tentative ear on her breast and listened. Her heart was still thumping.

Working there by himself was difficult and nerve-racking, not knowing who the woman was, not knowing whether she would live or die. It was hot in the grass at the base of the slope, and every time he brushed at the sweat dripping into his eyes, he left a streak of her blood on his face. Off and on he would lift the compress and take a look. And each time he would stare in frustration at the blood that refused to stop. Then he would replace the compress.

But he stayed with it.

Finally, when the blood had slowed to a trickle, he went into action. The thigh wound need to be sewn shut, but that was impossible. He cut a leg off the long underwear, folded it into a dressing, and laid it flat on the wound. Then, working as fast as he could, the lieutenant cut another strip from the flag and tied it securely around the bandage. He repeated this process with the lesser arm wounds.

As he worked, Stands With A Fist began to groan. She opened her eyes a few times but was too weak to make a fuss, even when he took up his canteen and poured a sip or two of water into her mouth.

After he had done all he could as a doctor, Dunbar put his uniform back on, wondering what to do as he buttoned his trousers and tunic.

He saw her pony out on the prairie and thought of catching it. But when he looked at the woman in the grass, it didn't make sense. She might be able to ride, but she would need help.

Dunbar glanced at the western sky. The smoky cloud was nearly gone. Only a few wisps remained. If he hurried, he could point himself in that direction before the cloud vanished.

He slipped his arms under Stands With A Fist, picked her up, and piled her as smoothly as he could onto Cisco's back, intending to lead while she rode. But the girl was semiconscious and started to keel over as soon as she was on.

With one hand holding her in place, he managed to jump up behind. Then he turned her around, and looking like a father cradling his stricken daughter, Dunbar steered his horse in the direction of the smoky cloud.

As Cisco carried them across the prairie, the lieutenant thought about his plan to impress the wild Indians. He didn't look very mighty or very official now. There was blood on his tunic and his hands. The girl was bandaged with his underwear and a United States flag.

It had to be better this way. When he thought about what he had done, cavorting stupidly around the countryside with polished boots and a silly red sash and, of all things, a flag flying at his side, the lieutenant smiled sheepishly.

I must be an idiot, he thought.

He looked at the cherry hair under his chin and wondered what this poor woman must have thought when she saw him in his dandy getup.

Stands With A Fist wasn't thinking at all. She was in twilight. She was only feeling. She felt the horse swaying under her, she felt the arm across her back, and she felt the strange fabric against her face. Most of all Stands With A Fist felt safe, and all the way back she kept her eyes closed, afraid that if she opened them, the feeling would be gone.

CHAPTER XIII

one

Smiles A Lot was not a reliable boy.

No one would have characterized him as a troublemaker, but Smiles A Lot disliked work, and unlike most Indian boys, the idea of shouldering responsibility left him cold.

He was a dreamer, and as a dreamer often does, Smiles A Lot had learned that one of the better stratagems for avoiding the boredom of work was to keep to himself.

It followed, then, that the shiftless boy spent as much time as possible with the band's large pony herd. He drew the assignment regularly, in part because he was always ready to go and in part because he had, at the age of twelve become an expert with horses.

Smiles A Lot could predict to within hours the foaling time for mares. He had a knack for controlling unruly stallions. And when it came to doctoring, he knew as much or more about tending to equine ailments as any grown man in the band. The horses just seemed to fare better when he was around.

All of this was second nature to Smiles A Lot . . . second nature and secondary. What he liked most about being with the horses was that they grazed away from camp, sometimes as far as a mile, and this placed Smiles A Lot far away, too; away from the omnipotent eyes of his father, away from the potential chore of minding his little brothers and sisters, and away from the never-ending work of maintaining camp.

Usually there were other boys and girls lolling around the herd, but unless something special came up, Smiles A Lot rarely joined their games and socializing.

He much preferred climbing onto the back of some calm gelding, stretching out along the horse's spine, and dreaming, sometimes for hours, as the ever-changing sky drifted by.

He'd been dreaming like this most of the afternoon, happy to be away from the village, which was still reeling from the tragic return of the party that had gone against the Utes. Smiles A Lot knew that, though he had little interest in fighting, sooner or later he would have to take up the warpath, and already he'd made a mental note to watch out for parties going against the Utes.

For the last hour he'd been enjoying the uncommon luxury of being alone with the herd. The other children had been called back for one reason or another, but no one had come for Smiles A Lot, and this made him the happiest of dreamers. With luck, he wouldn't have to go back until dark, and sunset was still several hours off.

He was smack in the middle of the big herd, daydreaming about being the owner of a herd all his own, one that would be like a great assembly of warriors whom no one would dare to challenge, when he picked up a movement on the ground.

It was a large, yellow gopher snake. Somehow he'd managed to get himself lost in the midst of all these shifting hooves and was slithering along at a desperate clip, looking for a way out.

Smiles A Lot was fond of snakes, and this one was surely big enough and old enough to be a grandfather. A grandfather in trouble. He spilled off his horsey couch with the idea of catching the old fellow and carrying him away from this dangerous place.

The big snake was not easy to run down. He was moving very fast, and Smiles A Lot kept getting hemmed in by the tightly bunched ponies. The boy was constantly ducking under necks and bellies, and it was only through the dogged determination of a Good Samaritan that he was able to keep the yellow body twisting along the ground in sight.

It ended well. Near the edge of the herd the big snake finally found a hole to crawl into, and the only thing Smiles A Lot caught was a last glimpse of the tail as it disappeared underground.

Then, while he was standing over the hole, several of the horses whinnied and Smiles A Lot saw their ears go up. He saw all the heads around him suddenly arch in the same direction.

They'd seen something coming.

A shiver ran through the boy, and the buoyancy of being alone turned against him in a single stroke. He was afraid, but he moved forward stealthily, staying low amongst the ponies, hoping to see before being seen.

When he could see empty patches of prairie opening in front of him, Smiles A Lot dropped down and duck-walked alongside the horses' legs. They hadn't panicked and that made him feel a little less scared. But they were still watching with as much curiosity as ever, and the boy was careful not to make a sound.

He stopped when the horse flashed by, twenty or thirty yards away. He couldn't get a good look because his view was blocked, but he was sure he'd seen legs, too.

Slowly he rose up and peeked over a pony's back. Every hair on Smiles A Lot's head tingled. A racket went off in his head like buzzing bees. The boy's mouth froze, and so did his eyes. He didn't blink. He'd never seen one before, but he knew exactly what he was looking at.

It was a white man. A white soldier man with blood on his face.

And he had somebody. He had that strange one, that Stands With A Fist woman.

She looked hurt. Her arms and legs were wrapped with a funny-looking cloth. Maybe she was dead.

The white soldier's horse started into a trot as he passed. They were headed straight for the village. It was too late to run ahead and raise the alarm. Smiles A Lot shrank back into the herd and started to work his way back to the center. He would get into trouble for this. What could he possibly do?

The boy couldn't think clearly; everything was tumbling in his head, like seeds in a rattle. If he'd been a little steadier, he would have known from the look on his face that the white soldier could not be on a hostile mission. Nothing in his bearing said so. But the only words banging around in Smiles A Lot's brain were "White soldier, white soldier."

Suddenly he thought, Maybe there are more. Maybe there is an army of hair mouths out on the prairie. Maybe they're close by.

Thinking only of atoning for his carelessness, Smiles A Lot pulled off the willow bridle he kept around his neck, slipped it onto the face of a strong-looking pony, and led it as quietly as he could out of the herd.

Then he jumped up and whipped the pony into a run, racing away in the opposite direction of the village, anxiously squinting at the horizon for any sign of white soldiers.

two

Lieutenant Dunbar's adrenaline was running. That pony herd . . . At first he'd thought the prairie was moving. Never had he seen horses in such numbers. Six, maybe seven hundred of them. It was so awe-inspiring that he'd been tempted to stop and watch. But of course he couldn't.

There was a woman in his arms.

She'd held up fairly well. Her breathing was regular and she hadn't bled much. She'd been very quiet, too, but tiny as she was, the woman was breaking his back. He'd carried her for more than an hour, and now that he was close, the lieutenant wanted more than ever to get there. His fate would be decided shortly, and that kept his adrenaline running, but more than anything, he thought of the monstrous ache between his shoulder blades. It was killing him.

The land up ahead was dropping away, and as he drew closer, he could see pieces of the stream cutting across the prairie, then the tips of something; and then, as he reached the brow of the slope, the encampment rose into view before his eyes, rising as the moon had done the night before.

Unconsciously, the lieutenant squeezed the reins. He had to stop now. He was gazing on a sight for all time.

There were fifty or sixty conical, hide-covered houses pitched along the stream. They looked warm and peaceful in the late afternoon sun, but the shadows they cast also made them look larger than life, like ancient, still-living monuments.

He could see people working around the houses. He could hear some of their voices as they walked along the tamped-down avenues between lodges. He heard laughter, and somehow that surprised him. There were more people up and down the stream. Some of them were in the water.

Lieutenant Dunbar sat on Cisco, holding the woman he had found, his senses crushed by the power of the ageless tableau spread out before him, spread out like the unraveling of a living canvas. A primal, completely untouched civilization.

And he was there.

It was beyond the reach of his imagination, and at the same time he knew that this was why he'd come, this was at the core of his urge to be posted on the frontier. This, without his knowing it before, was what he had yearned to see.

These fast-moving moments on the brow of the slope would never come again in his mortal life. For these fleeting moments he became part of something so large that he ceased to be a lieutenant or a man or even a body of working parts. For these moments he was a spirit, hovering in the timeless, empty space of the universe. For these precious few seconds he knew the feeling of eternity.

The woman coughed. She stirred against his chest and Dunbar tenderly patted the back of her head.

He made a short kissing sound with his lips, and Cisco started down the slope. They'd only gone a few feet when he saw a woman and two children come out of the breaks along the river.

And they saw him.

three

The woman screamed as she let go of the water she was hauling, scooped up her children, and broke for the village, crying, "White soldier, white soldier," at the top of her lungs. Scores of Indian dogs went off like firecrackers, women shrieked for their children, and horses stampeded around the lodges, neighing wildly. It was full-scale pandemonium.

The entire band thought it was under attack.

As he drew closer to the village Lieutenant Dunbar could see men running everywhere. Those who had gotten hold of weapons were going for their horses with a whooping that reminded him of game birds in a panic. The village in upheaval was just as otherworldly as the village in repose. It was like a great nest of hornet people into which a stick had been poked.

The men who had reached their horses were swarming into a force that would momentarily race out to meet him, perhaps to kill him. He had not expected to create such a stir, nor had he expected these people to be so primitive. But there was something else that weighed on him as he moved close to the village, something that blotted out all else. For the first time in his life Lieutenant Dunbar knew what it felt like to be an invader. It was a feeling he didn't like, and it had a lot to do with the action he took next. The last thing he wanted was to be regarded as an intruder, and when he reached the bare ground of a clearing at the mouth of the village, when he was close enough to see through the curtain of dust that had been raised by the clamor and into the eyes of the people inside, he squeezed the reins once more and came to a stop.

Then he dismounted, taking the woman into his arms, and walked a pace or two in front of his horse. There he stood still, his eyes closed, holding the wounded girl like some strange traveler bearing a strange gift.

The lieutenant listened hard as the village, in stages that lasted only a few seconds each, grew oddly quiet. The dusty curtain began to settle, and Dunbar perceived with his ears that the mass of humanity that had raised such a fearful howling only moments before was now creeping toward him. In the eerie quiet he could hear the occasional clank of some item of gear, the rustling of footsteps, the snort of a horse as it pawed and jostled impatiently.

He opened his eyes to see that the whole band had gathered at the village entrance, warriors and young men in front, women and children behind them. It was a dream of wild people, clothed in skins and colored fabric, a whole separate race of humans watching him breathlessly not a hundred yards away.

The girl was heavy in his arms, and when Dunbar shifted his stance, a buzz rose and died in the crowd. But no one moved forward to meet him.

A group of older men, apparently men of importance, went into a huddle as their people stood by, whispering amongst themselves in guttural tones so foreign to the lieutenant's ear that they hardly seemed to be talking.

He let his attention wander during this lull, and when he glanced on a knot of about ten horsemen, the lieutenant's eyes fell on a familiar face. It was the same man, the warrior who had barked at him so ferociously on the day of the raid at Fort Sedgewick. Wind In His Hair was staring back with such intensity that Dunbar almost turned around to see if someone was standing at his back.

His arms were so leaden that he wasn't sure if he could move them anymore, but with the warrior's glare still fixed on him, Dunbar lifted the woman a little higher, as if to say, "Here . . . please take her."

Thrown by this sudden, unexpected gesture, the warrior hesitated, his eyes darting about the crowd, obviously wondering if this silent exchange had been noticed by anyone else. When he looked back, the lieutenant's eyes were still on his and the gesture had not been withdrawn.

With an inward sigh of relief Lieutenant Dunbar saw Wind In his Hair leap off the pony and start across the clearing, a stone war club swinging loosely in his hand. He was coming over, and if the warrior had any fear at all, it was well masked, for his face was ungiving and uncaring, set, it seemed, on doling out a punishment.

The assembly fell silent as the space between the immobile Lieutenant Dunbar and the fast-striding Wind In His Hair shrank steadily to nothing. It was too late to stop whatever was going to happen. Everyone stood still and watched.

In the face of what was closing on him, Lieutenant Dunbar could not have been braver. He stood his ground unblinking, and though there was no pain in his face, he wore no fear there either.

When Wind In His Hair was within a few feet and slowing his pace, the lieutenant said in a clear, strong voice:

"She's hurt."

He shifted his load a little as the warrior stared into the woman's face, and Dunbar could see that he recognized her. In fact, Wind In His Hair's shock was so plain that, for a moment, the awful idea that she might have died flashed through his head. The lieutenant looked down at her, too.

And as he did, she was torn from his arms. In one strong, sure motion she'd been ripped from his grasp, and before

Dunbar knew it, the warrior was walking back toward the village, hauling Stands With A Fist roughly along, like a dog would a pup. As he went he called something out that prompted a collective exclamation of surprise from the Comanches. They rushed forward to meet him.

The lieutenant stood motionless in front of his horse, and as the village swirled around Wind In His Hair, he felt the spirit run out of him. These were not his people. He would never know them. He might as well have been a thousand miles away. He wanted to be small, small enough to crawl into the smallest, darkest hole.

What had he expected of these people? He must have thought they would run out and throw their arms around him, speak his language, have him to supper, share his jokes, without so much as a how-do-you-do. How lonely he must be. How pitiful he was to entertain any expectations at all, grasping at these outlandish straws, hoping hopes that were so far-flung that he could not be honest with himself. He had managed to fool himself about everything, fool himself into thinking he was something when he was nothing.

These terrible thoughts were going off in his head like a storm of incoherent sparks, and where he stood now, in front of this primeval village, mattered not at all. Lieutenant Dunbar was swaying under the crush of a morbid personal crisis. Like so much chalk wiped from a board with one swipe, his heart and his hope had deserted him all at once. Somewhere deep inside, a switch had been thrown and Lieutenant Dunbar's light had gone out.

Oblivious to all but the hollowness he felt, the unhappy lieutenant swung onto Cisco, reined him around, and started back the way he had come at a brisk walk. This happened with so little fanfare that the already occupied Comanches didn't realize he was going until he had covered some distance.

Two teenage braves started after him but were held back by the coolheaded men of Ten Bears's inner circle. They were wise enough to know that a good deed had been done,

that the white soldier had brought back one of their own, and
that nothing was to be gained by chasing after him.

four

The ride back was the longest and most agonizing of Lieutenant Dunbar's life. For several miles he rode in a daze, his
mind churning away with thousands of negative thoughts.
He resisted the temptation to cry in the way one resists vom-
iting, but self-pity bore in on him relentlessly, in wave after
wave, and at last he broke down.

He slumped forward, letting his shoulders bunch up at first,
and his tears fell without a sound. But when he began to sniffle,
the floodgates swung wide. His face twisted grotesquely and
he began to moan with the abandon of a hysteric. In the midst
of these first convulsions he gave Cisco his head, and as the
miles piled up unrecorded, he let his heart bleed free, sobbing
as piteously as an inconsolable child.

five

He never saw the fort. When Cisco stopped, the lieutenant
looked up and saw that they had halted in front of his quarters.
The strength had been wrung from him, and for a few seconds
it was all he could do to sit comatose on his horse's back. When
he finally lifted his head again, he saw Two Socks, stationed
at his usual place on the bluff across the river. The sight of the
wolf, sitting so patiently, like a royal hunting dog, his face so
sweetly inquisitive, brought a new lump of sorrow into Dunbar's throat. But all of his tears had been spent.

He tumbled off Cisco, slipped the bit out of his mouth,
and lurched through the door. Dropping the bridle on the

floor, he flopped onto his bunk, pulled a blanket over his head, and rolled into a ball.

Exhausted as he was, the lieutenant could not sleep. For some reason he kept thinking of Two Socks, waiting out there so patiently. With a superhuman effort he dragged himself off the bed, staggered into the twilight, and squinted across the river.

The old wolf was still sitting in his place, so the lieutenant sleepwalked his way to the supply house and carved a big hunk of bacon off the slab. He carried the meat out to the bluff and, with Two Socks watching intently, dropped it on the grassy ground near the top of the bluff.

Then, thinking of sleep with every step, he threw some hay for Cisco and retreated to his quarters. Like a soldier hitting the dirt, he pitched onto the pallet, pulled up the blanket, and covered his eyes.

A woman's face came to him, a face out of the past that he knew well. There was a shy smile on her lips and her eyes shone with a light that can only come from the heart. In times of trouble he had always called upon the face, and it had come to comfort him. There was much more behind the face, a long story with an unhappy ending, but Lieutenant Dunbar didn't get into that. The face and the wonderful look it wore were all he wanted to remember, and he clung to it tenaciously. He used it like a drug. It was the most powerful painkiller he knew. He didn't think of her often, but he carried the face around with him, using it only when he was close to scraping bottom.

He lay unmoving on the bed, like an opium smoker, and eventually the image he held in his mind began to take effect. He was already snoring by the time Venus appeared, leading a long parade of stars across the endless prairie sky.

CHAPTER XIV

one

Minutes after the white man's departure, Ten Bears called another council. Unlike the recent meetings, which had begun and ended in confusion, Ten Bears knew exactly what he wanted to do now. He was set on a plan before the last of the men had seated themselves in his lodge.

The white soldier with blood on his face had brought back Stands With A Fist, and Ten Bears was convinced that this surprise was a bright omen, one that should be followed through on. The issue of the white race had troubled his thoughts too long. For years he had not been able to see anything good in their coming. But he wanted to desperately. Today he'd seen something good at last, and now he was determined not to let what he considered a golden opportunity slip past.

The white soldier had showed extreme bravery in coming alone to their camp. And he had obviously come with a single intention . . . not to steal or cheat or fight but to return something he had found, something that belonged to them. This talk of gods was probably wrong, but one thing was abundantly clear to Ten Bears. For the good of everyone, this soldier should be investigated. A man who behaved like this was bound to be positioned high with the whites. It was possible that he already carried great weight and influence. A man like this was someone with whom agreements might be reached. And without agreements, war and suffering were sure to come.

So Ten Bears was encouraged. The overture he had witnessed that afternoon, though it was only a single event, appeared to him as a light in the night, and as the men filed in, he was thinking of the best way to put his plan into action.

While he listened to the preliminaries, throwing in an occasional comment of his own, Ten Bears sifted through a mental roster of reliable men, trying to decide who would be best for his idea.

It wasn't until Kicking Bird arrived, having been held up by attending to Stands With A Fist, that the old man realized it should not be a one-man job. He should send two men. Once that was decided, the individuals came to him quickly. He should send Kicking Bird for his powers of observation and Wind In His Hair for his aggressive nature. Each man's character was representative of him and his people, and they complemented each other perfectly.

Ten Bears kept the council short. He didn't want the kind of protracted discussions that could lead to indecision. When the time was right, he made an eloquent, beautifully reasoned speech, recounting the many stories of white numerical superiority and white riches, especially in terms of guns and horses. He concluded with the notion that the man at the fort was surely an emissary and that his good actions should be cause for talking, not fighting.

There was a long silence at the end of his speech. Everyone knew he was right.

Then Wind In His Hair spoke up.

''I do not think it is right for you to go and speak to this white man,'' he said. ''He is not a god, he is just another white man lost in his way.''

A tiny twinkle flashed in the old man's eyes as he made his reply.

"I will not go. But good men should. Men who can show what a Comanche is."

Here he paused, shutting his eyes for dramatic effect. A minute passed, and some of the men thought he might have fallen asleep. But at the last second he opened them long enough to say to Wind In His Hair:

"You should go. You and Kicking Bird."

Then he closed his eyes again and dozed off, ending the council at just the right place.

two

The first big thunderstorm of the season came that night, a miles-long front marching to the hollow boom of thunder and the brilliant crackle of forked lightning. The rain it brought swept over the prairie in great rolling curtains, driving everything that lived to shelter.

It woke Stands With A Fist.

The rain was drumming against the lodge's hide walls like deadened fire from a thousand rifles, and for a few moments, she didn't know where she was. There was light, and she turned slowly on her side for a look at the little fire that was still popping in the center of the lodge. As she did, one of her hands drifted over the wound on her thigh and accidently brushed against something foreign. She felt carefully and discovered that her leg had been sewn.

Everything came back to her then.

She glanced sleepily around the lodge, wondering who lived here. She knew it was not hers.

Her mouth was dry as cotton, so she slid a hand from under the covers to explore with her fingers. The first thing they bumped into was a little bowl half-filled with water. She lifted herself to one elbow, took several long swallows, and lay back down.

There were things she wanted to know, but thinking was difficult now. It was warm as summer under the robe. The fire's shadows were dancing happily above her head, the rain was singing its strong lullaby in her ears, and she was very weak.

Maybe I am dying, she thought as her eyelids began to lower, shutting down the last of the firelight. Just before she fell asleep she said to herself, It is not so bad.

But Stands With A Fist was not dying. She was recovering, and what she had suffered, once it was healed, would make her stronger than ever.

Good would be coming out of the bad. In fact, the good had already begun. She was lying in a good place, a place that would be her home for a long time to come.

She was lying in Kicking Bird's lodge.

three

Lieutenant Dunbar slept like the dead, only vaguely aware of the spectacular show in the sky overhead. Rain punished the little sod hut for hours, but he was so snug and secure under the pile of army-issue blankets that Armageddon could have come and gone without his knowing it.

He never stirred, and it wasn't until well after sunup, long after the storm had passed on, that the carefree, persistent singsong of a meadowlark finally brought him around. The rain had freshened every square inch of the prairie, and the sweetness of its smell was shooting up his nose before he could open his eyes. At first flutter he realized he was lying on his back, and when they opened he was looking directly over his toes at the hut's entrance.

There was a flash of movement as something low and hairy

ducked away from the door. The lieutenant sat up, blinking.
A moment later the blankets were thrown aside and he was
tiptoeing unsteadily to the entrance. Standing inside, he
peered around the jamb with one eye.

Two Socks had just trotted clear of the awning and was
turning around to settle himself in the sun of the yard. He
saw the lieutenant and stiffened. They watched each other
for a few seconds. Then the lieutenant rubbed at the sleep in
his eyes, and when he dropped his hands, Two Socks
stretched out prone, his muzzle resting on the ground between his outstretched legs, like a dutiful dog waiting for his
master.

Cisco whinnied shrilly in the corral, and the lieutenant's
head jerked in that direction. He caught a simultaneous flash
from the corner of his eye and turned back in time to see
Two Socks galloping out of sight over the bluff. Then, as his
eyes panned back to the corral, he saw them.

They were sitting on ponies, not a hundred yards in front
of him. He didn't make a count, but there were eight of them.

Two men suddenly started forward. Dunbar didn't move,
but unlike previous encounters, he held his ground in a relaxed way. It was in the way they were coming. The ponies'
heads were drooping as they plodded in, casual as workers
coming home after a long, routine day.

The lieutenant was anxious, but his anxiety had little to do
with life or death.

He was wondering what he would say and how he could
possibly communicate his first words.

four

Kicking Bird and Wind In His Hair were wondering exactly
the same thing. The white soldier was as alien as anything
they had ever met, and neither one knew how this was going

to turn out. Seeing that blood was still smeared on the white soldier's face didn't make them feel any better about the meeting that was about to begin. In terms of roles, however, each man was different. Wind In His Hair rode forward as a warrior, a fighting Comanche. Kicking Bird was much more the statesman. This was an important moment in his life, the life of the band, and the life of the whole tribe. For Kicking Bird a whole new future was beginning, and he was sitting in on history.

five

When their faces were close enough to be distinct, Dunbar instantly recognized the warrior who had taken the woman from his arms. There was something familiar about the other man, too, but he couldn't place him. He didn't have time.

They had stopped a dozen feet in front of him.

They looked all lit up, resplendent in the glittering sunshine. Wind In His Hair was wearing a breastplate of bone, and a large metal disk hung around Kicking Bird's neck. These things were reflecting in the light. There was even a glint coming off their deep brown eyes, and each man's shiny, black hair was shimmering with sun streams.

Despite having just awakened, there was a certain sheen about Lieutenant Dunbar as well, though it was much more subtle than that of his visitors.

His crisis of the heart had passed, leaving him as the storm of the night before had left the prairie: fresh and full of vigor.

Lieutenant Dunbar tipped forward in the suggestion of a bow and tapped his hand against the side of his head in a slow and deliberate salute.

A moment later Kicking Bird returned this overture with a strange movement of his own hand, turning it over, from back to palm.

The lieutenant didn't know what it meant, but he interpreted it correctly as a friendly gesture. He glanced around, as if to make sure the place was still there, and said, "Welcome to Fort Sedgewick."

What the words meant were a complete mystery to Kicking Bird, but as Lieutenant Dunbar had done, he took them for some kind of greeting.

"We have come from Ten Bears's camp to make a peaceful talk," he said, drawing a blank look of ignorance from the lieutenant.

Since it was now established that neither one would be able to converse, a silence fell over the two parties. Wind In His Hair took advantage of the lull to study the details of the white man's buildings. He looked sharp and long at the awning, which was now beginning to roll in the breeze.

Kicking Bird sat impassively on his pony as the seconds dragged. Dunbar tapped his toe against the ground and stroked his chin. As time ticked away he grew nervous, and his nervousness reminded him of the morning coffee he'd missed and how much he wanted a cup. He wanted a cigarette, too.

"Coffee?" he asked Kicking Bird.

The medicine man tilted his head curiously.

"Coffee?" the lieutenant repeated. He curled his hand around an imaginary cup and made a drinking motion. "Coffee?" he said again. "To drink?"

Kicking Bird merely stared at the lieutenant. Wind In His Hair asked a question and Kicking Bird answered. Then they both looked through their host. After what seemed an eternity to Dunbar, Kicking Bird finally nodded his assent.

"Good, good," said the lieutenant, patting the side of his leg. "Come along then." He motioned them off their horses and waved them forward as he walked under the awning.

The Comanches trailed along cautiously. Everything their eyes fell on had an air of mystery, and the lieutenant cut something of a ludicrous figure, fidgeting like a man whose guests had caught him off guard by arriving an hour early.

There was no fire going in the pit, but luckily he'd laid in enough dry wood for coffee. He squatted next to the pile of kindling and started making up the fire.

"Sit down," he asked. "Please."

But the Indians didn't understand and he had to repeat himself, pantomiming the act of sitting as he spoke.

When they were down he rushed over to the supply hut and returned just as quickly carrying a five-pound sack of beans and a grinder. Once he had the fire going, Lieutenant Dunbar poured beans into the rim of the grinder's funnel and started cranking the handle.

As the beans began to disappear down the grinder's metal cone, he could see that Kicking Bird and Wind In His Hair were leaning forward curiously. He hadn't realized that something so ordinary as grinding coffee could be magic. But it was magic to Kicking Bird and Wind In His Hair. Neither one had ever seen a coffee grinder.

Lieutenant Dunbar was thrilled to be with people after all this time and was anxious for his guests to stay awhile, so he milked the grinding operation for all it was worth. Stopping abruptly, he moved the machine a couple of feet closer to the Indians, providing them with a clearer view of the process. He cranked slowly, letting them watch the beans descend. When there were only a few left he finished with a flourish, cranking with a wild, theatrical flair. Then he paused with the dramatic effect of a magician, allowing his audience to react.

Kicking Bird was intrigued with the machine itself. He ran his fingertips lightly against one of the grinder's slick wooden sides. True to his nature, Wind In His Hair found the crushing mechanism most to his liking. He stuck one of his long, dark fingers into the funnel and felt around the little hole at the bottom, hoping to find out what had happened to the beans.

It was time for the finale, and Dunbar interrupted these inspections by holding up a hand. Turning the machine around, he squeezed the little knob at its base between his fingers. The Indians bent their heads, more curious than ever.

At the last possible moment and in the way someone might reveal a fabulous jewel, Lieutenant Dunbar's eyes widened, a smile sprang up on his face, and out came the drawer, filled with fresh black grounds.

Both Comanches were mightily impressed. Each took little dabs of pulverized beans and sniffed. Then they sat quietly as their host hung his pot over the fire and let the water come to a boil, awaiting the next development.

Dunbar served up the coffee, handing each of his guests a steaming black cup. The men let the aroma climb into their faces and exchanged knowing looks. This smelled like good coffee, much better than what they raided from the Mexicans for so many years. Much stronger.

Dunbar watched expectantly as they began to sip and was surprised when they screwed up their faces. Something was wrong. They both spoke a few words at once, a question, it seemed.

The lieutenant shook his head. ''I don't understand,'' he said, shrugging his shoulders.

The Indians held a brief but inconclusive conference. Then Kicking Bird had an idea. He made a fist, held it over the cup, and opened his hand, as if he were letting something drop into the coffee. He pretended to stir what he had dropped with a twig.

Lieutenant Dunbar said something he didn't understand and then Kicking Bird watched as the white man jumped up, walked to the badly made house of earth, returned with another sack, and handed it around the fire.

Kicking Bird looked inside, grunting when he saw the brown crystals.

Lieutenant Dunbar saw a smile flicker on the Indian's face

and knew he had guessed right. Sugar was what they had wanted.

six

Kicking Bird was especially encouraged by the white soldier's enthusiasm. He wanted to make talk, and when they introduced themselves, Loo Ten Nant asked for the names several times, until he could speak them in the right way. He looked odd and he did some odd things, but the white man was eager to listen and seemed to have large stores of energy. Perhaps because he himself was so inclined toward peace, Kicking Bird greatly appreciated the force of energy in others.

He talked more than Kicking Bird was used to. When he thought about it, it seemed the white man never stopped talking the whole time.

But he was entertaining. He did strange dances and made strange signals with his hands and face. He even did some impressions that made Wind In His Hair laugh. And that was hard to do.

Aside from his general impressions, Kicking Bird had found out some things. Loo Ten Nant could not be a god. He was far too human. And he was alone. No one else was living there. But he did not learn why he was alone. Nor did he learn if more white men were coming and what their plans might be. Kicking Bird was anxious for the answers to these questions.

Wind In His Hair was just ahead. They were riding single file along a trail winding through a stand of cottonwoods close by the river. There was only the mushy plop of the ponies' hooves in the wet sand, and he wondered what Wind In His Hair thought. They had not yet compared notes on the meeting. It worried him a little.

Kicking Bird needn't have worried, for Wind In His Hair was also favorably impressed. This despite the fact that killing the white solider had crossed his mind several times. He had long thought white men were no more than useless irritations, coyotes getting around the meat. But more than once this white soldier had showed some bravery. He was friendly, too. And he was funny. Very funny.

Kicking Bird looked down at the two bags, the coffee and sugar flopping against his horse's shoulders, and the idea came into his mind that he actually liked the white soldier. It was a strange idea and he had to think about it.

Well, what if I do? the medicine man thought at last.

He heard the muffled sound of laughter. It seemed to be coming from Wind In His Hair. Again there was a laugh out loud and the stern warrior turned on his pony, speaking over his shoulder.

"That was funny," he sputtered, "when the white man became a buffalo."

Without waiting for a reply, he turned back to the trail. But Kicking Bird could see Wind In His Hair's shoulders bouncing to the beat of stifled giggles.

It was funny. Loo Ten Nant walking around on his knees, his hands growing out of his head for horns. And that blanket, that blanket stuffed under his shirt for a hump.

No, Kicking Bird smiled to himself, nothing is stranger than a white man.

seven

Lieutenant Dunbar spread the heavy robe out on his bunk and marveled at it.

I have never seen a buffalo, he thought pridefully, and already I have a buffalo robe.

Then he sat down rather reverently on the edge of the bed,

fell onto his back, and swept his hands across the soft, thick hide. He lifted one of the edges hanging over the bunk and inspected the curing. He pressed his face against the fur and savored the wild smell.

How quickly things can change. A few hours before, he'd been rocked off his foundations, and now he was floating.

He frowned slightly. Some of his deportment, that buffalo thing, for instance, might have gone overboard. And he seemed to have done most of the talking, perhaps too much. But these were tiny doubts. As he ruminated on the great robe, he couldn't help but be encouraged by his first real encounter.

He liked both Indians. The one with the smooth, dignified manner he liked most. There was something strong about him, something in his peaceful, patient manner that was appealing. He was quiet but manly. The other one, the hot-tempered one who had taken the girl from his arms, was certainly nobody to fool with. But he was fascinating.

And the robe. They had given it to him. The robe was really something.

The lieutenant played back other remembrances as he relaxed on his beautiful souvenir. With all these fresh thoughts flying through his head there was no room and no inclination to delve into the true source of his euphoria.

He had made good use of his time alone, time he had shared only with a horse and a wolf. He had done a good job with the fort. All of that was a mark in his favor. But the waiting and the worrying had clung to him like grease in a wrinkle, and the weight of this load had been considerable.

Now it was gone, lifted by two primitive men whose language he did not speak, whose likes he had not seen, whose entire state of being was alien.

Unwittingly they had done a great service by coming. The root of Lieutenant Dunbar's euphoria could be found in deliverance. Deliverance from himself.

He was no longer alone.

CHAPTER XV

one

May 17, 1863

I've written nothing in this record for many days. So much has happened that I hardly know where to begin.

The Indians have come to visit on three occasions thus far, and I have no doubt there will be more. Always the same two with their escort of six or seven other warriors. (I am amazed that all these people are warriors. Have not seen a man yet who is not a fighter.)

Our meetings have been highly amicable, though greatly hampered by the language barrier. Whatever I have learned to date is so little compared to what I could know. I still don't know what type of Indians they are but suspect them to be Comanche. I believe I have heard a word that sounds like Comanche more than once.

I know the names of my visitors but could not begin to spell them. I find them agreeable and interesting men. They are different as night and day. One is exceedingly fiery and is no doubt a leading warrior. His physique (which is something to behold) and his sullen, suspicious disposition must make him a formidable fighter. I sincerely hope I never have to fight him, for I should be hard-pressed if it came to that. This fellow, whose eyes are rather close-set but must be called handsome nonetheless, greatly covets my horse and never fails to engage me in conversation about Cisco.

We converse in made-up signs, a sort of pantomime which both Indians are starting to get the hang of. But it is very slow going, and most of our common ground has been established on the basis of failure rather than success in communication.

The fierce one dumps extraordinary amounts of sugar into his coffee. It won't be long before that ration is exhausted. Luckily, I do not take sugar. Ha! The fierce one (as I call him) is likable despite his taciturn manner, rather like a king of street toughs who, by virtue of his physical prowess, commands respect. Having spent some time on the streets myself, I respect him in this way.

Beyond that, there is a crude honesty and intent which I like.

He is a direct fellow.

I call the other man the quiet one and like him immensely. Unlike the fierce one, he is patient and inquisitive.

I think he is as frustrated as I with the language difficulties. He has taught me a few words of their speech, and I have done the same for him. I know the Comanche words for head, hand, horse, fire, coffee, house, and several others, as well as hello and goodbye. I don't know enough yet to make a sentence. It takes a long time to get the sounds right. I have no doubt it is hard for him as well.

The quiet one calls me Loo Ten Nant and for some reason does not use Dunbar. I am sure he doesn't forget to use it (I have reminded him several times), so there must be another reason. It certainly has a distinctive ring . . . Loo Ten Nant.

He strikes me as being possessed of a first-rate intelligence. He listens with care and seems to notice everything. Every shift in the wind, every random call of a bird, is as likely to catch his attention as something much more dramatic. Without language I am reduced to reading his reactions with my senses, but by all appearances he is favorably inclined toward me.

There was an incident concerning Two Socks which aptly illustrates this point. It occurred at the end of their most recent visit. We'd drunk a substantial amount of coffee and I had just introduced my guests to the wonders of slab bacon. The quiet one suddenly noticed Two Socks on the bluff across the river. He said a few words to the fierce one and they both watched the wolf. Being anxious to show them what I knew of Two Socks, I took knife and bacon in hand and went to the edge of the bluff on our side of the river.

The fierce one was occupied with sugaring his coffee and tasting the bacon, and watched from where he sat. But the quiet one got up and followed me. I usually leave Two Socks scraps on my side of the river, but after I had cut away his ration, something got into me and I hurled it across the river. It was a good toss, landing only a few feet from Two Socks. He just sat there, however, and for a time I thought he would do nothing. But bless the old man's heart if he didn't walk over and sniff around the bacon and then pick it up. I'd never seen him take the meat before, and felt a certain pride in him as he trotted off with the goods.

To me it was a happy event and nothing more. But the quiet one seemed unduly affected by this display. When I turned back to him, his face seemed more peaceful than ever. He nodded at me several times, then walked up and put his hand on my shoulder as though he approved.

Back at the fire he performed a series of signs which I was finally able to discern as an invitation to visit his home on the next day. I readily accepted, and they departed soon after.

It would be impossible to give a full account of all my impressions of the Comanche camp. I should be writing forever were that the case. But I shall try to give a brief sketch in hopes that my observations may prove of some use in future dealings with these people.

I was met a mile out by a small delegation with the quiet one at its head. We proceeded on to the village without delay. The people had turned out in their best wardrobes to meet us. The color and beauty of these costumes is something to see. They were strangely subdued, and so, I must admit, was I. A few of the smaller children broke ranks and ran up to tap me about the legs with their hands. Everyone else held back.

We dismounted in front of one of the conical houses and there was a brief moment of doubt when a boy of about twelve ran up and tried to lead Cisco away. We had a short tug-of-war with the bridle, but the quiet one interceded. Again he placed a hand on my shoulder, and the look in his eyes told me I had nothing to fear. I let the boy take Cisco away. He seemed delighted.

Then the quiet one showed me into his abode. The place was dark but not uncheerful. It smelled of smoke and meat. (The entire village has a distinct odor, which I find not distasteful. As close as I can describe it, it is the smell of a wild life.) There were two women and several children inside. The quiet one bade me to sit down, and the women brought food in bowls. Everyone disappeared then, leaving us alone.

We ate in silence for a time. I thought of making

inquiries about the girl I found on the prairie. I had not seen her, and whether she still lived, I did not know. (I still do not know.) But it seemed far too complicated a subject considering our limitations, so we talked as best we could about the food (a kind of sweet meat I found delicious).

When we had finished I made a cigarette and smoked it while the quiet one sat across from me. His attention was constantly diverted to the entrance. I felt sure we were waiting for someone or something. My assumption was correct, for it was not long before the flap of hide opened and two Indians appeared. They spoke something to the quiet one and he immediately rose, making a sign for me to follow.

A considerable crowd of onlookers was waiting outside, and I was jostled in the crush of humanity as we made our way past several other homes before stopping at one which was decorated with a large, solid-colored bear. Here I was pushed gently inside by the quiet one.

There were five older men sitting in a rough circle around the customary fire pit, but my gaze fell immediately on the oldest among them. He was a powerfully built man whom I guessed to be past sixty though still remarkably fit. His leather shirt was adorned with beadwork of intricate beauty, the designs being precise and colorful. Attached to a lock of his graying hair was a huge claw, which I judged, owing to the design outside, had once belonged to a bear. Hair was hanging at intervals along his shirtsleeves, and I realized a moment later that these must be scalps. One of them was light brown. That was unsettling.

But the most salient feature of all was his face. Never have I seen such a face. His eyes were of a brightness that might only be compared to fever. His cheekbones were extremely high and round, and his nose was

*curved like a beak. His chin was very square. Lines
ran in such heavy profusion along the skin of his face
that to call them wrinkles hardly seems adequate. They
were on the order of crevices. One side of his forehead
carried a distinct dent, probably the result of some
long-ago battle injury.*

*He was altogether a stunning image of aged wisdom
and strength. But for all this I never felt threatened
during my short stay.*

*It seemed clear that I was the reason for this con-
ference. I was certain that I had been produced for the
sole purpose of allowing the old man a close look at
me.*

*A pipe appeared and the men began to smoke. It
was long-stemmed, and from what I could tell, the tobacco was a harsh, native blend, for I alone was ex-
cluded from the smoking.*

*I was eager to make a good impression, and being
in want of a cigarette of my own, I took out the fixings
and offered them to the old man. The quiet one said
something to him, and the chieftain reached across
with one of his gnarled hands and took the pouch and
papers. He made a careful inspection of my things.
Then he looked at me sharply with his heavy-lidded,
rather cruel-looking eyes and handed the fixings back.
Not knowing if my offer had been accepted, I rolled a
smoke anyway. The old man seemed interested as I
went about it.*

*I held the cigarette out and he took it. The quiet one
said something again and the old man handed it back.
With signs, the quiet one asked me to smoke and I
complied with his request.*

*As they all watched, I lit up, inhaled, and blew out
the smoke. Before I could have another puff the old
man was reaching out. I gave it to him. He looked at
it with some caution at first, then inhaled as I had*

done. And as I had done, he exhaled in a stream. Then he drew the cigarette close to his face.

To my chagrin, he began to roll his fingers to and fro in a rapid way. The ember fell off and the tobacco spilled out. He rolled the empty paper into a ball and carelessly tossed it into the fire.

Slowly he began to smile, and in short order all the men around the fire were laughing.

Perhaps I had been insulted, but their good humor was such that I was swept up in the contagion of it.

Afterwards I was shown to my horse and escorted a mile or so from the village, where the quiet one bid me a curt good-bye.

That is the essential record of my first visit to the Indian camp. I do not know what they are thinking now.

It was good to see Fort Sedgewick again. It is my home. And yet, I look forward to another visit with my "neighbors."

When I look at the eastern horizon I rarely fail to wonder if a column might be out there. I can only hope that my vigilance here and my "negotiations" with the wild people of the plains will, in the meantime, bear fruit.

                              Lt. John J. Dunbar, U.S.A.

CHAPTER XVI

one

A few hours after Lieutenant Dunbar's first visit to the village, Kicking Bird and Ten Bears held a high-level talk. It was short and to the point.

Ten Bears liked Lieutenant Dunbar. He liked the look in his eyes, and Ten Bears put great stock in what he saw in a person's eyes. He also liked the lieutenant's manners. He was humble and courteous, and Ten Bears placed considerable value on these traits. The matter of the cigarette was amusing. How someone could make smoke out of something with so little substance defied logic, but he didn't hold it against Lieutenant Dunbar and agreed with Kicking Bird that, as an intelligence-gathering source, the white man was worth knowing.

The old chief tacitly approved Kicking Bird's idea for breaking the language barrier. But there were conditions. Kicking Bird would have to orchestrate his moves unofficially. Loo Ten Nant would be his responsibility, and only his. Already there was talk that the white man might be responsible in some way for the scarcity of game. No one knew how people would take to the white soldier if he made repeated visits to the village. The people might turn against him. It was entirely possible that someone would kill him.

Kicking Bird accepted the conditions, assuring Ten Bears that he would do everything in his power to conduct the plan in a quiet way.

This settled, they took up a more important subject.

The buffalo were way overdue.

Scouts had been ranging far and wide for days, but so far they had seen only one buffalo. That was an aging, solitary bull being torn apart by a large pack of wolves. His carcass had hardly been worth picking over.

The band's morale was sinking along with its meager food reserves, and it would not be many days before the shortage would become critical. They'd been living on the meat of local deer, but this source was playing out fast. If the buffalo didn't come soon, the promise of an abundant summer would be broken by the sound of crying children.

The two men decided that in addition to sending out more scouts, a dance was urgently needed. It should be held within a week's time.

Kicking Bird would be in charge of the preparations.

two

It was a strange week, a week in which time was jumbled for the medicine man. When he needed time, the hours would fly by, and when he was intent on time passing, it would crawl, minute by minute. Trying to balance everything out was a struggle.

There were myriad sensitive details to consider in mounting the dance. It was to be an invocation, very sacred, and the whole band would be participating. The planning and delegating of various responsibilities for an event of this importance amounted to a full-time job.

Plus there were the ongoing duties of being a husband to two wives, a father to four children, and a guide to his newly adopted daughter. Added to it all were the routine problems and surprises that cropped up each day: visits to the sick, impromptu councils with drop-in visitors, and the making of his own medicine.

Kicking Bird was the busiest of men.

And there was something else, something that nipped constantly at his concentration. Like a low-grade, persistent headache, Lieutenant Dunbar preyed on his mind. Wrapped up as he was in the present, Loo Ten Nant was the future, and Kicking Bird could not resist its call. The present and the future occupied the same space in the medicine man's day. It was a crowded time.

Having Stands With A Fist around did not make it easier for him. She was the key to his plan, and Kicking Bird could not look at her without thinking of Loo Ten Nant, an act that inevitably sent him wandering down new trails of speculative thought. But he had to keep an eye on her. It was important to approach the matter at the right time and place.

She was healing fast, moving without trouble now, and had picked up the rhythm of life at his lodge. Already a favorite with the children, she worked as long and as hard as anyone in camp. When left to herself, she was withdrawn, but that was understandable. In fact, it had always been her nature.

Sometimes, after watching her a while, Kicking Bird would heave a private sigh of burden. At those times he would pull up at the edge of questions, the main one being whether or not Stands With A Fist truly belonged. But he could not presume an answer, and an answer would not help him anyway. Only two things mattered. She was here and he needed her.

By the day of the dance he still had not found an opportunity to speak to her in the way he wanted. That morning he woke with the realization that he, Kicking Bird, would have to put his plan in motion if he ever wanted it to happen.

He dispatched three young men to Fort Sedgewick. He was too busy to go himself, and while they were gone he would find a way to have a talk with Stands With A Fist.

Kicking Bird was spared the drudgery of manipulation when his entire family set off on an expedition to the river at midmorning, leaving Stands With A Fist behind to dress out a fresh-shot deer.

Kicking Bird watched her from inside the lodge. She never looked up as the knife flew along in her hand, peeling away hide with the same ease that tender flesh falls away from the bone. He waited until she paused in her work, taking a few moments to watch a group of children playing tag in front of a lodge across the way.

"Stands With A Fist," he said softly, bending through the entrance to the lodge.

She looked up at him with her wide eyes but said nothing.

"I would talk with you," he said, disappearing into the darkness of the lodge.

She followed.

three

It was tense inside. Kicking Bird was going to say things she probably would not want to hear, and it made him uneasy.

As she stood in front of him, Stands With A Fist felt the kind of foreboding that comes before questioning. She had done nothing wrong, but her life had become a day-to-day proposition. She never knew what was going to befall her next, and since the death of her husband, she had not felt up to meeting challenges. She took solace in the man standing before her. He was respected by everyone and he had taken her in as one of his own. If there was anyone she could trust, it was Kicking Bird.

But he seemed nervous.

"Sit," he said, and they both dropped to the floor. "How is the wound?" he began.

"It is healing," she replied, her eyes barely meeting his.

"The pain is gone?"

"Yes."

"You have found strength again."

"I am stronger now; I am working well."

She toyed with a patch of dirt at her feet, scraping it into a little pile while Kicking Bird tried to find the words he wanted. He didn't like rushing, but he didn't want to be interrupted either, and someone might come by at any time.

She looked up at him suddenly, and Kicking Bird was struck by the sadness of her face.

"You are unhappy here," he said.

"No." She shook her head. "I am glad for it."

She played with the dirt halfheartedly, flicking at it with her fingers.

"I am sad without my husband."

Kicking Bird thought for a moment, and she began to build another pile of dirt.

"He is gone now," the medicine man said, "but you are not. Time is moving and you are moving with it, even if you go unhappily. Things will be happening."

"Yes," she said, pursing her lips, "but I am not much interested in what will happen."

From his vantage point facing the entrance Kicking Bird saw several shadows pass in front of the lodge flap and then move on.

"The whites are coming," he said suddenly. "More of them will be coming through our country each year."

A shiver ran up Stands With A Fist's spine. It spread across her shoulders. Her eyes hardened and her hands involuntarily rolled themselves into fists.

"I won't go with them," she said.

Kicking Bird smiled. "No," he said, "you won't go. There is not a warrior among us who would not fight to keep you from going."

Hearing these words of support, the woman with the dark cherry hair leaned forward slightly, curious now.

"But they will be coming," he continued. "They are a strange race in their habits and beliefs. It is hard to know what to do. People say they are many, and that troubles me. If they come as a flood, we will have to stop them. Then we will lose many of our good men, men like your husband. There will be many more widows with long faces."

As Kicking Bird drew closer to the point, Stands With A Fist dropped her head, contemplating the words.

"This white man, the one who brought you home. I have seen him. I have been to his lodge downriver and drunk his coffee and talked with him. He is strange in his ways. But I have watched him and I think his heart is a good one. . . ."

She lifted her head and glanced fleetingly at Kicking Bird.

"This white man is a soldier. He may be a person of influence among the whites. . . ."

Kicking Bird stopped. A common sparrow had found its way through the open flap and fluttered into the lodge. Knowing it had trapped itself, the young bird beat its wings frantically as it bounced off one hide wall after another. Kicking Bird watched as the sparrow climbed closer to the smoke hole and suddenly disappeared to freedom.

He looked now at Stands With A Fist. She had ignored the intrusion and was staring at the hands folded in her lap. The medicine man thought, trying to pick up the thread of his monologue. Before he could start, however, he again heard the soft *whir* of little wings.

Looking overhead, he saw the sparrow, hovering just inside the smoke hole. He followed its flight as it dived deliberately toward the floor, pulled up in a graceful swoop, and lighted quietly on the cherry-colored head. She didn't move, and the bird began preening, as natural as if it were nesting in the branches of a tall tree. She passed an absent hand over her head, and like a child skipping rope, the sparrow hopped a foot into the air, hovered as the hand swept under its feet, and landed once more. Stands With A Fist sat oblivious as the tiny visitor fluffed its wings, threw out its chest, and took off like a shot, making a beeline for the entrance. It was gone in the blink of an eye.

With time Kicking Bird would have made certain conclusions concerning the import and meaning of the sparrow's arrival and Stands With A Fist's role in its performance. There was no time to take a walk and mull it over, but somehow Kicking Bird felt reassured by what he had seen.

Before he could speak again, she was lifting her head.

"What do you want of me?" she asked.

"I want to hear the white soldier's words, but my ears cannot understand them."

Now it was done. Stands With A Fist's face dropped.

"I am afraid of him," she said.

"A hundred white soldiers coming on a hundred horses with a hundred guns . . . that is something to fear. But he is only one man. We are many and this is our country."

She knew he was right, but rightness didn't make her feel any more secure. She shifted uncomfortably.

"I do not remember the white tongue," she said halfheartedly. "I am Comanche."

Kicking Bird nodded.

"Yes, you are Comanche. I do not ask for you to become something else. I am asking you to put your fear behind and your people ahead. Meet the white man. Try to find your white tongue with him, and when you do, we three will make a talk that will serve all the people. I have thought on this for a long time."

He lapsed into silence and the whole lodge became still.

She looked around, letting her eyes linger here and there, as if it would be a long time before she saw this place again.

She wasn't going anywhere, but in her mind Stands With A Fist was taking another step toward giving up the life she loved so dearly.

"When will I see him?" she asked.

Stillness filled the lodge again.

Kicking Bird got to his feet.

"Go to a quiet place," he instructed, "away from our camp. Sit for a time and try to think back the words of your old tongue."

Her chin was tilted at her chest as Kicking Bird walked her to the entrance.

"Put your fear behind and it will be a good thing," he said as she ducked out of the lodge.

He didn't know if she heard this last bit of advice. She hadn't turned back to him, and now she was walking away.

four

Stands With A Fist did as she was asked.

With an empty water jug resting on her hip, she made her way down the main track to the river. It was close to noon, and the morning traffic, water haulers and horses and washers and beaming children, had thinned out. She walked slowly, eyeing each side of the trail for a seldom-traveled rut that would take her to a place of solitude. Her heart quickened as she spotted an overgrown path that cut away from the main trail and ran through the breaks a hundred yards from the river.

No one was about, but she listened carefully for anyone who might be coming. Hearing nothing, she hid the cumbersome jug under a chokecherry bush and slipped into the heavy cover of the old path just as voices started up near the water's edge.

She hurried through the tangle hanging over the path and

was relieved when, after only a few yards, the footpath swelled into a full-fledged trail. Now she was moving with ease, and the voices along the main trail soon died out.

The morning was beautiful. Light breezes bent the willows into swaying dancers, the patches of sky overhead were a brilliant blue, and the only sounds were those of an occasional rabbit or lizard, startled by her step. It was a day for rejoicing, but there was no joy in Stands With A Fist's heart. It was marbled with long veins of bitterness, and as she slowed her pace, the white girl of the Comanches gave in to hate.

Some of it was directed at the white soldier. She hated him for coming to their country, for being a soldier, for being born. She hated Kicking Bird for asking her to do this and for knowing that she could not refuse him. And she hated the Great Spirit for being so cruel. The Great Spirit had wrecked her heart. But it wasn't enough to kill someone's heart.

Why do you keep hurting me? she asked. I am already dead.

Gradually her head began to cool. But her bitterness didn't diminish; it hardened into something cold and brittle.

Find your white tongue. Find your white tongue.

It came to her that she was tired of being a victim, and it made her angry.

You want my white tongue, she thought in Comanche. You see some worth in me for that? I will find it then. And if I am to become no one for doing that, I will be the greatest of all the no ones. I will be a no one to remember.

As her moccasins scraped softly over the grass-tufted path, she began to cast herself back, trying to find a place at which to start, a place where she could begin to remember the words.

But everything was blank. No matter how much she concentrated, nothing came to mind, and for several minutes she suffered the terrible frustration of having a whole language on the tip of her tongue. Instead of lifting, the mist of her past had closed in like fog.

She was worn out by the time she came to a small clearing that opened into the river a mile upstream from the village. It was a spot of rare beauty, a grassy porch shaded by a sparkling cottonwood tree and surrounded on three sides by natural screens. The river was wide and shallow and dotted with sandbars crowned with reeds. On days past she would have delighted in finding such a place. Stands With A Fist had always been keen for beauty.

But today she barely noticed. Wanting only to rest, she sat heavily in front of the cottonwood and leaned back against its trunk. She crossed her legs in the Indian way and hiked her shift to let the cool air from the river play around her thighs. Finally she closed her eyes and resolved herself to remembering.

But still she could remember nothing. Stands With A Fist gritted her teeth. She raised her hands and ground the palms into her tired eyes.

It was while she rubbed her eyes that the image came.

It struck her like a bright splash of color.

five

Images had come to her the preceding summer, when it was discovered that white soldiers were in the vicinity. One morning while she lay in bed, her doll had appeared on the wall. In the middle of a dance she had seen her mother. But both images were opaque.

The ones she was seeing now were alive and moving as if in a dream. There was white-man talk all the way through. And she understood every word.

What appeared first had startled her with its clarity. It was the torn hem of a blue gingham dress. A hand was on the hem, playing about the fringe. As she watched through closed eyes, the image grew larger. The hand belonged to a girl in her early teens. She was standing in a rough earthen room, furnished only with a small, hard-looking bed, a framed spray of flowers mounted next to the only window, and a sideboard over which hung a mirror with a large chip at one edge.

The girl was facing away, her unseen face bent toward the hand that held the hem as she inspected the tear.

In making the inspection, the dress had been lifted high enough to expose the girl's short, skinny legs.

A woman's voice suddenly called from outside the room. "Christine . . ."

The girl's head turned, and in a rush of realization, Stands With A Fist recognized her old self. Her old face listened, and then the old mouth made the words: "Coming, Mother."

Stands With A Fist opened her eyes then. She was frightened by what she had seen, but like a listener at the feet of a storyteller, she wanted more.

She closed her eyes again, and from the limb of an oak tree a scene opened through a mass of rustling leaves. A long-fronted sod house, shaded by a pair of cottonwoods, was built against the bank of a draw. A crude table thrown together with planking sat in front of the house. And seated at the table were four grown-up people, two men and two women. The four were talking, and Stands With A Fist could understand every word.

Three children were playing blindman's bluff farther out in the yard, and the women kept an eye on them as they chatted about a fever one of the children had recently conquered.

The men were smoking pipes. On the table in front of them were scattered the remains of a late afternoon Sunday lunch: a bowl of boiled potatoes, several dishes of greens, a pile of cornless cobs, a turkey skeleton, and a half-full pitcher of milk. The men were talking about the likelihood of rain.

She recognized one of them. He was tall and stringy. His cheeks were hollow and high-boned. His hair was pushed straight back over his head. A short, wispy beard clung to his jaw. It was her father.

Up above she could make out the forms of two people lying in the buffalo grass growing out of the roof. At first she didn't know who they were, but suddenly she was closer and could see them clearly.

She was with a boy about her age. His name was Willy. He was raw and skinny and pale. They were side by side on their backs, holding hands as they watched a line of high clouds spreading across the spectacular sky.

They were talking about the day they would be married.

"I would rather there was nobody," Christine said dreamily. "I would rather you came to the window one night and took me away."

She squeezed his hand, but Willy didn't squeeze back. He was watching the clouds intently.

"I don't know about that part," he said.

"What don't you know?"

"We could get in trouble."

"From who?" she asked impatiently.

"From our parents."

Christine turned her face to his and smiled at the concern she saw.

"But we'd be married. Our business would be our own, not someone else's."

"I suppose," he said, his brow still knitted.

He didn't offer anything more, and Christine went back to watching the sky with him.

At length the boy sighed. He looked at her from the corner of his eye, and she at him.

"I guess I don't care what kind of fuss there is . . . so long as we get married."

"I don't either," she said.

Without embracing, their faces were suddenly moving toward one another, their lips making ready for a kiss. Christine changed her mind at the last moment.

"We can't," she whispered.

Hurt passed across his eyes.

"They'll see us," she whispered again. "Let's scoot down."

Willy was smiling as he watched her slide a little farther down the back side of the roof. Before he went after her he threw a backward glance at the people in the yard below.

Indians were coming in from the prairie. There were a dozen of them, all on horseback. Their hair was roached and their faces were painted black.

"Christine," he hushed, grabbing her.

They squirmed forward on their bellies, edging close for the best possible view. Willy pulled up his squirrel gun as they craned their necks.

The women and children must have gone inside already, for her father and his friend were alone in the yard. Three Indians had come all the way up. The others were waiting at a respectful distance.

Christine's father began to talk in signs to one of the three emissaries, a big Pawnee with a scowl on his face. She could see right away the talk was not good. The Indian kept motioning toward the house, making the sign for drinking. Christine's father kept shaking his head in denial.

Indians had come before, and Christine's father had always shared what he had on hand. These Pawnee wanted something he didn't have . . . or something he wouldn't part with.

Willy whispered in her ear.

"They look sore. . . . Maybe they want whiskey."

That might be it, she thought. Her father didn't approve of strong drink in any form, and as she watched, she could see he was losing patience. And patience was one of his hallmarks.

He waved them off, but they didn't move. Then he threw his hands into the air, and the ponies tossed their heads. Still the Indians did not move, and now all three were scowling.

Christine's father said something to the white friend standing by his side, and showing their backs, they turned for the house.

There was no time for anyone to yell a warning. The big Pawnee's hatchet was on a downward arc before Christine's father had fully turned away. It struck deep under his shoulder, driving the length of the blade. He grunted as if he'd had the wind knocked out of him and hopped sideways across the yard. Before he'd gone even a few steps, the big Pawnee was on his back, hacking furiously as he drove him to ground.

The other white man tried to run, but singing arrows knocked him down halfway to the door of the sod house.

Terrible sounds flooded Christine's ears. Screams of despair were coming from inside the house, and the Indians who had held back were whooping madly as they dashed forward at a gallop. Someone was roaring in her face. It was Willy.

"Run, Christine . . . run!"

Willy planted one of his boots on her behind and sent the girl rolling down to the spot where the roof ended and the prairie began. She looked back and saw the raw, skinny boy standing on the edge of the roof, his squirrel gun pointed down at the yard. It fired, and for a moment Willy stood motionless. Then he turned the rifle around, held it like a club, jumped quietly into space, and disappeared.

She ran then, wild with fear, her skinny fourteen-year-old legs churning up the draw behind the house like the wheels of a machine.

The sun was slanting into her eyes and she fell several times, scraping the skin off her knees. But she was up in a wink each time, the fear of dying pushing her past pain. If a brick wall had suddenly sprung up in the draw, she would have run right into it.

She knew she couldn't keep this pace, and even if she could, they would be coming on horseback, so as the draw began to curve and its banks grew steeper, she looked for a place to hide.

Her frantic search had yielded nothing and the pain in her lungs was starting to stab when she spotted a dark opening partially obscured by a thick growth of bunchgrass halfway up the slope on her left.

Grunting and crying, she scrambled up the rock-strewn embankment and, like a mouse diving for cover, threw herself into the hole. Her head went in, but her shoulders didn't. It was too small. She rocked back onto her knees and banged at the sides of the hole with her fists. The earth was soft. It began to fall away. Christine dug deliriously, and after a few moments there was enough room to wriggle inside.

It was a very tight fit. She was curled in a fetal ball and, almost at once, had the sickening feeling that she had somehow stuffed herself into a jar. Her right eye could see over the lip of the hole's entrance for several hundred yards down the draw. No one was coming. But black smoke was rising from the direction of the house. Her hands were drawn up against her throat and one of them discovered the miniature crucifix she'd worn ever since she could remember. She held it tight and waited.

six

When the sun began to sink behind her, the young girl's hopes rose. She was afraid one of them had seen her run away, but with each passing hour her chances got better. She prayed for night to come. It would be all but impossible for them to find her then.

An hour after sundown she held her breath as horses passed by down in the draw. The night was moonless and she couldn't make out any forms. She thought she heard a child crying. The hoofbeats slowly died away and didn't return.

Her mouth was so dry that it hurt to swallow, and the throbbing of her skinned knees seemed to be spreading over the whole of her body. She would have given anything to stretch. But she couldn't move more than an inch or two in any direction. She couldn't turn over, and her left side, the side she was lying on, had gone numb.

As the young girl's longest night ground slowly on, her discomfort would build and break like a fever and she would have to steel herself against sudden rushes of panic. She might have died of shock had she given in, but each time Christine found a way to beat back these swells of hysteria. If there was a saving grace, it was that she thought little of what had happened to her family and friends. Now and again she would hear her father's death grunt, the one he made when the Pawnee hatchet sliced through his back. But each time she heard the grunt she managed to stop there, shutting the rest of it out of her mind. She'd always been known as a tough little girl, and toughness was what saved her.

Around midnight she dropped off to sleep only to wake minutes later in a claustrophobic frenzy. Like the slipknot on a rope, the more she struggled, the tighter she wedged herself.

Her pitiful screams rang up and down the draw.

At last she could scream no more and settled down to a long, cleansing cry. When that, too, was spent, she was calm, weak with the exhaustion an animal feels after hours in the trap.

Forsaking escape from the hole, she concentrated on a series of tiny activities to make herself more comfortable. She moved her feet back and forth, counting off each toe only when she could wiggle it separate from the rest. Her hands were relatively free and she pressed her fingertips together until she had run through every combination she could think of. She counted her teeth. She recited the Lord's Prayer, spelling each word. She composed a long song about being in the hole. Then she sang it.

seven

When first light came she began to cry again, knowing she could not possibly make it through the coming day. She'd had enough. And when she heard horses in the draw the prospect of dying at someone's hand seemed much better than dying in the hole.

"Help," she cried. "Help me."

She heard the hoofbeats come to an abrupt halt. People were coming up the slope, scuffling over the rocks. The scuffling stopped and an Indian face loomed in front of the hole. She couldn't bear to look at him, but it was impossible to turn her head away. She closed her eyes to the puzzled Comanche.

"Please . . . get me out," she murmured.

Before she knew it strong hands were pulling her into the sunshine. She couldn't stand at first, and as she sat on the ground, stretching out her swollen legs an inch at a time, the Indians conferred amongst themselves.

They were split. The majority could see no value in taking her. They said she was skinny and small and weak. And if they took this little bundle of misery, they might be blamed for what the Pawnee had done to the white people in the earth house.

Their leader argued against this. It was unlikely that the people at the earth house, so far from any other whites, would be found right away. They would be well out of the country by then. The band had only two captives now, both Mexicans, and captives were always of value. If this one died on the long trip home, they would leave her by the trail and no one would be the wiser. If she survived, she would be useful as a worker or as something to bargain with if the need arose. And the leader reminded the others that there was a tradition of captives becoming good Comanches, and there was always a need for more good Comanches.

The matter was settled quick enough. Those who were for

killing her on the spot might have had the better argument, but the man who was for keeping her was a fast-rising young warrior with a future, and no one was eager to go against him.

eight

She survived all the hardships, largely through the benevolence of the young warrior with a future whose name she eventually learned was Kicking Bird.

In time she came to understand that these people were her people and that they were vastly different from those who had murdered her family and friends. The Comanches became her world and she loved them as much as she hated the Pawnee. But while the hate of the killers remained, memories of her family sank steadily, like something trapped in quicksand. In the end, the memories had sunk completely from sight.

Until this day, the day she had unearthed her past.

As vivid as the recollection had been, Stands With A Fist was not thinking of it as she got up from her spot in front of the cottonwood and waded into the river. When she squatted in the water and splashed some on her face, she was not thinking of her mother and father. They were long gone, and the remembrance of them was nothing she could use.

As her eyes scanned the opposite bank, she was thinking only of the Pawnee, wondering if they would be raiding into Comanche territory this summer.

Secretly, she hoped they would. She wanted another opportunity for revenge.

There had been an opportunity several summers before, and she had made the most of that one. It came in the form of an arrogant warrior who had been taken alive for the purpose of ransom.

Stands With A Fist and a delegation of women had met the men bringing him in at the edge of camp. She herself had led the ferocious charge that the returning war party had been powerless to turn back. They'd pulled him from his horse and cut him to pieces on the spot. Stands With A Fist had been first to drive in her knife, and she'd stayed until only shreds remained. Striking back at last had been deeply satisfying, but not so satisfying that she didn't dream regularly of another chance.

The visit with her past was a tonic, and she felt more Comanche than ever as she walked back on the little-used path. Her head was high and her heart was very strong.

The white soldier seemed a trifling thing now. She resolved that if she talked to him at all, it would only be as much as pleased Stands With A Fist.

CHAPTER XVII

one

The appearance of three strange young men on ponies was a surprise. Shy and respectful, they carried the appearance of messengers, but Lieutenant Dunbar was very much on his guard. He had not yet learned to tell tribal differences, and to his unpracticed eye they could have been anybody.

With the rifle tipped over his shoulder, he walked a hundred yards behind the supply house to meet them. When one of the young men made the sign of greeting used by the quiet one, Dunbar answered with his usual short bow.

The hand talk was short and simple. They asked him to come with them to the village, and the lieutenant agreed. They stood by as he bridled Cisco, talking in low tones about the little buckskin horse, but Lieutenant Dunbar paid them little mind.

He was anxious to find out what was up and was glad when they left the fort at a gallop.

two

It was the same woman, and though she was sitting away from them, toward the back of the lodge, the lieutenant's eyes kept roving in her direction. The deerskin dress was drawn over her knees and he couldn't tell if she had recovered from the bad leg wound.

Physically she looked fine, but he could read no clues in her expression. It was a shade sullen but mainly blank. His eyes kept going to her because he was sure now that she was the reason for his being summoned to the village. He wished they could get on with it, but his limited experience with the Indians had already taught him to be patient.

So he waited as the medicine man meticulously packed his pipe. The lieutenant glanced again at Stands With A Fist. For a split second her eyes linked with his and he was reminded of how pale they were compared to the deep brown eyes of the others. Then he remembered her saying "Don't" that day on the prairie. The cherry-colored hair suddenly sprang at him with new meaning, and a tingling started at the base of his neck.

Oh my God, he thought, that woman is white.

Dunbar could tell that Kicking Bird was more than casually aware of the woman in the shadows. When, for the first time, he offered the pipe to his special visitor, he did it with a sidelong glance in her direction.

Lieutenant Dunbar needed help with the smoking, and Kicking Bird politely obliged, positioning his hands on the long, smooth stem and adjusting the angle. The tobacco was as harsh as it smelled, but he found it to be full of aroma. A good smoke. The pipe itself was fascinating. Heavy to pick up, it felt extraordinarily light once he began to smoke, as if it might float away if he eased his grip.

They puffed it back and forth for a few minutes. Then Kicking Bird laid the pipe carefully at his side. He looked squarely at Stands With A Fist and made a little flick of his wrist, motioning her forward.

She hesitated for a moment, then planted a hand on the ground and started to her feet. Lieutenant Dunbar, ever the gentleman, instantly jumped up and, in so doing, ignited a wild ruckus.

It all happened in a violent flash. Dunbar didn't see the knife until she'd covered half the distance between them. The next thing he knew, Kicking Bird's forearm slammed into his chest and he was falling backward. As he went down he saw the woman coming in a crouch, punctuating the words she was hissing with wicked stabbing motions.

Kicking Bird was on her just as quickly, twisting the knife away with one hand while he shoved her to the ground with the other. As the lieutenant sat up, Kicking Bird was turning on him. There was a fearsome glare on the medicine man's face.

Desperate to defuse this awful situation, Dunbar hopped to his feet. He waved his hands back and forth as he said "No" several times. Then he made one of the little bows he used as a greeting when Indians came to Fort Sedgewick. He pointed to the woman on the floor and bowed again.

Kicking Bird understood then. The white man was only trying to be polite. He had meant no harm. He spoke a few words to Stands With A Fist and she came to her feet again. She kept her eyes on the floor, avoiding any contact with the white soldier.

For a moment each member of the trio in the lodge stood motionless.

Lieutenant Dunbar waited and watched as Kicking Bird slowly stroked the side of his nose with a long, dark finger, thinking things over. Then he muttered softly to Stands With A Fist and the woman raised her eyes. They seemed paler than before. And blanker. Now they were staring straight into Dunbar's.

With signs Kicking Bird asked the lieutenant to resume his

seat. They sat as they had before, facing each other. More soft words were directed at Stands With A Fist and she came forward, settling light as a feather only a foot or two from Dunbar.

Kicking Bird looked at both of them expectantly. He placed his fingers on his lips, prodding the lieutenant with this sign until Dunbar understood that he was being asked to speak, to say something to the woman sitting next to him.

The lieutenant dipped his head in her direction, waiting until he caught a little slice of her eye.

"Hello," he said.

She blinked.

"Hello," he said again.

Stands With A Fist remembered the word. But her white tongue was as rusty as an old hinge. She was afraid of what might come out, and her subconscious was still resisting the very idea of this talk. She made several soundless attempts before it came out.

"Hulo," she answered, quickly dropping her chin.

Kicking Bird's delight was such that he uncharacteristically slapped the side of his leg. He reached over and patted the back of Dunbar's hand, urging him on.

"Speak?" the lieutenant asked, mixing his words with the sign Kicking Bird had used. "Speak English?"

Stands With A Fist tapped the side of her temple and nodded, trying to tell him the words were in her head. She placed a pair of fingers against her lips and shook her head, trying to tell him of the trouble with her tongue.

The lieutenant didn't fully understand. Her expression was still blankly hostile, but there was an ease in her movements now that gave him the feeling she was willing to communicate.

"I am . . ." he started, poking a finger at his tunic. "I am John. I am John."

Her flat eyes were trained on his mouth.

"I am John," he said again.

Stands With A Fist moved her lips silently, practicing the word. When she finally said it out loud the word rang with perfect clarity. It shocked her. It shocked Lieutenant Dunbar.

She said, ''Willie.''

Kicking Bird knew there had been a misfire when he saw the stunned expression on the lieutenant's face. He watched helplessly as Stands With A Fist went through a series of muddled gyrations. She covered her eyes and rubbed her face. She covered her nose as if she were trying to stifle a smell and shook her head wildly. Finally she placed her hands palm down on the ground and sighed deeply, again forming silent words with her little mouth. At that moment Kicking Bird's heart sagged. Perhaps he had asked too much in mounting this experiment.

Lieutenant Dunbar didn't know what to make of her, either. He thought it possible that the poor girl's long captivity had made her a lunatic.

But Kicking Bird's experiment, though terribly difficult, was not too much. And Stands With A Fist was not a lunatic. The white soldier's words and her memories and the confusion of her tongue were all jumbled together. Sorting through the tangle was like trying to draw with her eyes closed. She was struggling to get hold of it as she stared into space.

Kicking Bird started to say something, but she cut him off sharply with a flurry of Comanche.

Her eyes remained closed a few seconds longer. When they opened again she looked through her tangled hair at Lieutenant Dunbar and he could see that they had softened. With a calm beckoning of her hand she asked him in Comanche to speak again.

Dunbar cleared his throat.

''I am John,'' he said, and pronounced the word carefully. ''John . . . John.''

Once more her lips worked at the word, and once more she tried to speak it.

''Jun.''

"Yes." Dunbar nodded ecstatically. "John."

"Jun," she said again.

Lieutenant Dunbar tilted his head back. It was a sweet sound to him, the sound of his own name. He had not heard it for months.

Stands With A Fist smiled in spite of herself. Her recent life had been so filled with frowns. It was good to have something, no matter how small, to smile about.

Simultaneously, they glanced at Kicking Bird.

There was no smile on his mouth. But in his eyes, though it was ever so faint, was a happy light.

three

The going was slow that first afternoon in Kicking Bird's lodge. The time was eaten up by Stands With A Fist's painstaking attempts to repeat Lieutenant Dunbar's simple words and phrases. Sometimes it took a dozen or more repetitions, all of them excruciatingly tedious, to produce a single one-syllable word. And even then the pronunciation was far from perfect. It was not what would be called talking.

But Kicking Bird was greatly encouraged. Stands With A Fist had told him that she remembered the white words well. She was only having difficulty with her tongue. The medicine man knew that practice would bring the rusty tongue around, and his mind galloped with the happy prospects of the time when conversation between them would be free and full of information.

He felt a twinge of irritation when one of his assistants arrived with the news that he would shortly be needed to oversee final preparations for the dance that evening.

But Kicking Bird smiled as he took the white man's hand and bid him good-bye with hair-mouth words.

"Hulo, Jun."

four

It was tough to figure. The meeting had ended so abruptly. And so far as he knew, it had been going well. Something must have taken priority.

Dunbar stood outside Kicking Bird's lodge and looked down the wild avenue. People seemed to be congregating in an open space at the end of the street near the tipi that carried the mark of the bear. He wanted to stay, to see what was going to happen.

But the quiet one had already disappeared into the steadily growing crowd. He spotted the woman, so small among the already smallish Indians, walking between two women. She didn't look back at him, but as the lieutenant's eyes followed her receding form, he could see the two people in her carriage: white and Indian.

Cisco was coming toward him, and Dunbar was surprised to see that the boy with the constant smile was riding his horse. The youngster pulled up, rolled off, patted Cisco's neck, and chattered something that Lieutenant Dunbar correctly interpreted as praise for his horse's virtues.

People were streaming into the clearing now and they were taking little notice of the man in uniform. The lieutenant thought again of staying, but much as he wanted to, he knew that without a formal invitation he would not be welcome. There had been no invitation.

The sun was beginning to sink and his stomach was starting to growl. If he was going to get home before dark and thus avoid a lot of fumbling just to get dinner together, he would have to make quick time. He swung up, turned Cisco around, and started out of the village at an easy canter.

As he passed the last of the lodges he chanced upon a strange assembly. Perhaps a dozen men were gathered behind one of the last lodges. They were draped in all kinds of finery and their bodies were painted with loud designs. Each man's head was covered with the head of a buffalo, complete with curly hair and horns. Only the dark eyes and prominent noses were visible beneath the strange helmets.

Dunbar held up a hand as he cantered past. Some of them glanced in his direction, but none of them returned the wave, and the lieutenant rode on.

five

Two Socks's visits were no longer limited to late afternoon or early morning. He was likely to pop up anytime now, and when he did, the old wolf made himself at home, roaming the little confines of Lieutenant Dunbar's world as if he were a camp dog. The distance he once kept had shrunk as his familiarity grew. More often than not he was no more than twenty or thirty feet away as the solitary lieutenant went about his little tasks. When he made journal entries Two Socks would usually stretch out and lie down, his yellow eyes blinking curiously as he watched the lieutenant scratch on the pages.

The ride back had been a lonely one. The untimely end of his meeting with the woman who was two people and the mysterious excitement in the village (of which he was not a part) saddled Dunbar with his old nemesis, the morose feeling of being left out. All his life he'd been hungry to participate, and as with every other human, loneliness was something that constantly had to be handled. In the lieutenant's case loneliness had become the dominant feature of his life, so it was reassuring to see the tawny form of Two Socks rise up under the awning when he rode in at twilight.

The wolf trotted out into the yard and sat down to watch as the lieutenant slipped off Cisco's back.

Dunbar noticed immediately that something else was under the awning. It was a large prairie chicken, lying dead on the ground, and when he stooped to examine it, he found the bird fresh-killed. The blood on its neck was still sticky. But aside from the punctures about its throat, the guinea fowl was undisturbed. Hardly a feather was out of place. It was a puzzle for which there was only one solution, and the lieutenant looked pointedly at Two Socks.

"Is this yours?" he said out loud.

The wolf raised his eyes and blinked as Lieutenant Dunbar studied the bird a moment longer.

"Well, then"—he shrugged—"I guess it's ours."

six

Two Socks stood by, his narrow eyes following Dunbar as the bird was plucked, gutted, and roasted over the open fire. While it was on the spit he trailed the lieutenant to the corral and waited patiently as Cisco's grain ration was doled out. Then back to the fire to await the feast.

It was a good bird, tender and full of meat. The lieutenant ate slowly, carving off the plump flesh a strip at a time and tossing a piece out to Two Socks every now and then. When he'd eaten his fill he lobbed the carcass into the yard and the old wolf carried it off into the night.

Lieutenant Dunbar sat in one of the camp chairs and smoked, letting the nighttime sounds entertain him. He thought it amazing how far he had come in such a short time. Not so long ago these same sounds had kept him on edge. They'd stolen his sleep. Now they were so familiar as to be comforting.

He thought back over the day and decided it had been a very good one. As the fire burned down with his second cigarette he realized how unique it was for him to be dealing singly and directly with the Indians. He allowed himself a pat on the back, thinking that he had done a credible job thus far as a representative of the United States of America. And without any guidelines, to boot.

Suddenly he thought of the Great War. It was possible that he was no longer a representative of the United States. Perhaps the war was over. The Confederate States of America . . . He couldn't imagine such a thing. But it could be. He'd been without any information for a long time now.

These musings brought him to his own career, and he admitted inwardly that he'd been thinking less and less about the army. That he was in the midst of a great adventure had much to do with these omissions, but as he sat by the dwindling fire and listened to the yip of coyotes down by the river, it crossed his mind that he might have stumbled on to a better life. In this life he wanted for very little. Cisco and Two Socks weren't human, but their unwavering loyalty was satisfying in ways that human relationships had never been. He was happy with them.

And of course there were the Indians. They held a distinct pull for him. At the least they made for excellent neighbors, well mannered, open, and sharing. Though he was much too white for aboriginal ways, he felt more than comfortable with them. There was something wise about them. Maybe that was why he'd been drawn from the start. The lieutenant had never been much of a learner. He'd always been a doer, sometimes to a fault. But he sensed that this facet of his personality was shifting.

Yes, he thought, that's it. There is something to learn from them. They know things. If the army never comes, I don't suppose the loss would be so great.

Dunbar felt suddenly lazy. Yawning, he flipped the butt of his smoke into the embers glowing at his feet and stretched his arms high over his head.

"Sleep," he said. "I will now sleep like a dead man the whole night through."

seven

Lieutenant Dunbar woke with alarm in the dark of early morning. His sod hut was trembling. The earth was trembling, too, and the air was filled with a hollow rumbling sound.

He swung out of bed and listened hard. The rumble was coming from somewhere close, just downriver.

Pulling on his pants and boots, the lieutenant slipped outside. The sound was even louder here, filling the prairie night with a great, reverberating echo.

He felt small in its midst.

The sound was not coming toward him, and without knowing precisely why, he ruled out the idea that some freak of nature, an earthquake or a flood, was producing this enormous energy. Something alive was making the sound. Something alive was making the earth tremble, and he had to see.

The light of his lantern seemed tiny as he walked toward the rush of sound somewhere in front of him. He hadn't gone a hundred yards along the bluff before the feeble light he was holding picked up something. It was dust: a great, billowing wall of it rising into the night.

The lieutenant slowed to a creep as he got closer. All at once he knew that hooves were making the thunderous sound and that the dust was being raised by a movement of beasts so large that he could never have believed what he was now seeing with his own eyes.

The buffalo.

One of them swerved out of the dusty cloud. And another. And another. He only glimpsed them as they roared past, but the sight of them was so magnificent that they may as well have been frozen. At that moment they froze forever in Lieutenant Dunbar's memory.

In that moment, all alone with his lantern, he knew what they meant to the world he lived in. They were what the ocean meant to fishes, what the sky meant to birds, what air meant to a pair of human lungs.

They were the life of the prairie.

And there were thousands of them pouring over the embankment and down to the river, which they crossed with no more care than a train would a puddle. Then up the other side and out onto the grasslands, thundering to a destination known only to them, a torrent of hooves and horns and meat cutting across the landscape with a force beyond all imagining.

Dunbar dropped the lantern where he stood and broke into a run. He stopped for nothing except Cisco's bridle, not even a shirt. Then he jumped up and kicked his horse into a gallop. He laid his bare chest close on the little buckskin's neck and gave Cisco his head.

eight

The village was ablaze with firelight as Lieutenant Dunbar raced into the depression where the lodges were pitched and pounded up the camp's main avenue.

Now he could see the flames of the biggest fire and the crowd gathered around it. He could see the buffalo-headed dancers and he could hear the steady roll of the drums. He could hear deep, rhythmic chanting.

But he was barely aware of the spectacle opening before him, just as he had been barely aware of the ride he'd made, tearing across the prairie at full speed for miles. He wasn't conscious of the sweat that coated Cisco from head to tail. Only one thing was in his head as he rushed his horse up the avenue . . . the Comanche word for buffalo. He was turning it over and over, trying to remember the exact pronunciation.

Now he was shouting out the word. But with all the drumming and chanting, they hadn't yet heard his approach. As he neared the fire he tried to pull Cisco up, but the horse was high on runaway speed and didn't answer the bit.

He charged into the very center of the dance, scattering Comanches in every direction. With a supreme effort the lieutenant pulled him up, but as Cisco's hindquarters brushed against the ground, his head and neck rose straight up. His front legs clawed madly at empty space. Dunbar couldn't keep his seat. He slid off the sweat-slicked back and crashed to earth with an audible thud.

Before he could move, a half-dozen infuriated warriors pounced on him. One man with a club might have ended everything, but the six men were tangled together and no one could get a clear shot at the lieutenant.

They rolled over the ground in a chaotic ball. Dunbar was screaming "Buffalo" as he fought against the punches and kicks. But no one could understand what he was saying, and some of the blows were now finding their mark.

Then he was dimly aware of a lessening of the weight pressing against him. Someone was shouting above the tumult, and the voice sounded familiar.

Suddenly there was no one on him. He was lying alone on the ground, staring up through half-stunned eyes at a multitude of Indian faces. One of the faces bent closer.

Kicking Bird.

The lieutenant said, "Buffalo."

His body was heaving as it sucked for air, and his voice had been a whisper.

Kicking Bird's face leaned closer.

"Buffalo," the lieutenant gasped.

Kicking Bird grunted and shook his head. He turned his ear to within a whisker of Dunbar's mouth and the lieutenant said the word once more, struggling with all his might for the right accent.

"Buffalo."

Kicking Bird's eyes were back in front of Lieutenant Dunbar's.

''Buffalo?''

''Yes,'' Dunbar said, a wan smile flaring on his face. ''Yes . . . buffalo . . . buffalo.''

Exhausted, he closed his eyes for a moment and heard Kicking Bird's deep voice bellow over the stillness as he shouted the word.

It was answered with a roar of joy from every Comanche throat, and for a split second the lieutenant thought the power of it was carrying him away. Blinking away the glaze on his eyes, he realized that strong Indian arms were bringing him to his feet.

When the erstwhile lieutenant looked up, he was greeted with scores of beaming faces. They were pressing in around him.

CHAPTER XVIII

one

Everyone went.

The camp by the river was left virtually deserted when the great caravan moved out at dawn.

Flankers were sent in every direction. The bulk of mounted warriors rode at the front. Then came the women and children, some mounted, some not. Those on foot marched alongside ponies dragging travois piled with gear. Some of the very old rode on the drags. The huge pony herd brought up the rear.

There was much to be amazed at. The sheer size of the column, the speed with which it traveled, the incredible racket it made, the marvel of organization that gave everyone a place and a job.

But what Lieutenant Dunbar found most extraordinary of all was his own treatment. Literally overnight he had gone from one who was eyed by the band with suspicion or indifference to a person of genuine standing. The women smiled openly at him now and the warriors went so far as to share their jokes with him. The children, of which there were many,

158

constantly sought out his company and occasionally made themselves a nuisance.

In treating him this way the Comanches revealed an altogether new side of themselves, reversing the stoic, guarded appearance they had presented to him in the past. Now they were an unabashed, thoroughly cheerful people, and it made Lieutenant Dunbar the same.

The arrival of the buffalo would have brightened the lagging Comanche spirits in any event, but the lieutenant knew as the column struck out across the prairie that his presence added a certain luster to the undertaking, and he rode a little taller at the thought of that.

Long before they reached Fort Sedgewick, scouts brought word that a big trail had been found where the lieutenant said it would be, and more men were immediately dispatched to locate the main herd's grazing area.

Each scout took several fresh mounts in tow. They would ride until they found the herd, then come back to the column to report its size and how many miles away it was. They would also report the presence of any enemies who might be lurking around the Comanche hunting grounds.

As the column passed by, Dunbar made a brief stop at the fort. He gathered a supply of tobacco, his revolver and rifle, a tunic, a grain ration for Cisco, and was back at the side of Kicking Bird and his assistants within a matter of minutes.

After they'd crossed the river, Kicking Bird motioned him forward and the two men rode beyond the head of the column. It was then that Dunbar got his first look at the buffalo trail: a gigantic swath of torn-up ground a half-mile wide, sweeping over the prairie like some immense, dung-littered highway.

Kicking Bird was describing something in signs that the lieutenant couldn't fully grasp when two puffs of dust appeared on the horizon. The dust swirls gradually became riders. A pair of returning scouts.

Leading spare mounts, they came in at a gallop and pulled

up directly in front of Ten Bears's entourage to make their report.

Kicking Bird rode over to confer, and Dunbar, not knowing what was being said, watched the medicine man closely, hoping to divine something from his expression.

What he saw didn't help him much. If he'd known the language, he would have understood that the herd had stopped to graze in a great valley about ten miles south of the column's present position, a place they could easily reach by nightfall.

The conversation suddenly became animated and the lieutenant leaned reflexively forward as if to hear. The scouts were making long, sweeping gestures, first to the south and then to the east. The faces of their listeners grew markedly more somber, and after questioning the scouts a few moments more, Ten Bears held a council on horseback with his closest advisers.

Shortly, two riders broke away from the meeting and galloped back down the line. While they were gone Kicking Bird glanced once at the lieutenant, and Dunbar knew his face well enough now to know that this expression meant not all was as it should be.

Hoofbeats sounded behind him, and the lieutenant turned to see a dozen warriors charging to the front of the line. The fierce one was leading them.

They stopped next to Ten Bears's group, held a brief consultation, and, taking one of the scouts with them, flew off in an easterly direction.

The column began to move again, and as Kicking Bird came back to his place next to the white soldier, he could see that the lieutenant's eyes were full of questions. It was not possible to explain this thing to him, this bad omen.

Enemies had been discovered in the neighborhood, mysterious enemies from another world. By their deeds they had proved themselves to be people without value and without soul, wanton slaughterers with no regard for Comanche rights. It was important to punish them.

So Kicking Bird avoided the lieutenant's questioning eyes. Instead, he watched the dust of Wind In His Hair's party trail off to the east and said a silent prayer for the success of their mission.

two

From the moment he saw the little rose-colored bumps rising in the distance, he knew he was coming on to something ugly. There were black specks on the rose-colored bumps, and as the column drew closer, he could see that they were moving. Even the air seemed suddenly closer and the lieutenant loosened another button on his tunic.

Kicking Bird had brought him to the front with a purpose. But his intention was not to punish. It was to educate, and the education could best be served by seeing rather than talking. The impact would be greater in front. It would be greater for both of them. Kicking Bird had never seen this sight, either.

Like mercury in a thermometer, a bilious mixture of revulsion and lament climbed steadily in Lieutenant Dunbar's throat. He had to swallow constantly to keep it from coming out as he and Kicking Bird led the column through the center of the killing ground.

He counted twenty-seven buffalo. And though he couldn't count them, he figured there were at least as many ravens swarming over each body. In some cases the heads of the buffalo were covered with the battling black birds, screaming and twisting and flopping as they fought for the eyeballs. Those whose eyes had already been swallowed played host to larger swarms, which pecked ravenously as they strolled back and forth on the carcasses, defecating every so often as if to accent the richness of their feast.

Wolves were appearing from all directions. They would be crouching at the shoulders and haunches and bellies as soon as the column passed.

But there would be more than enough for every wolf and bird within miles. The lieutenant calculated roughly and came up with a figure of fifteen thousand. Fifteen thousand pounds of dead flesh decaying in the hot afternoon sun.

All this left to rot, he thought, wondering if some arch-enemy of his Indian friends had left this as a macabre warning.

Twenty-seven hides had been stripped away from neck to buttocks, and as he passed within feet of a particularly large animal, he saw that its open mouth held no tongue. Others had been robbed of their tongues, too. But that was all. Everything else had been left.

Lieutenant Dunbar suddenly thought of the dead man in the alley. Like these buffalo, the man had been lying on his side. The bullet that had been fired into the base of his skull had taken the right side of the man's jaw out when it exited.

He had been just John Dunbar then, a fourteen-year-old boy. In succeeding years he'd seen scores of dead men: with whole faces missing, men whose brains leaked onto the ground like spilled mush. But the first dead man was the one he remembered best. Mainly because of the fingers.

He'd been standing right behind the constable when it was discovered that two of the dead man's fingers had been sliced off. The constable had looked around and said to no one in particular, ''This fella got killed for his rings.''

And now these buffalo lying dead on the ground, their guts spread all over the prairie just because someone wanted their tongues and hides. It struck Dunbar as the same kind of crime.

When he saw an unborn calf, half hanging from its mother's slit abdomen, the same word he'd first heard that evening in the alley jumped into his mind like a glowing sign.

Murder.

He glanced at Kicking Bird. The medicine man was staring at the wreckage of the unborn calf, his face a long, sober mask.

Lieutenant Dunbar turned away then and looked back along the column. The whole band was weaving its way through the carnage. Hungry as they were after weeks of scraps, no one had stopped to help himself or herself to the bounty spread out around them. The voices that had been so raucous all morning were now stilled, and he could see in their faces the melancholy that comes from knowing a good trail has suddenly turned bad.

three

The horses were casting giant shadows by the time they reached the hunting grounds. While the women and children set to work pitching camp in the lee of a long ridge, most of the men rode ahead to scout the herd before night fell.

Lieutenant Dunbar went with them.

About a mile from the new camp they rendezvoused with three scouts who had made a little camp of their own a hundred yards from the mouth of a wide draw.

Leaving their horses below, sixty Comanche warriors and one white man started quietly up the long western slope leading out of the draw. As they neared the crest, everyone dropped close to the ground and crawled the final yards.

The lieutenant looked expectantly at Kicking Bird and was met with a shallow smile. The medicine man pointed ahead and put a finger to his lips. Dunbar knew they had arrived.

A few feet in front of him the earth fell away to nothing but sky, and he realized they had surmounted the back side of a cliff. The stiff prairie breeze bit into his face as he lifted his head and peered into a great depression a hundred feet below.

It was a magnificent dish of a valley, four or five miles wide and at least ten miles across. Grass of the most luxuriant variety was rippling everywhere.

But the lieutenant barely noticed the grass or the valley or its dimensions. Even the sky, now building with clouds, and the sinking sun, with its miraculous display of cathedral rays, could not compare with the great, living blanket of buffalo that covered the valley floor.

That this many creatures existed, let alone occupied the same immediate space, set the lieutenant's mind spinning with incalculable figures. Fifty, seventy, a hundred thousand? Could there be more? His brain backed away from the enormity of it.

He didn't shout or jump or whisper to himself in awe. Witnessing this put everything but that which he was seeing in suspension. He didn't feel the little, odd-sized rocks pinching against his body. When a blue wasp landed on the point of his slackened jaw he didn't brush at it. All he could do was blink at the coating of wonder that glazed his eyes.

He was watching a miracle.

When Kicking Bird tapped him on the shoulder, he realized that his mouth had been open the whole time. It was parched dry by the prairie wind.

He swung his head dully and looked back along the slope.

The Indians had started down.

four

They had been riding in darkness for half an hour when the fires appeared, like faraway dots. The strangeness of it was like a dream.

Home, he thought. That's home.

How could it be? A temporary camp of fires on a distant plain, peopled by two hundred aborigines whose skin was different than his, whose language was a tangle of grunts and shouts, whose beliefs were yet a mystery and probably always would be.

But tonight he was very tired. Tonight it promised the comfort of a birthplace. It was home and he was glad to see it.

The others, the scores of half-naked men with whom he'd been riding the last few miles, were glad to see it, too. They had begun talking again. The horses could smell it. They were walking high on their toes now, trying to break into a trot.

He wished he could see Kicking Bird among the vague shapes around him. The medicine man said a lot with his eyes, and out here in the darkness, bunched so intimately with these wild men as they approached their wild camp, he felt helpless without Kicking Bird's telling eyes.

A half mile out he could hear voices and the beat of drums. A buzzing swept the ranks of his fellow riders and suddenly the horses surged into a run. They were packed so tightly and moving at such a good clip that, for a moment, Lieutenant Dunbar felt part of an unstoppable energy, a breaking wave of men and horses that no one would dare to oppose.

The men were yipping, high and shrill, like coyotes, and Dunbar, caught up as he was in the excitement, let out a few barks of his own.

He could see the flames of the fires and the silhouettes of people milling about the camp. They were aware of the returning riders now and some were running onto the prairie to meet them.

He had a funny feeling about the camp, a feeling that told him it was unusually agitated, that something out of the ordinary had happened during their absence. His eyes widened as he rode closer, trying to pick up some clue that would tell him what was different.

Then he saw the wagon, parked at the fringes of the largest

fire, as out of place as a fine carriage floating on the surface of the sea.

There were white people in camp.

He pulled Cisco up hard, letting the other riders blow past while he hung back to collect his thoughts.

The wagon looked crude to him, a thing of ugliness. As Cisco danced nervously under him, the lieutenant was startled by his own thoughts. When he imagined the voices that had come with it, he didn't want to hear them. He didn't want to see the white faces that would be so eager to see his. He didn't want to answer their questions. He didn't want to hear the news he'd missed.

But he knew he had no choice. There was no place else to go. He fed Cisco a little rein and they walked forward slowly.

He paused when he was within fifty yards. The Indians were dancing about exuberantly as the men who had scouted the herd jumped off their horses. He waited for the ponies to clear out, then he scanned all the faces in his line of sight.

There were no white ones.

They came closer and once again Dunbar paused, his gaze searching the camp carefully.

No white people.

He spotted the fierce one and the men of his little party that had left them in the afternoon. They seemed to be the center of attention. This was definitely more than a greeting. It was a celebration of some sort. They were passing long sticks back and forth. They were yelling. The villagers who had gathered to watch them were yelling, too.

He and Cisco edged still closer and the lieutenant saw right away that he was wrong. They weren't passing sticks around. They were passing lances. One of them came back to Wind In His Hair, and Dunbar saw him lift it high into the air. He wasn't smiling, but he was surely happy. As he let out a long, vibrating howl, Dunbar caught a glimpse of the hair tied near the lance's point.

At the same moment, he realized it was a scalp. A fresh scalp. The hair was black and curly.

His eyes darted to the other lances. Two more of them held scalps; one was light brown and the other was sandy, almost blond. He looked quickly at the wagon and saw what he had not seen before. A load of stacked buffalo hides was peeking over the rails.

Suddenly it was clear as a cloudless day.

The skins belonged to the murdered buffalo and the scalps belonged to the men who had killed them, men who had been alive that very afternoon. White men. The lieutenant was numb with confusion. He couldn't participate in this, not even as a watcher. He had to leave.

As he was turning away he happened to catch sight of Kicking Bird. The medicine man had been smiling widely, but when he saw Lieutenant Dunbar in the shadows just beyond the firelight, his smile vanished. Then, as though he wanted to relieve the lieutenant of some embarrassment, he turned his back.

Dunbar wanted to believe that Kicking Bird's heart was with him, that in some vague way it knew his confusion. But he couldn't think now. He had to go off by himself.

Skirting the camp, he located his gear on the far side and went out onto the prairie with Cisco. He went until he could no longer see the fires. Then he spread his bedroll on the ground and lay looking at the stars, trying to believe that the men who had been killed were bad people and deserved to die. But it was no good. He could not know that for certain, and even if he did . . . well, it was not for him to say. He tried to believe that Wind In His Hair and Kicking Bird and all the other people who shared in the killing were not so happy for having done it. But they were.

More than anything he wanted to believe that he was not in this position. He wanted to believe he was floating toward the stars. But he wasn't.

He heard Cisco lie down in the grass with a heavy sigh. It

was quiet then and Dunbar's thought turned inward, toward himself. Or rather his lack of self. He did not belong to the Indians. He did not belong to the whites. And it was not time for him to belong to the stars.

He belonged right where he was now. He belonged no-where.

A sob rose in his throat. He had to gag to stifle it. But the sobs kept coming up and it was not long before he ceased to see the sense in trying to keep them down.

five

Something tapped him. As he came awake he thought he'd dreamed the little nudge he felt in his back. The blanket was heavy and damp with dew. He must have pulled it over his head during the night.

He lifted the edge of the blanket and peered out at the hazy light of morning. Cisco was standing alone in the grass a few feet in front of him. His ears were up.

There it was again, something kicking him lightly in the back. Lieutenant Dunbar threw off the blanket and looked into the face of a man standing directly over him.

It was Wind In His Hair. His stern face was painted with bars of ocher. A sparkling new rifle was hanging from one of his hands. He started to move the rifle and the lieutenant held his breath. This might be his time. He pictured his hair, dangling from the fierce one's lance.

But as Wind In His Hair lifted the rifle a little higher, he smiled. He jabbed his toe gently into the lieutenant's side and said a few words in Comanche. Lieutenant Dunbar lay still as Wind In His Hair sighted down his rifle at some imag-ined game. Then he shoved a hunk of imaginary food into his mouth, and like one friend playfully rousting another, he tickled Dunbar's ribs with the toe of his moccasin once again.

six

They came from downwind, every able-bodied man in the band, riding in a great, hornlike formation, a moving crescent half a mile wide. They rode slowly, taking care not to startle the buffalo until the last possible moment, until it was time to run.

As a novice among experts Lieutenant Dunbar was absorbed in trying to piece together the strategy of the hunt as it unfolded. From his position close to the center of the formation he could see that they were moving to isolate one small section of the gigantic herd. The riders comprising the right part of the moving horn had nearly succeeded in closing off the small section while the middle was pressuring its rear. Off to his left the hunting formation was swinging into an ever-straightening line.

It was a surround.

He was close enough to hear sounds: the random bawling of calves, the lowing of mothers, and an occasional snort from one of the massive bulls. Several thousand animals were straight ahead.

The lieutenant glanced to his right. Wind In His Hair was the next rider over, and he was all eyes as they closed on the herd. He seemed unaware of the horse moving under him or of the rifle rocking in his hand. His keen eyes were everywhere at once: on the hunters, on the quarry, and on the shrinking ground between them. If the air could be seen, he would have noticed every subtle shift. He was like a man listening to the countdown tick of some unseen clock.

Even Lieutenant Dunbar, so unpracticed at such things, could feel the tension bristling about him. The air had gone absolutely dead. Nothing was carrying. He could no longer hear the hooves of the hunter's ponies. Even the herd ahead had gone suddenly silent. Death was settling over the prairie with the surety of a descending cloud.

When he was within a hundred yards a handful of the

shaggy beasts turned as a unit and faced him. They lifted their great heads, nosing the dead air for a hint of what their ears had heard but their weak eyes were as yet unable to identify. Their tails went up, curling above their rumps like little flags. The largest among them pawed at the grass, shook his head, and snorted gruffly, challenging the intrusion of the approaching riders.

Dunbar understood then that for every hunter, the killing about to take place would not be a foregone conclusion, that it would not be a lying-in-wait thing, that to perform death on these animals, each man was going to chance his own.

A commotion broke out along the right flank, far up the line at the tip of the horn. The hunters had struck.

With astonishing speed this first strike set off a chain re-action that caught Dunbar in the same way an ocean breaker slams into an unsuspecting wader.

The bulls that had been facing him turned and ran. At the same time every Indian pony shot forward. It happened so fast that Cisco nearly ran out from under the lieutenant. He reached back as his hat blew off, but it tumbled past his fingertips. It didn't matter. There was no stopping now, not if he had used all his strength. The little buckskin was surging ahead, chewing up the ground as if flames were tickling his heels, as if his life depended on running.

Dunbar looked at the line of riders to his right and left and was appalled to see that no one was there. He glanced over his shoulder and saw them, flat on the backs of their straining ponies. They were going as fast as they could, but compared to Cisco they were dawdlers, hopelessly struggling to keep up. They were falling farther behind with each passing sec-ond, and suddenly the lieutenant was occupying a space all to himself. He was between the pursuing hunters and the fleeing buffalo.

He tugged on Cisco's reins, but if the buckskin felt it at all, he paid it no mind. His neck was stretched out straight, his ears were flat, and his nostrils were flared to their fullest, gobbling the wind that fueled him ever closer to the herd.

Lieutenant Dunbar had no time to think. The prairie was flying past his feet, the sky was rolling overhead, and between the two, spread out in a long line directly ahead, was a wall of stampeding buffalo.

He was close enough now to see the muscles of their hindquarters. He could see the bottoms of their hooves. In seconds he would be close enough to touch them.

He was rushing into a deathly nightmare, a man in an open boat floating helplessly toward the lip of the falls. The lieutenant didn't scream. He didn't say a prayer or make the sign of the cross. But he did close his eyes. The faces of his father and mother popped into his head. They were doing something he had never seen them do. They were kissing passionately. There was a pounding all about them, a great, rolling rumble of a thousand drums. The lieutenant opened his eyes and found himself in a dreamlike landscape, a valley filled with gigantic brown and black boulders hurtling in a single direction.

They were running with the herd.

The tremendous thunder of tens of thousands of cloven hooves carried the curious silence of a deluge, and for a few moments Dunbar was serenely adrift in the crazy quiet of the stampede.

As he clung to Cisco he looked out over the massive, moving carpet of which he was now a part and imagined that, if he wanted, he could slip off his horse's back and make it to the safety of empty ground by hopping from one hump to another, as a boy might skip across the rocks in a stream.

The rifle slipped, nearly falling out of his sweaty hand, and as it did, the bull running on his left, no more than a foot or two away, veered in sharply. With a thrust of his shaggy head he tried to gore Cisco. But the buckskin was too deft. He jumped away and the horn only grazed his neck. The move nearly dumped Lieutenant Dunbar. He should have fallen to his death. But the buffalo were packed so tightly around him that he bounced against the back of a buffalo running along the other side and somehow righted himself.

Panicked, the lieutenant lowered his rifle and fired at the buffalo who had tried to gore Cisco. It was a bad shot, but the bullet shattered one of the beast's front legs. Its knees buckled and Dunbar heard the snap of its neck as the bull somersaulted.

Suddenly there was open space all around him. The buffalo had shied away from the report of his gun. He pulled hard at Cisco's reins and the buckskin responded. In a moment they had stopped. The rumble of the herd was receding.

As he watched the herd fall away in front of him he saw that his fellow hunters had caught them. The sight of naked men on horseback, running with all these animals, like corks bobbing in high seas, held him spellbound for several minutes. He could see the bend of their bows and the puffs of dust as one after another of the buffalo went down.

But not many minutes had passed before he turned back. He wanted to see his kill with his own eyes. He wanted to confirm what seemed too fantastic to be true.

Everything had happened in less time than it took to shave.

seven

It was a big animal to begin with, but in death, lying still and alone in the short grass, it looked bigger.

Like a visitor at an exhibit, Lieutenant Dunbar circled the body slowly. He paused at the bull's monstrous head, took one of the horns in hand, and tugged at it. The head was very heavy. He ran his hand the length of the body: through the wooly thatch on the hump, down the sharply sloping back, and over the fine-coated rump. He held the tufted tail between his fingers. It seemed ridiculously small.

Retracing his steps, the lieutenant squatted in front of the bull's head and squeezed the long, black beard hanging from its chin. It reminded him of a general's goatee, and he wondered if this fellow had been a high-standing member of the herd.

He stood up then and back up a step or two, still taken with the sight of the dead buffalo. How just one of these remarkable creatures could exist was a beautiful mystery. And there were thousands of them.

Maybe there are millions, he thought.

He felt no pride in having taken the bull's life, but it brought him no remorse, either. Aside from a strong sensation of respect, he felt no emotion. He did feel something physical, however. He could feel his stomach twisting. He heard it grumble. His mouth had begun to water. For several days his meals had been skimpy, and now, gazing down at this large pile of meat, he was acutely aware of his hunger.

Barely ten minutes had passed since the furious charge, and already the hunt was over. Leaving their dead behind, the herd had vanished. The hunters were hanging about their kills, waiting as the women and children and elderly poured onto the plains, hauling their butchering equipment along with them. Their voices were ringing with excitement, and Dunbar was struck by the idea that some kind of festival had begun.

Wind In His Hair suddenly galloped up with two cronies. Flush with success, he was smiling broadly as he vaulted off his heaving pony. The lieutenant noticed an ugly, leaking gash just below the warrior's knee.

But Wind In His Hair didn't notice. He was still beaming grandly as he sidled up to the lieutenant and whacked him on the back with a well-intentioned greeting that sent Dunbar sprawling onto the ground.

Laughing good-naturedly, Wind In His Hair pulled the stunned lieutenant to his feet and pressed a thick-bladed knife into his palm. He said something in Comanche and pointed at the dead bull.

Dunbar stood flatfooted, staring sheepishly at the knife in his hand. He smiled helplessly and shook his head. He didn't know what to do.

Wind In His Hair muttered an aside that made his friends laugh, smacked the lieutenant on the shoulder, and took back the knife. Then he dropped to one knee at the belly of Dunbar's buffalo.

With the aplomb of a seasoned carver he drove the knife deep into the buffalo's chest and, using both hands, dragged the blade back, opening it up. As the guts spilled out, Wind In His Hair stuck a hand into the cavity, groping about like a man feeling for something in the dark.

He found what he wanted, gave it a couple of stiff tugs, and rose to his feet with a liver so large that it flopped over both his hands. Mimicking the white soldier's well-known bow, he presented this prize to the dumbstruck lieutenant. Gingerly, Dunbar accepted the steaming organ, but having no idea what to do, he fell back on his trusty bow and, politely as he could, handed the liver back.

Normally, Wind In His Hair might have taken offense, but he reminded himself that "Jun" was white and therefore ignorant. He made yet another bow, stuffed one end of the still warm liver into his mouth, and tore off a substantial chunk.

Lieutenant Dunbar watched incredulously as the warrior passed the liver to his friends. They also gnawed off pieces of the raw meat. They were eating it greedily, as if it were fresh apple pie.

By now a little crowd, some mounted, some on foot, had gathered around Dunbar's buffalo. Kicking Bird was there, and so was Stands With A Fist. She and another woman had already begun to skin the dead bull.

Once again Wind In His Hair offered him the half-eaten meat and once again Dunbar took it. He held it dumbly as his eyes searched for an expression or a sign from someone in the crowd that would let him off the hook.

He got no help. They were watching him silently, waiting expectantly, and he realized it would be foolishly transparent to try to pass it off again. Even Kicking Bird was waiting.

So as Dunbar lifted the liver to his mouth he told himself how easy this was, that it would be no more difficult than forcing down a spoonful of something he hated, like lima beans.

Hoping he wouldn't gag, he bit into the liver.

The meat was incredibly tender. It melted in his mouth. He watched the horizon as he chewed, and for the moment Lieutenant Dunbar forgot about his silent audience as his taste buds sent a surprising message to his brain.

The meat was delicious.

Without thinking, he took another bite. A spontaneous smile broke across his face and he lifted what was left of the meat triumphantly over his head.

His fellow hunters answered his gesture with a chorus of wild cheers.

CHAPTER XIX

one

Like many people, Lieutenant Dunbar had spent most of his life on the sidelines, observing rather than participating. At the times when he was a participant, his actions were distinctly independent, much like his experience in the war had been.

It was a frustrating thing, always standing apart.

Something about this lifelong rut changed when he enthusiastically lifted the liver, the symbol of his kill, and heard the cries of encouragement from his fellows. Then he had felt the satisfaction of belonging to something whose whole was greater than any of its parts. It was a feeling that ran deep from the start. And in the days he spent on the killing plain and the nights he spent in the temporary camp, the feeling was solidly reinforced.

The army had tirelessly extolled the virtues of service, of individual sacrifice in the name of God or country or both. The lieutenant had done his best to adopt these tenets, but the feeling of service to the army had dwelled mostly in his head. Not in his heart. It never lasted beyond the fading, hollow rhetoric of patriotism.

The Comanches were different.

They were primitive people. They lived in a big, lonely, alien world that was written off by his own people as nothing more than hundreds of worthless miles to be crossed.

But the facts of their lives had grown less important to him. They were a group who lived and prospered through service. Service was how they controlled the fragile destiny of their lives. It was constantly being rendered, faithfully and without complaint, to the simple, beautiful spirit of the way they lived, and in it Lieutenant Dunbar found a peace that was to his liking.

He did not deceive himself. He did not think of becoming an Indian. But he knew that so long as he was with them, he would serve the same spirit.

He was made a happier man by this revelation.

two

The butchering was a colossal enterprise.

There were perhaps seventy dead buffalo, scattered like chocolate drops across a great earthen floor, and at each body families set up portable factories that worked with amazing speed and precision in transforming animals into usable products.

The lieutenant could not believe the blood. It soaked into the killing ground like juice spilled on a tablecloth. It covered the arms and faces and clothing of the butcherers. It dripped from the ponies and travois transporting the flesh back to camp.

They took everything: hides, meat, guts, hooves, tails, heads. In the space of a few hours it was all gone, leaving the prairie with the appearance of a gigantic, recently cleared banquet table.

Lieutenant Dunbar passed the butchering time lolling

around with the other warriors. Spirits were high. Only two men had been hurt, neither one of them seriously. One veteran pony had snapped a foreleg, but that was little to lose when compared with the abundance the hunters had produced.

They were delighted, and it showed in their faces as they hobnobbed through the afternoon, smoking and eating and swapping stories. Dunbar didn't understand the words, but the stories were easy enough to pick up. They were tales of close calls and broken bows and the ones who had gotten away.

When the lieutenant was called upon to relate his story, he mimed the adventure with a theatricality that drove the warriors crazy with laughter. It became the day's most sought-after testimonial, and he was forced to repeat it a half-dozen times. The result was the same with every telling. By the time he was halfway through, his listeners would be hugging themselves, trying to hold back the ache of unbridled laughter.

Lieutenant Dunbar didn't mind. He was laughing, too. And he didn't mind the role that luck had played in his deeds, for he knew that they were real. And he knew that through them he had accomplished something marvelous.

He had become "one of the boys."

three

The first thing he saw when they returned to camp that evening was his hat. It was riding on the head of a middle-aged man whom he did not know.

There was a brief moment of tension as Lieutenant Dunbar strode directly over, pointed at the army-issue hat, which fitted the man rather badly, and said, in a matter-of-fact way, "That's mine."

The warrior looked at him curiously and removed the hat. He turned it around in his hands and placed it back on his head. Then he slipped the knife off his belt, handed it to the lieutenant, and went on his way without saying a word.

Dunbar watched his hat bob out of sight and stared down at the knife in his hand. Its beaded sheath looked like a treasure, and he walked off to find Kicking Bird, thinking he'd gotten much the best part of the exchange.

He moved freely through the camp, and everywhere he went he found himself the object of cheerful salutations.

Men nodded acknowledgments, women smiled, and giggling children tottered after him. The band was delirious with the prospect of the great feast to come, and the lieutenant's presence was an added source of joy. Without a formal proclamation or consensus they had come to think of him as a living good-luck charm.

Kicking Bird took him directly to Ten Bears's lodge, where a little ceremony of thanks was being held. The old man was still remarkably fit, and the hump from his kill was being roasted first. When it was ready Ten Bears himself cut away a piece, said a few words to the Great Spirit, and honored the lieutenant by handing him the first piece.

Dunbar made his short bow, took a bite, and gallantly handed the slab back to Ten Bears, a move that impressed the old man greatly. He fired up his pipe and further honored the lieutenant by offering him the first puff.

The smoking in front of Ten Bears's lodge marked the beginning of a wild night. Everyone had a fire going, and over every fire fresh meat was roasting: humps, ribs, and a wide array of other choice cuts.

Lit like a small city, the temporary village twinkled long into the night, its smoke trailing into the darkened sky with an aroma that could be smelled for miles.

The people ate like there was no tomorrow. When they were stuffed full they took short breaks, drifting off into little groups to make idle talk or to play at games of chance. But once the last meal had settled, they would return to the fires and gorge themselves again.

Before the night was very far along Lieutenant Dunbar felt like he had eaten an entire buffalo. He'd been touring the camp with Wind In His Hair, and at each fire the pair was treated like royalty.

They were en route to still another group of merrymakers when the lieutenant stopped in the shadows behind a lodge and told Wind In His Hair with signs that his stomach was hurting and that he wanted to sleep.

But at this moment Wind In His Hair wasn't listening too closely. His attention was riveted on the lieutenant's tunic. Dunbar looked down his chest at the row of brass buttons, then back into the face of his hunting pal. The warrior's eyes were slightly glazed as he stuck out a finger and let it come to rest on one of the buttons.

"You want this?" the lieutenant asked, the sound of his words wiping the glaze from Wind In His Hair's eyes.

The warrior said nothing. He inspected his fingertip to see if anything had come off the button.

"If you want it," the lieutenant said, "you can have it."

He loosed the buttons, slipped his arms free of the sleeves, and handed it to the warrior.

Wind In His Hair knew it was being offered, but he didn't take it right away. Instead he began to undo the magnificent breastplate of shiny pipe-bone that was tied at his neck and waist. This he handed to Dunbar as his other brown hand closed around the tunic.

The lieutenant helped with the buttons, and when it was on he could see that Wind In His Hair was as delighted as a kid at Christmas.

Dunbar handed back the beautiful breastplate and was met with rejection. Wind In His Hair shook his head violently and waved his hands. He made motions that told the white soldier to put it on.

"I can't take this," the lieutenant stammered. "This is not . . . it's not a fair trade. . . . You understand?"

But Wind In His Hair wouldn't hear of it. To him it was more than fair. Breastplates were full of power and took time to make. But the tunic was one of a kind.

He turned Dunbar around, draped the decorative armor over his chest, and fastened the ties securely.

So the trade was made and each man was happy. Wind In His Hair grunted a good-bye and started for the nearest fire. The new acquisition was tight and it itched against his skin. But that was of little import. He was certain that the tunic would prove to be a solid addition to his supply of charms. In time it might show itself to possess strong medicine, particularly the brass buttons and the golden bars on the shoulders.

It was a great prize.

four

Eager to avoid the food he knew he would be foisted on him were he to cut through camp, Lieutenant Dunbar stole onto the prairie and circled the temporary village, hoping he could spot Kicking Bird's lodge and go straightaway to sleep.

On his second full revolution he caught sight of the lodge marked with a bear, and knowing that Kicking Bird's tepee would be pitched nearby, he reentered the camp.

He'd not gone far when a sound gave him pause, and he stopped behind a nondescript lodge. Light from a fire was splashing across the ground just in front of him, and it was from this fire that the sound was coming. It was singing, high and repetitive and distinctly feminine.

Hugging the wall of the lodge, Lieutenant Dunbar peered ahead in the manner of a Peeping Tom.

A dozen young women, their chores behind them for the

moment, were dancing and singing in a ragged circle close to the fire. As far as he could tell, there was nothing ceremonial involved. The singing was punctuated by light laughter, and he figured that this dance was impromptu, something designed purely for fun.

His eyes accidentally fell on the breastplate. It was lit now with the orangish glow of the fire, and he couldn't resist running a hand over the double row of tubelike bones that now covered the whole of his chest and stomach. What a rare thing it was to see such beauty and such strength residing in the same place at the same time. It made him feel special.

I will keep this forever, he thought dreamily.

When he looked up again several of the dancers had broken away to form a little knot of smiling, whispering women whose current topic was obviously the white man wearing the bone breastplate. They were looking straight at him, and though he didn't perceive it, there was a touch of the devil in their eyes.

Having been a constant subject of discussion for many weeks, the lieutenant was well known to them: as a possible god, as a clown, as a hero, and as an agent of mystery. Unbeknownst to the lieutenant, he had achieved a rare status in Comanche culture, a status that was perhaps most appreciated by its women.

He was a celebrity.

And now, his celebrity and his natural good looks had been greatly enhanced in the eyes of the women by the addition of the stunning breastplate.

He made the suggestion of a bow and stepped self-consciously into the firelight, intending to pass through without further interrupting their fun.

But as he went by, one of the women reached out impulsively and took his hand gently in hers. The contact stopped him cold. He stared at the women, who were now giggling nervously, and wondered if some trick was about to be played on him.

Two or three of them began to sing, and as the dance picked up, several of the women tugged at his arms. He was being asked to join them.

There weren't many people in the vicinity. He wouldn't have an audience looking over his shoulder.

And besides, he told himself, a little exercise would be good for the digestion.

The dance was slow and simple. Raise one foot, hold it, put it down. Raise the other foot, hold it, put it down. He slipped into the circle and tried out the steps. He got them down quickly and it was no time before he was in sync with the other dancers, smiling just as broadly and enjoying himself enormously.

Dancing had always been easy to embrace. It was one of his favorite releases. As the music of the women's voices carried him along, he lifted his feet ever higher, picking them up and dropping them with newly invented flair. He began to drive his arms like wheels, involving more and more of himself in the rhythm. At last, when he was really going good, the still-smiling lieutenant closed his eyes, losing himself fully in the ecstasy of motion.

This made it impossible for him to detect that the circle had begun to shrink. It was not until he bumped the rump of the woman in front of him that the lieutenant realized how close the quarters had become. He glanced apprehensively at the women in the circle, but they reassured him with cheerful smiles. Dunbar went right on dancing.

Now he could feel the occasional touch of breasts, unmistakably soft, on his back. His waist was regularly contacting the rump in front of him. When he tried to hold up, the breasts would press in again.

None of this was as arousing as it was startling. He'd not felt a woman's touch in so long that it seemed a thing brand-new, too new to know what to do.

There was nothing overt in the women's faces as the circle

closed tighter. Their smiles were constant. So was the pressure of buttocks and breasts.

He was no longer lifting his feet. They were jammed too close together and he was reduced to bobbing up and down.

The circle fell apart and the woman surged in against him. Their hands were touching him playfully, toying with his back and his stomach and his rear end. Suddenly they were brushing his most private spot, at the front of his pants.

In another second the lieutenant would have bolted, but before he could make a move, the women melted away.

He watched them skip into the darkness like embarrassed schoolgirls. Then he turned to see what had frightened them off.

He was standing alone at the edge of the fire, resplendent and ominous in an owl's-head cap. Kicking Bird grunted something at him, but the lieutenant couldn't tell whether or not he was displeased.

The medicine man turned away from the fire, and like a puppy who thinks he may have done something wrong but has yet to be punished, Lieutenant Dunbar followed.

five

As it turned out, there were no repercussions from his encounter with the dancing women. But to his despair Dunbar found the fire in front of Kicking Bird's lodge crowded with still-feasting celebrants who insisted he take first crack at the roasted ribs just coming off the fire.

So the lieutenant sat a while longer, basking in the good cheer of the people around him, while he stuffed more meat into his swollen stomach.

An hour later he could barely hold his eyes open, and when they met Kicking Bird's, the medicine man rose up from his seat. He took the white soldier into the lodge and led him to a pallet that had been specially made up for him against a far wall.

Lieutenant Dunbar plopped down on the robe and began to pull off his boots. He was so sleepy that he didn't think to say good night and only caught a glimpse of the medicine man's back as he left the lodge.

Dunbar let the last boot flop carelessly on the floor and rolled into bed. He threw an arm over his eyes and floated off toward sleep. In the twilight before unconsciousness his mind began to fill with a steady-flowing stream of warm, unfocused, and vaguely sexual images. Women were moving around him. He couldn't make out their faces, but he could hear the murmur of their soft voices. He could see their forms passing close, swirling like the folds of a dress dancing in the breeze.

He could feel them touching him lightly, and as he drifted, he felt the press of bare flesh against his own.

six

Someone was giggling in his ear and he couldn't open his eyes. They were too heavy. But the giggling persisted and soon he was aware of a smell in his nose. The buffalo robe. Now he could hear that the giggling was not in his ear. But it was close by. It was in the room.

He forced his eyes open and turned his head to the sound. He couldn't see anything and raised up slightly. The lodge was quiet and the dim forms of Kicking Bird's family were unmoving. Everyone seemed to be asleep.

Then he heard the giggle again. It was high and sweet, definitely a woman's, and it was coming from a spot directly across the floor. The lieutenant raised up a little more, enough to let his gaze clear the dying fire in the center of the room.

The woman giggled again, and a man's voice, low and

gentle, floated across to him. He could see the strange bundle that always hung over Kicking Bird's bed. The sounds were coming from there.

Dunbar could not guess what was going on and, giving his eyes a quick rub, raised himself a notch higher.

Now he could make out the forms of two people; their heads and shoulders were jutting out of the bedding, and their lively movement seemed out of place for so late an hour. The lieutenant narrowed his eyes, trying to pierce the darkness.

The bodies shifted suddenly. One rose over the other and they settled into one. There was a moment of absolute silence before a long, low moan, like exhaled breath, swept into his ears, and Dunbar realized they were having sex.

Feeling like an ass, he sank quickly down, hoping neither lover had seen his stupid, gawking face staring across at them.

More awake than asleep now, he lay on the robe, listening to the steady, urgent sounds of their lovemaking. His eyes had grown accustomed to the dark and he could make out the shape of the sleeper closest to him.

The regular rise and fall of her bedding told him it was a deep sleep. She was lying on her side, her back turned to him. But he knew the shape of her head and the tangled, cherry-colored hair.

Stands With A Fist was sleeping alone and he began to wonder about her. She might be white by blood, but by all else she was one of these people. She spoke their language as if it were her native tongue. English was foreign to her. She didn't act as if she were under any duress. There was not the slightest hint of the captive about her. She seemed to be an absolute equal in the band now. He guessed correctly that she had been taken when young.

As he wondered his way back to sleep, the questions about the woman who was two people gradually wove together until only one remained.

I wonder if she's happy in her life, he asked himself.

The question stayed in his head, commingling lazily with the sounds of Kicking Bird and his wife making love.

Then, without any effort, the question began to spin, starting a slow whirl that gained speed with every turn. It circled faster and faster until at last he could see it no longer, and Lieutenant Dunbar fell asleep again.

CHAPTER XX

one

They spent less than three full days in the temporary camp, and three days is a short time in which to undergo extensive change.

But that's what happened.

Lieutenant Dunbar's course in life shifted.

There was no single, bombastic event to account for the shift. He had no mystic visions. God did not make an appearance. He was not dubbed a Comanche warrior.

There was no moment of proof, no obvious relic of evidence a person could point to and say it was here or there, at this time or that.

It was as if some beautiful, mysterious virus of awakening that had been long in incubation finally came to the forefront of his life.

The morning after the hunt he woke with rare clarity. There was no hangover of sleep, and the lieutenant thought consciously about how long it had been since he'd woken like this. Not since he was a boy.

His feet were sticky, so he picked up his boots and crept past the sleepers in the lodge, hoping he would find a place outside to wash between his toes. He found the spot as soon as he stepped out of the tipi. The grass-covered prairie was soaked with dew for miles.

Leaving his boots next to the lodge, the lieutenant walked toward the east, knowing that the pony herd was out there somewhere. He wanted to check on Cisco.

The first rosy streaks of dawn had broken through the darkness and he watched them in awe as he walked, oblivious to the pant legs that were already sopping with dew.

Every day begins with a miracle, he thought suddenly.

The streaks were growing larger, changing colors by the second.

Whatever God may be, I thank God for this day.

He liked the words so much that he said them out loud.

"Whatever God may be, I thank God for this day."

The heads of the first horses appeared, their pricked ears silhouetted against the dawn. He could see the head of an Indian, too. It was probably that boy who smiled all the time.

He found Cisco without much trouble. The buckskin nickered at his approach and the lieutenant's heart swelled a little. His horse laid his soft muzzle against Dunbar's chest and the two of them stood still for a few moments, letting the morning cool hang over them. The lieutenant gently lifted Cisco's chin and blew breath into each of his nostrils.

Overcome with curiosity, the other horses began to press in around them, and before they could become annoying, Lieutenant Dunbar slipped a bridle over Cisco's head and started back to camp.

Going in the opposite direction was just as impressive as coming out. The temporary village was tuned perfectly to nature's clock, and like the day, it was slowly coming to life.

A few fires had started, and in the short time he'd been gone, it seemed as though everyone had gotten up. As the light grew brighter, like the gradual turning of a lamp, the figures moving about the camp did, too.

''What harmony,'' the lieutenant said flatly as he walked with one arm slung over Cisco's withers.

Then he lapsed into a deep and complex line of abstract thought concerning the virtues of harmony, which stuck to him all the way through breakfast.

two

They went out again that morning, and Dunbar killed another buffalo. This time he held Cisco well in check during the charge, and instead of plunging into the herd, he searched the fringe for a likely animal and rode it down. Though he took great care with his aim, the first shot was high and a second bullet was needed to finish the job.

The cow he took was large, and he was complimented on his good selection by a score of warriors who rode by to inspect his kill. There wasn't the same kind of excitement that attended the first day's hunting. He didn't eat any fresh liver this day, but in every way, he felt more competent.

Once again women and children flooded onto the plain for the butchering, and by late afternoon the temporary camp was overflowing with meat. Uncounted drying racks, sagging under the weight of thousands of pounds of meat, sprang up like toadstools after a downpour, and there was more feasting on fresh-roasted delicacies.

The youngest warriors and a number of boys not ready for the warpath organized a horse-racing tournament shortly after they returned to camp. Smiles A Lot had his heart set on riding Cisco. He made his request with such respect that the lieutenant could not refuse him, and several races had been run before he realized to his horror that the winners were being given the horses of the losers. He rooted for Smiles A Lot with the fingers of both hands crossed, and fortunately for the lieutenant, the boy had won all three of his races.

Later on there was gambling, and Wind In His Hair got the lieutenant into a game. Except for being played with dice, it was unfamiliar, and learning the ropes cost Dunbar his whole tobacco supply. Some of the players were interested in the pants with the yellow stripes, but having already traded away his hat and tunic, the lieutenant thought he should retain some pretense of being in uniform.

Besides, the way things were going, he would lose the pants and have nothing to wear.

They liked the breastplate, but that, too, was out. He offered the old pair of boots he was wearing, but the Indians could see no value in them. Finally the lieutenant produced his rifle, and the players were unanimous in accepting it. Wagering a rifle created a big stir, and the game instantly became a high-stakes affair, drawing many observers.

By now the lieutenant knew what he was doing, and as the game continued, the dice took a liking to him. He hit a hot streak, and when the dust of his run had settled, he not only had held on to the rifle, but was now the new owner of three excellent ponies.

The losers gave up their treasures with such grace and good humor that Dunbar was moved to reply in kind. He immediately made presents of his winnings. The tallest and strongest of the three he gave to Wind In His Hair. Then, with a throng of the curious trailing in his wake, he led the remaining two horses through camp and, on reaching Kicking Bird's lodge, handed both sets of reins to the medicine man.

Kicking Bird was pleased but bewildered. When someone explained where the horses had come from, he glanced around, caught sight of Stands With A Fist, and called her over, indicating that he wished her to speak for him.

She was a gruesome sight as she stood listening to the medicine man. The butchering had splattered her arms and face and apron with blood.

She pleaded ignorance, shaking him off with her head, but

Kicking Bird persisted, and the little assembly in front of the lodge fell silent, waiting to see if she could perform the English Kicking Bird had asked for.

She stared at her feet and mouthed a word several times. Then she looked at the lieutenant and tried it.

"Tankus," she said.

The lieutenant's face twitched.

"What?" he replied, forcing a smile.

"Tank."

She poked his arm with a finger and swung her arm toward the ponies.

"Horz."

"Thank?" the lieutenant guessed. "Thank me?"

Stands With A Fist nodded.

"Yes," she said clearly.

Lieutenant Dunbar reached out to shake with Kicking Bird, but she stopped him. She wasn't finished, and holding a finger aloft, she stepped between the ponies.

"Horz," she said, pointing to the lieutenant with her free hand. She repeated the word and pointed at Kicking Bird.

"One for me?" the lieutenant queried, using the same hand signs. "And one for him?"

Stand With A Fist sighed happily, and knowing he understood her, she smiled thinly.

"Yes," she said, and without thinking, another old word, perfectly pronounced, popped out of her mouth. "Correct."

It sounded so odd, this rigid, proper English word, that Lieutenant Dunbar laughed out loud, and like a teen-ager who has just said something silly, Stands With A Fist covered her mouth with a hand.

It was their joke. She knew the word had flown out like an inadvertent burp, and so did the lieutenant. Reflexively they looked to Kicking Bird and the others. The Indian faces were blank, however, and when the eyes of the cavalry officer and the woman who was two people came together again, they were dancing with the laughter of an inside thing only they could share. There was no way to adequately explain it to the others. It wasn't funny enough to go to the trouble.

Lieutenant Dunbar didn't keep the other pony. Instead he led it to Ten Bears's lodge and, without knowing it, elevated his status even further. Comanche tradition called for the rich to spread their wealth among the less fortunate. But Dunbar reversed that, and the old man was left with the thought that this white man was truly extraordinary.

That night, as he was sitting around Kicking Bird's fire, listening to a conversation he didn't understand, Lieutenant Dunbar happened to see Stands With A Fist. She was squatting a few feet away and she was looking at him. Her head was tilted and her eyes seemed lost in curiosity. Before she could look away, he tipped his head in the direction of the warrior's conversation, put on an official face, and laid a hand against the side of his mouth.

"Correct," he whispered loudly.

She turned away quickly then. But as she did, he heard the distinct sound of a giggle.

three

To stay any longer would have been useless. They had all the meat they could possibly carry. Just after dawn everything was packed, and the column was on the march by midmorning. With every travois piled high, the return trip took twice as long, and it was getting dark by the time they reached Fort Sedgewick.

A travois loaded with several hundred pounds of jerked meat was brought up and unloaded into the supply house. A flurry of good-byes followed, and with Lieutenant Dunbar watching from the doorway of his sod hut, the caravan marched off for the permanent camp upstream.

Without forethought his eyes searched the semidarkness surrounding the long, noisy column for a glimpse of Stands With A Fist.

He couldn't find her.

four

The lieutenant had mixed feelings about being back.

He knew the fort as his home, and that was reassuring. It was good to pull his boots off, lie down on the pallet, and stretch out unobserved. With half-closed eyes he watched the wick flicker in his lamp, and drifted lazily in the quiet surrounding the hut. Everything was in its place, and so was he.

Not many minutes had passed, however, before he realized his right foot was jiggling with aimless energy.

What are you doing? he asked himself as he stilled the foot. You're not nervous.

It was only a minute more before he discovered the fingers of his right hand drumming impatiently at his chest.

He wasn't nervous. He was bored. Bored and lonely.

In the past he would have reached for his cigarette fixings, made a smoke, and put himself to work puffing on it. But there was no more tobacco.

Might as well have a look at the river, he thought, and with that, got back into his boots and walked outside.

He stopped, thinking of the breastplate that was already so precious to him. It was draped over the army-issue saddle he'd brought from the supply house. He went back inside, intending only to look at it.

Even in the weak light of the lamp it was shining brilliantly. Lieutenant Dunbar ran his hand over the bones. They were like glass. When he picked it up there was a solid clacking as bone kissed bone. He liked the cool, hard feel of it on his bare chest.

The "look at the river" turned into a long walk. The moon was nearly full again and he didn't need the lantern as he treaded lightly along the bluff overlooking the stream.

He took his time, pausing often to look at the river, or at a branch as it bent in the breeze, or at a rabbit nibbling at a shrub. Everything was unconcerned with his presence.

He felt invisible. It was a feeling he liked.

After almost an hour he turned around and started home. If someone had been there as he passed by, they would have seen that, for all his lightness of step and for all his attention to things other than himself, the lieutenant was hardly invisible.

Not during the times he stopped to look up at the moon. Then he would lift his head, turn his body full into the face of its magical light, and the breastplate would flash the brightest white, like an earthbound star.

five

An odd thing happened the next day.

He spent the morning and part of the afternoon trying to work around the place: re-sorting what was left of the supplies, burning a few useless items, finding a protective way to store the meat, and making some journal entries.

All of it was done with half a heart. He thought of shoring up the corral again but decided that he would just be manufacturing work for himself. He'd already made work for himself. It made him feel rudderless.

When the sun was well on its way down, he found himself wanting to take another stroll on the prairie. It had been a blistering day. Perspiration from doing his chores had soaked through his pants and produced patches of prickly heat on his upper thighs. He could see no reason why this unpleasantness should accompany his stroll. So, Dunbar walked onto the prairie without his clothes, hoping he might run into Two Socks.

Forsaking the river, he struck out across the immense grasslands, which rippled in every direction with a life of its own.

The grass had reached the peak of its growth, in some places grazing his hip. Overhead the sky was filled with fleecy, white clouds that stood against the pure blue like cutouts.

On a little rise a mile from the fort he lay down in the deep grass. With a windbreak on all sides, he soaked up the last of the sun's warmth and stared dreamily at the slow-moving clouds.

The lieutenant turned on his side to bake his back. When he moved in the grass, a sudden sensation swamped him, one he had not known for so long that at first he wasn't sure what he was feeling.

The grass above rustled softly as the breeze moved through it. The sun lay on his backside like a blanket of dry heat. The feeling welled higher and higher and Dunbar surrendered to it.

His hand fell downward, and as it did, the lieutenant ceased to think. Nothing guided his action, no visions or words or memories. He was feeling, and nothing more.

When he was conscious again he looked to the sky and saw the earth turning in the movement of the clouds. He rolled onto his back, placed his arms straight against his sides in the manner of a corpse, and floated awhile on his bed of grass and earth.

Then he closed his eyes and napped for half an hour.

six

He tossed and turned that night, his mind flitting from one subject to the next as though it were checking a long succession of rooms for a place to rest. Every room was either locked or inhospitable until at last he came to the place that, in the back of his mind, he knew he was bound for all the time.

The room was filled with Indians.

The idea was so right that he considered making the trip to Ten Bears's camp that instant. But it seemed too impetuous.

I'll get up early, he thought. Maybe I'll stay a couple of days this time.

He woke with anticipation before dawn but steeled himself against getting up, resisting the idea of a headlong rush to the village. He wanted to go without rash expectations, and stayed in bed until it was light.

When he had everything on but his shirt, he picked it up and slid an arm through one of the sleeves. He paused then, staring through the hut's window to assess the weather. It was already warm in the room, probably warmer outside.

It's going to be a scorcher, he thought as he pulled the sleeve off his arm.

The breastplate was hanging on a peg now, and as he reached for it, the lieutenant realized that he'd wanted to wear it all along, regardless of the weather.

He packed the shirt away in a haversack, just in case.

seven

Two Socks was waiting outside.

When he saw Lieutenant Dunbar come through the door he took two or three quick steps back, spun in a circle, side-stepped a few feet, and lay down, panting like a puppy.

Dunbar cocked his head quizzically.

"What's got into you?"

The wolf lifted his head at the sound of the lieutenant's voice. His look was so intent that it made Dunbar chuckle.

"You wanna go with me?"

Two Socks jumped to his feet and stared at the lieutenant, not moving a muscle.

"Well, c'mon then."

eight

Kicking Bird woke thinking of "Jun" down there at the white man's fort.

"Jun." What an odd name. He tried to think of what it might mean. Young Rider perhaps. Or Fast Rider. Probably something to do with riding.

It was good to have the season's first hunt ended. With the buffalo come at last, the problem of food had been solved, and that meant he could return to his pet project with some regularity. He would resume it this very day.

The medicine man went to the lodges of two close advisers and asked if they wanted to ride down there with him. He was surprised at how eager they were to go but took it as a good sign nonetheless. No one was afraid anymore. In fact, people seemed to be at ease with the white soldier. In the talk he'd heard the last few days there were even expressions of fondness for him.

Kicking Bird rode out of camp feeling especially good

about the day to come. Everything had gone well with the early stages of his plan. The cultivation was finally complete. Now he could get down to the real business of investigating the white race.

nine

Lieutenant Dunbar figured he'd made close to four miles. He had expected the wolf to be long gone at the two-mile mark. At three miles he'd really started to wonder. And now, at four miles, he was thoroughly stumped.

They'd entered a narrow, grassy depression wedged between two slopes, and the wolf was still with him. Never before had he followed so far.

The lieutenant scissored off Cisco's back and stared out at Two Socks. In his customary way the wolf had stopped, too. As Cisco lowered his head to chomp at the grass Dunbar began to walk in Two Socks's direction, thinking he would be pressured into withdrawing. But the head and ears peering above the grass didn't move, and when the lieutenant finally came to a halt, he was no more than a yard away.

The wolf tilted his head expectantly but otherwise stayed motionless as Dunbar squatted.

"I don't think you're going to be welcome where I'm going," he said out loud, as though he were chatting with a trusted neighbor.

He looked up at the sun. "It's gonna be hot; why don't you go on home?"

The wolf listened attentively, but still he did not move.

The lieutenant rocked to his feet.

"C'mon, Two Socks," he said irritably, "go home."

He made a shooing motion with his hands, and Two Socks scurried to one side.

He shooed again and the wolf hopped, but it was obvious that Two Socks had no intention of going home.

"All right then," Dunbar said emphatically, "don't go home. But stay. Stay right there."

He punctuated this with a wag of his finger and made an about-face. He'd just completed his turn when he heard the howl. It wasn't full-blown, but it was low and plaintive and definite.

A howl.

The lieutenant swung his head around and there was Two Socks, his muzzle up, his eyes trained on Lieutenant Dunbar, moaning like a pouty child.

To an objective observer it would have been a remarkable display, but to the lieutenant, who knew him so well, it was simply the last straw.

"You go home!" Dunbar roared, and he charged at Two Socks. Like a son who has pushed his father too far, the wolf flattened his ears and gave ground, scooting away with his tail tucked.

At the same time Lieutenant Dunbar took off at a run in the opposite direction, thinking he would get to Cisco, gallop off at full tilt, and ditch Two Socks.

He was tearing through the grass, thinking of his plan, when the wolf came bounding happily alongside.

"You go home," the lieutenant snarled, and veered suddenly at his pursuer. Two Socks hopped straight up like a scared rabbit, leaving his paws in the sudden panic to get away. When he came to ground the lieutenant was only a step behind. He reached out for the base of Two Socks's tail and gave it a squeeze. The wolf shot ahead as if a firecracker had gone off under him, and Dunbar laughed so hard that he had to stop running.

Two Socks skittered to a halt twenty yards away and stared back over his shoulder with an expression of such embarrassment that the lieutenant couldn't help but feel sorry for him.

He gave him a wave of good-bye and, still chortling to himself, turned around to find that Cisco had wandered back the way they'd come, browsing at the choicest grass.

The lieutenant started into an easy trot, unable to keep from laughing at the image of Two Socks running from his touch.

Dunbar jumped wildly as something grabbed at his ankle and then let go. He spun back, ready to face the unseen attacker.

Two Socks was right there, panting like a fighter between rounds.

Lieutenant Dunbar stared at him for a few seconds.

Two Socks glanced casually in the direction of home, as if thinking the game might be coming to a close.

"All right then," the lieutenant said gently, surrendering with his hands. "You can come, or you can stay. I don't have any more time for this."

It might have been a tiny noise or it might have been something on the wind. Whatever it was, Two Socks caught it. He whirled suddenly and stared up the trail with his hackles raised.

Dunbar followed suit and immediately saw Kicking Bird with two other men. They were close by, watching from the shoulder of a slope.

Dunbar waved eagerly and hollered, "Hello," as Two Socks began to slink away.

ten

Kicking Bird and his friends had been watching for some time, long enough to have seen the entire show. They had been greatly entertained. Kicking Bird also knew that he had witnessed something precious, something that had provided a solution to one of the puzzles surrounding the white man . . . the puzzle of what to call him.

A man should have a real name, he thought as he rode down to meet Lieutenant Dunbar, particularly when it is a white who acts like this one.

He remembered the old names, like The Man Who Shines Like Snow, and some of the new ones being bandied about, like Finds The Buffalo. None of them really fit. Certainly not Jun.

He felt certain that this was the right one. It suited the white soldier's personality. People would remember him by this. And Kicking Bird himself, with two witnesses to back him up, had been present at the time the Great Spirit revealed it.

He said it to himself several times as he came down the slope. The sound of it was as good as the name itself.

Dances With Wolves.

CHAPTER XXI

one

In a quiet way it was one of the most satisfying days of Lieutenant Dunbar's life.

Kicking Bird's family greeted him with a warmth and respect that made him feel like more than a guest. They were genuinely happy to see him.

He and Kicking Bird settled down for a smoke that, because of constant but pleasant interruptions, lasted well into the afternoon.

Word of Lieutenant Dunbar's name and how he got it spread through camp with the usual astonishing speed, and any nagging suspicions the people might have harbored toward the white soldier evaporated with this inspiring news.

He was not a god, but neither was he like any hair mouth they had encountered. He was a man of medicine. Warriors dropped by constantly, some of them wanting to say hello, others wanting nothing more than to lay eyes on Dances With Wolves.

The lieutenant recognized most of them now. At each arrival he would stand and make his short bow. Some of them bowed back. A few extended their hands, as they had seen him do.

There wasn't much they could talk about, but the lieutenant was getting good with signs, good enough to rehash some of the recent hunt's high points. This formed the basis for most of the visiting.

After a couple of hours the steady stream of visitors trickled away to no one, and Dunbar was just wondering why he hadn't seen Stands With A Fist, and if she was on the agenda, when Wind In His Hair suddenly walked in.

Before greetings could be exchanged, each man's attention was drawn to the items they had traded: the unbuttoned tunic and the gleaming breastplate. For both of them it was a subtly reassuring sight.

As they shook hands Lieutenant Dunbar thought, I like this fellow; it's good to see him.

The same sentiments were foremost in Wind In His Hair's thoughts, and they sat down together for an amicable chat, though neither man could understand what the other was saying.

Kicking Bird called to his wife for food, and the trio soon devoured a lunch of pemmican and berries. They ate without saying a word.

After the meal another pipe was packed and the two Indians fell into a conversation that the lieutenant could not divine. By their gestures and speech, however, he guessed they were dealing with something beyond idle chitchat.

They seemed to be planning some activity, and he was not surprised when, at the end of their talk, both men stood up and asked him to follow as they went outside.

Dunbar trailed them to the rear of Kicking Bird's tepee, where a cache of material was waiting for them. A neat stack of limber willow poles was sitting next to a high pile of dried brush.

The two men had another, even briefer discussion, then set to work. When the lieutenant saw what was taking shape, he lent a hand here and there, but before he could contribute much, the material had been transformed into a shady arbor four or five feet high.

A small portion had been left uncovered to afford an entrance, and Lieutenant Dunbar was shown inside first. There wasn't enough room to stand up, but once he was down, he found the place roomy and peaceful. The brush made good cover against the sun and was sheer enough to allow for a free flow of air.

It wasn't until he'd finished this quick inspection that he realized Kicking Bird and Wind In His Hair had vanished. A week ago he would have been uncomfortable with their sudden desertion. But, like the Indians, he was no longer suspicious. The lieutenant was content to sit quietly against the surprisingly strong back wall, listening to the now familiar sounds of Ten Bears's camp as he awaited developments.

They were not long in coming.

Only a few minutes had passed before he heard footsteps approaching. Kicking Bird duck-walked through the entrance and seated himself far enough away to leave a full space between them.

A shadow falling across the entrance told Dunbar that someone else was waiting to come inside. Without thinking, he assumed it was Wind In His Hair.

Kicking Bird called out softly. The shadow shifted to the accompaniment of tinkling bells, and Stands With A Fist stooped through the doorway.

Dunbar scooted to one side, making room as she maneuvered between them, and in the few seconds it took her to settle, he saw much that was new.

The bells were sewn on the sides of finely beaded moccasins. Her doeskin dress looked like an heirloom, something well cared for and not for every day. The bodice was sprinkled with small, thick bones arranged in rows. They were elk's teeth.

The wrist closest to him wore a bracelet of solid brass. Around her neck was a choker of the same pipe-bone he wore on his chest. Her hair, fresh and fragrant, hung down her back in a single braid, exposing more of the high-cheeked, distinctly browed face than he had seen before. She looked more delicate and feminine to him now. And more white.

It dawned on the lieutenant then that the arbor had been built as a place for them to meet. And in the time it took her to sit, he realized how much he had anticipated seeing her again.

She still wouldn't look at him, and while Kicking Bird mumbled something to her, he made up his mind to take the initiative and say hello.

It so happened that they turned their heads, opened their mouths, and said the word at precisely the same time. The two hellos collided in the space between them, and the speakers recoiled awkwardly at their accidental beginning.

Kicking Bird saw a favorable omen in the accident. He saw two people of like mind. Because this was exactly what he hoped for, it struck him as ironic.

The medicine man chuckled to himself. Then he pointed to Lieutenant Dunbar and grunted, as if saying, "Go ahead . . . you first."

"Hello," he said pleasantly.

She lifted her head. Her expression was businesslike, but he could see nothing of the hostility that had been there before.

"Hulo," she replied.

two

They sat a long time in the arbor that day, most of it spent reviewing the few simple words they had exchanged at their first formal session.

Toward sundown, when all three had wearied of the constant, stumbling repetitions, the English translation for her Indian name suddenly came to Stands With A Fist.

It so excited her that she began immediately to teach it to Lieutenant Dunbar. First she had to get across what she wanted. She pointed to him and said, "Jun," then pointed to herself and said nothing. In the same motion she held up a finger that said, "Stop. I will show you."

The pattern had been for him to perform whatever action she asked for, then guess the action's word in English. She wanted him to stand, but that was impossible in the arbor, so she hustled both men outside, where they would have full freedom of movement.

Lieutenant Dunbar guessed "rise," "rises," "gets up," and "on my feet" before he hit "stands." "With" was not so hard, "a" had already been covered, and he got "fist" on the first try. After he had it in English, she taught him the Comanche.

From there, in rapid succession, he mastered Wind In His Hair, Ten Bears, and Kicking Bird.

Lieutenant Dunbar was excited. He asked for something to make marks, and using a sliver of charcoal, he wrote the four names in phonetic Comanche on a strip of thin, white bark.

Stands With A Fist kept her reserve throughout. But inwardly she was thrilled. The English words were showering in her head like sparks as thousands of doors, locked up for so long, swung open. She was delirious with the excitement of learning.

Each time the lieutenant ran down the list written on his scrap of bark and each time he came close to pronouncing the names as they should be pronounced, she encouraged him with the suggestion of a smile and said the word "yes."

For his part, Lieutenant Dunbar did not have to see her little smile to know that the encouragement was heartfelt. He could hear it in the sound of the word and he could see it in the power of her pale brown eyes. To hear him say these words, in English and Comanche, meant something special to her. Her inward thrill was tingling all about them. The lieutenant could feel it.

She was not the same woman, so sad and lost, that he had found on the prairie. That moment was now something left behind. It made him happy to see how far she had come.

Best of all was the little piece of bark he held in his hands. He grasped it firmly, determined not to let it slip away. It was the first section of a map that would guide him into whatever future he had with these people. So many things would be possible from now on.

It was Kicking Bird, however, who was most profoundly affected by this turn of events. To him it was a miracle of the highest order, on a par with attending something all-consuming, like birth or death.

His dream had become reality.

When he heard the lieutenant say his name in Comanche, it was as though an impenetrable wall had suddenly turned to smoke. And they were walking through. They were communicating.

With equal force his view of Stands With A Fist had enlarged. She was no longer a Comanche. In making herself a bridge for their words, she had become something more. Like the lieutenant, he heard it in the sound of her English words and he saw it in the new power of her eyes. Something had been added, something that was missing before, and Kicking Bird knew what it was.

Her long-buried blood was running again, her undiluted white blood.

The impact of these things was more than even Kicking Bird could bear, and like a professor who knows when it is time for his pupils to take a rest, he told Stands With A Fist that this was enough for one day.

A trace of disappointment flashed on her face. Then she dropped her head and nodded submissively.

At that moment, however, a wonderful thought occurred to her. She caught Kicking Bird's eye and respectfully asked if they might do one more thing.

She wanted to teach the white soldier his name.

It was a good idea, so good that Kicking Bird could not refuse his adopted daughter. He told her to continue.

She remembered the word right away. She could see it, but she couldn't speak it. And she couldn't remember how she had done it as a girl. The men waited while she tried to remember.

Then Lieutenant Dunbar unwittingly raised his hand to brush at a gnat that was bothering his ear, and she saw it all again.

She grabbed the lieutenant's hand as it hung in space and let the fingertips of her other hand rest cautiously on his hip. And before either man could react, she led Dunbar into a creaky but unmistakable memory of a waltz.

After a few seconds she pulled away demurely, leaving Lieutenant Dunbar in a state of shock. He had to struggle to remember the point of the exercise.

A light went off in his head. Then it jumped into his eyes, and like the only boy in class who knows the answer, he smiled at his teacher.

three

From there it was easy to get the rest.

Lieutenant Dunbar went to one knee and wrote the name at the bottom of his bark grammar book. His eyes lingered on the way it looked in English. It seemed bigger than just a name. The more he looked at it, the more he liked it.

He said it to himself. Dances With Wolves.

The lieutenant came to his feet, bowed shortly in Kicking Bird's direction, and, as a butler might announce the arrival of a dinner guest, humbly and without fanfare, he said the name once more.

This time he said it in Comanche.

"Dances With Wolves."

CHAPTER XXII

one

Dances With Wolves stayed in Kicking Bird's lodge that
night. He was exhausted but, as sometimes happens, was too
tired to sleep. The day's events hopped about in his mind
like popcorn in a skillet.

When he finally began the drift into unconsciousness, the
lieutenant slipped into the twilight of a dream he had not had
since he was very young. Surrounded by stars, he was floating through the cold, silent void of space, a weightless little
boy alone in a world of silver and black.

But he was not afraid. He was snug and warm and under
the covers of a four-poster bed, and to drift like a single seed
in all the universe, even if for eternity, was not a hardship.
It was a joy.

That was how he fell asleep on his first night in the Comanches' ancestral summer camp.

two

In the months that followed, Lieutenant Dunbar would fall asleep many times in Ten Bears's camp.

He returned to Fort Sedgewick often, but the visits were prompted primarily by guilt, not desire. Even while he was there he knew he was maintaining the thinnest of appearances. Yet he felt compelled to do so.

He knew there was no logical reason to stay on. Certain now that the army had abandoned the post and him along with it, he thought of returning to Fort Hays. He had already done his duty. In fact, his devotion to the post and the U.S. Army had been exemplary. He could leave with his head held high.

What held him was the pull of another world, a world he had just begun to explore. He didn't know exactly when it happened, but it came to him that his dream of being posted on the frontier, a dream that he had concocted to serve the small boundaries of military service, had pointed from the beginning to the limitless adventure in which he was now engaged. Countries and armies and races paled beside it. He had discovered a great thirst and he could no more turn it down than a dying man could refuse water.

He wanted to see what would happen, and because of that, he gave up his idea of returning to the army. But he did not fully give up the idea of the army returning to him. Sooner or later it had to.

So on his visits to the fort he would putter about with trivialities: repairing an occasional tear in the awning, sweeping cobwebs from the corners of the sod hut, making journal entries.

He forced these jobs on himself as a farfetched way of staying in touch with his old life. Deeply involved as he was with the Comanches, he could not find it in himself to jettison everything, and the hollow motions he went through made it possible to hang on to the shreds of his past.

By visiting the fort on a semiregular basis, he preserved discipline where there was no longer a need, and in doing so he also preserved the idea of Lieutenant John J. Dunbar, U.S.A.

The journal entries no longer carried depictions of his days. Most of them were nothing more than an estimate of the date, a short comment on the weather or his health, and a signature. Even had he wanted, it would have been too large a job to essay the new life he was living. Besides, it was a personal thing.

Invariably he would walk down the bluff to the river, usually with Two Socks in tow. The wolf had been his first real contact, and the lieutenant was always glad to see him. Their silent time together was something he cherished.

He would pause for a few minutes at the stream's edge, watching the water flow. If the light was right, he could see himself with mirrorlike clarity. His hair had grown past his shoulders. The constant beating of sun and wind had darkened his face. He would turn from side to side, like a man of fashion, admiring the breastplate that he now wore like a uniform. With the exception of Cisco, nothing he could call his own exceeded its value.

Sometimes the vision on the water would make him tingle with confusion. He looked so much like one of them now. When that happened he would balance awkwardly on one foot and lift the other high enough for the water to send back a picture of the pants with the yellow stripes and the tall, black riding boots.

Occasionally he would consider discarding them for leggings and moccasins, but the reflection always told him that they belonged. In some way they were a part of the discipline, too. He would wear the pants and boots until they disintegrated. Then he would see.

On certain days, when he felt more Indian than white, he would trudge back over the bluff, and the fort would appear as an ancient place, a ghostly relic of a past so far gone that it was difficult to believe he was ever connected to it.

As time passed, going to Fort Sedgewick became a chore. His visits were fewer and farther between. But he continued making the ride to his old haunt.

three

Ten Bears's village became the center of his life, but for all the ease with which he settled into it, Lieutenant Dunbar moved as a man apart. His skin and accent and pants and boots marked him as a visitor from another world, and like Stands With A Fist, he quickly became a man who was two people.

His integration into Comanche life was constantly tempered with the vestiges of the world he had left behind, and when Dunbar tried to think of his true place in life, his gaze would suddenly become faraway. A fog, blank and inconclusive, would fill his mind, as if all his normal processes had been suspended. After a few seconds the fog would lift and he would go about his business, not knowing quite what had hit him.

Thankfully, these spells subsided as time went on.

The first six weeks of his time in Ten Bears's camp revolved around one particular place: the little brush arbor behind Kicking Bird's lodge.

It was here, in daily morning and afternoon sessions lasting several hours each, that Lieutenant Dunbar first conversed freely with the medicine man.

Stands With A Fist made steady progress toward fluency, and by the end of the first week the three of them were having long-running talks.

The lieutenant had thought all along that Kicking Bird was a good person, but when Stands With A Fist began to translate large blocks of his thoughts into English, Dunbar discovered he was dealing with an intelligence that was superior by any standard he knew.

In the beginning there were mostly questions and answers. Lieutenant Dunbar told the story of how he came to be at Fort Sedgewick and of his unexplained isolation. Interesting as the story was, it frustrated Kicking Bird. Dances With Wolves knew almost nothing. He did not even know the army's mission, much less its specific plans. Of military things there was nothing to learn. He had been a simple soldier.

The white race was a different matter.

"Why are the whites coming into our country?" Kicking Bird would ask.

And Dunbar would reply, "I don't think they want to come into the country, I think they only want to pass through."

Kicking Bird would counter, "The Texans are already in our country, chopping down the trees and tearing up the earth. They are killing the buffalo and leaving them in the grass. This is happening now. There are too many of these people already. How many more will be coming?"

Here the lieutenant would twist his mouth and say, "I don't know."

"I have heard it said," the medicine man would continue, "that the whites only want peace in the country. Why do they always come with hair-mouth soldiers? Why do these hair-mouth Texas Rangers come after us when all we want is to be left alone? I have been told of talks the white chiefs have had with my brothers. I have been told these talks are peaceful and that promises are made. But I am told that the promises are always broken. If white chiefs come to see us, how shall we know their true minds? Should we take their presents? Should we sign their papers to show that there will be peace between us? When I was a boy many Comanches went to a house of law in Texas for a big meeting with white chiefs and they were shot dead.''

The lieutenant would try to provide reasoned answers to Kicking Bird's questions, but they were weak theories at best, and when pressed, he would inevitably end by saying, ''I don't know actually.''

He was being careful, for he could see the deep concern behind Kicking Bird's queries and could not bring himself to tell what he really thought. If the whites ever came out here in real force, the Indian people, no matter how hard they fought, would be hopelessly overmatched. They would be defeated by armaments alone.

At the same time he could not tell Kicking Bird to disregard his concerns. He needed to be concerned. The lieutenant simply could not tell him the truth. Nor could he tell the medicine man lies. It was a standoff, and finding himself cornered, Dunbar hid behind a wall of ignorance, hoping for the arrival of new, more palatable subjects.

But each day, like a stain that refuses to be washed out, one overriding question always remained.

''How many more are coming?''

four

Gradually Stands With A Fist began to look forward to the hours she spent in the brush arbor.

Now that he had been accepted by the band, Dances With Wolves ceased to be the great problem he had once been. His connection with white society had paled, and while what he represented was still a fearful thing, the soldier himself was not. He didn't even look like a soldier anymore.

At first the notoriety surrounding activities in the arbor bothered Stands With A Fist. The schooling of Dances With Wolves, his presence in camp, and her key role as go-between were constant topics of conversation around the village. The celebrity of it made her feel uneasy, as though she was being watched. She was especially sensitive to the possibility of criticism for shirking the routine duties expected of every Comanche woman. It was true that Kicking Bird himself had excused her, but she still worried.

After two weeks, however, none of these fears had materialized, and the new respect she enjoyed was having a beneficial effect on her personality. Her smile was quicker and her shoulders were squarer. The importance of her new role charged her step with a sense of authority that everyone could see. Her life was becoming bigger, and inside herself she knew it was a good thing.

Other people knew it, too.

She was gathering wood one evening when a woman friend stooping next to her suddenly said with a touch of pride: "People are talking about you."

Stands With A Fist straightened, unsure of how to take the remark.

"What are they saying?" she asked flatly.

"They say that you are making medicine. They say that maybe you should change your name."

"To what?"

"Oh, I don't know," the friend replied. "Medicine Tongue maybe, something like that. It's just some talk."

As they walked together in the twilight Stands With A Fist rolled this around in her head. They were at the edge of camp before she spoke again.

"I like my name," she said, knowing that word of her wishes would quickly filter through camp. "I will keep it."

A few nights later she was returning to Kicking Bird's tipi after relieving herself when she heard someone start to sing in a lodge close by. She paused to listen and was astounded at what she heard.

"The Comanches have a bridge
That passes to another world
The bridge is called Stands With A Fist."

Too embarrassed to hear more, she hurried along to bed.
But as she tucked the covers under her chin, she was not
thinking bad thoughts about the song. She was thinking only
of the words she had heard, and on reflection, they seemed
quite good.

She slept deeply that night. It was already light when she
woke the next morning. Scrambling to catch up with the day,
she hurried out of the lodge and stopped short.

Dances With Wolves was riding out of camp on the little
buckskin horse. It was a sight that made her heart sink a
little further than she might have imagined. The thought of
him going did not disturb her so much, but the thought of
him not coming back deflated her to the extent that it showed
on her face.

Stands With A Fist blushed to think that someone might
see her like this. She glanced around quickly and turned a
brighter shade of red.

Kicking Bird was watching her.

Her heart beat wildly as she struggled to compose herself.
The medicine man was coming over.

"There will be no talk today," he said, studying her with
a care that made her insides squirm.

"I see," she said, trying to keep her voice neutral.

But she could see curiosity in his eyes, curiosity that called
for an explanation.

"I like to make the talk," she went on. "I am happy to
make the white words."

"He wants to see the white man's fort. He will come back
at sundown."

The medicine man gave her another close look and said,
"We will make more talk tomorrow."

five

Her day passed minute by minute.

She watched the sun like a bored office worker watches each tick of the clock. Nothing moves slower than watched time. She had great difficulty concentrating on her duties because of this.

When she wasn't watching time she was daydreaming.

Now that he had emerged as a real person, there were things in him she found to admire. Some of them might be traced to their mutual whiteness. Some of them were his alone. All of them held her interest.

She felt a mysterious pride when she thought of the deeds he had performed, deeds that were known by all her people.

Remembering his playacting made her laugh. Sometimes he was very funny. Funny but not foolish. In every way he seemed sincere and open and respectful and full of good humor. She was convinced that these qualities were genuine.

The sight of him with the breastplate on had seemed out of place at first, like a Comanche would be out of place in a top hat. But he wore it day after day without paying the least attention to it. And he never took it off. It was obvious that he loved it.

His hair was tangled like hers, not thick and straight like the others. And he hadn't tried to change it.

He hadn't changed the boots and pants either but wore them in the same natural way he took to the breastplate.

These musings led her to the conclusion that Dances With Wolves was an honest person. Every human being finds certain characteristics above all others to cherish, and for Stands With A Fist it was honesty.

This thinking about Dances With Wolves did not subside, and as the afternoon wore on, bolder thoughts came to her. She pictured him coming back at sundown. She pictured them together in the arbor the following day.

One more image came to her as she knelt by the edge of

the river in the late afternoon, filling a jug with water. They were together in the arbor. He was talking about himself and she was listening. But it was only the two of them.

Kicking Bird was gone.

six

Her daydream became real on the very next day.

The three of them had just gotten down to talking when word was brought that a faction of young warriors had declared their intention to make a war party against the Pawnee. Because there had been no previous talk about this and because the young men in question were inexperienced, Ten Bears had hastily organized a council.

Kicking Bird was called away and suddenly they were alone.

The silence in the arbor was so heavy that it made both of them nervous. Each wanted to talk, but considerations of what to say and how to say it held them up. They were speechless.

Stands With A Fist finally decided on her opening words, but she was too late.

He was already turning to her, saying the words in a shy but forceful way.

"I want to know about you," he said.

She turned away, trying to think. The English was still hard for her. Fractured by the effort of thought, it came out in clear but half-stuttered words.

"Whaa . . . what you know . . . want to know?" she asked.

seven

For the rest of the morning she told him about herself, holding the lieutenant's eager attention with the stories of her time as a white girl, her capture, and her long life as a Comanche.

When she tried to end a story he would ask another question. Much as she might have wanted, she could not get off the subject of herself.

He asked how she came to be named, and she told the story of her arrival in camp so many years ago. Memories of her first months were hazy, but she well remembered the day she got her name.

She had not been officially adopted by anyone, nor had she been made a member of the band. She was only working. As she carried out her assignments successfully the work became less menial and she was given more instruction in the various ways of living off the prairie. But the longer she worked, the more resentful she became of her lowly status. And some of the women picked on her unmercifully.

Outside a lodge one morning she took a swing at the worst of these women. Being young and unskilled, she had no hope of winning a fight. But the punch she threw was hard and perfectly timed. It cracked against the point of the woman's chin and knocked her cold. She kicked her unconscious tormentor for good measure and stood facing the other women with her fists balled, a tiny white girl ready to take on all comers.

No one challenged her. They only watched. In moments everyone had returned to what they were doing, leaving the mean woman lying where she had dropped.

No one picked on the little white girl after that. The family that had been taking care of her became open with their kindnesses, and the road to becoming a Comanche was smoothed for her. She was Stands With A Fist from then on.

A special kind of warmth filled the arbor as she told the story. Lieutenant Dunbar wanted to know the exact spot where her fist struck the woman's chin, and Stands With A Fist unhesitatingly grazed his jaw with her knuckles.

The lieutenant stared at her after this was done.

His eyes slowly rolled under his lids and he keeled over.

It was a good joke and she extended it, bringing him to by gently jiggling his arm.

This little exchange produced a new ease between them, but good as it was, the sudden familiarity also caused Stands With A Fist some worry. She didn't want him to ask her personal questions, questions about her status as a woman. She could feel the questions coming, and the specter of this broke her concentration. It made her nervous and less communicative.

The lieutenant sensed her pulling back. It made him nervous and less communicative as well.

Before they knew it, silence had fallen between them once again.

The lieutenant said it anyway. He didn't know precisely why, but it was something he had to ask. If he let it pass now, he might never ask. So he did.

Casually as he could, he stretched out a leg and yawned.

"Are you married?" he asked.

Stands With A Fist dropped her head and fixed her eyes on her lap. She shook her head in a short, uncomfortable way and said, "No."

The lieutenant was on the verge of asking why when he noticed that her head was falling slowly into her hands. He waited a moment, wondering if something was wrong.

She was perfectly still.

Just as he was about to speak again she suddenly clambered to her feet and left the arbor.

She was gone before Dunbar could call after her. Devastated, he sat numbly in the arbor, damning himself for having asked the question and hoping against hope that whatever had gone wrong could be put right again. But there was nothing he could do on that account. He couldn't ask Kicking Bird's advice. He couldn't even talk to Kicking Bird.

For ten frustrating minutes he sat alone in the arbor. Then he started for the pony herd. He needed a walk and a ride.

Stands With A Fist went for a ride, too. She crossed the river and meandered down a trail though the breaks, trying to sort her thoughts.

She didn't have much luck.

Her feelings about Dances With Wolves were in a terrible jumble. Not so long ago she hated the thought of him. For the last several days she hadn't thought of anything but him. And there were so many other contradictions.

With a start she realized she had given no thought to her dead husband. He had been the center of her life so recently, and now she had forgotten him. Guilt bore down on her.

She turned her pony about and started back, forcing Dances With Wolves out of her head with a long string of prayers for her dead husband.

She was still out of sight of the village when her pony lifted his head and snorted in the way horses do when they're afraid.

Something large crashed in the brush behind her, and knowing the sound was too large to be anything but a bear, Stands With A Fist hurried her pony home.

She was recrossing the river when the idle thought hit her.

I wonder if Dances With Wolves has ever seen a bear, she said to herself.

Stands With A Fist stopped herself then. She could not let this happen, this constant thinking of him. It was intolerable.

By the time she reached the opposite bank the woman who was two people had resolved that her role as a translator would heretofore be a thing of business, like trading. It would go no further, not even in her mind.

She would stop it.

CHAPTER XXIII

one

Lieutenant Dunbar's solo ride carried him along the river, too. But while Stands With A Fist rode south, he went north.

Despite the day's intense heat, he swung away from the river after a mile or two. He broke into open country with the idea that, surrounded by space, he might start to feel better.

The lieutenant's spirits were very low.

He ran the picture of her leaving the arbor over and over in his mind, trying to find something in it to hang on to. But there was a finality about their departure, and it gave him that dreadful feeling of having let something wonderful slip from his hand just as he was picking it up.

The lieutenant chastised himself mercilessly for not having gone after her. If he had, they might be talking happily at this moment, the tender issue, whatever it was, settled and behind them.

He'd wanted to tell her something of himself. Now it might never happen. He wanted to be back in the arbor with her. Instead he was stumbling around out here, wandering like a lost soul under a broiling sun.

He'd never been this far north of the camp and was surprised at how radically the country was changing. These were real hills rising in front of him, not mere bumps on the grassland. Running out of the hills were deep, jagged canyons.

The heat, coupled with his constant self-criticism, had set his mind to simmering, and feeling suddenly dizzy, he gave Cisco a little squeeze with his knees. A half mile ahead he had spotted the shady mouth of a dark canyon spilling onto the prairie.

The walls on either side climbed a hundred feet or more and the darkness that fell over horse and rider was instantly refreshing. But as they picked their way carefully over the canyon's rock-strewn floor, the place grew ominous. Its walls were pressing tighter against them. He could feel Cisco's muscles bunching nervously, and in the absolute quiet of the afternoon he was increasingly aware of the hollow thump in his own heart.

He was struck with the certainty that he had entered something ancient. Perhaps it was evil.

He had begun to think of turning back when the canyon bottom suddenly started to widen. Far ahead, in the space between the canyon walls, he could see a stand of cottonwoods, their tops twinkling in bright sunlight.

After managing a few more twists and turns he and Cisco burst all at once into the large, natural clearing where the cottonwoods stood. Even at the height of summer the place was remarkably green, and though he could see no stream, he knew there must be water here.

The buckskin arched his neck and sniffed the air. He would have to be thirsty, too, and Dunbar gave him his head. Cisco skirted the cottonwoods and walked another hundred yards to the base of a sheer rock wall that marked the canyon's end. There he stopped.

At his feet, covered with a film of leaves and algae, was a small spring about six feet across. Before the lieutenant could jump off, Cisco's muzzle had thrust through the surface's coating and he was drinking in long gulps.

As the lieutenant knelt next to his horse, going to his hands at the edge of the spring, something caught his eye. There was a cleft at the base of the rock wall. It ran back into the cliff and was tall enough at its entrance for a man to walk into without stooping.

Lieutenant Dunbar buried his face next to Cisco's and drank quickly. He slipped the bridle off his horse's head, dropped it next to the spring, and walked into the darkness of the cleft.

It was wonderfully cool inside. The soil beneath his feet was soft, and as far as he could see, the place was empty. But as his eyes passed over the floor he knew that man was a fixture here. Charcoal from a thousand fires was scattered over the ground like plucked feathers.

The ceiling began to shrink, and when the lieutenant touched it, the soot of the thousand fires coated his fingertips.

Still feeling light-headed, he sat down, his bottom hitting the ground so heavily that he groaned.

He was facing the way he had come, and the entrance, a hundred yards away, was now a window to the afternoon. Cisco was grazing contentedly on the bunchgrass next to the spring. Behind him the cottonwood leaves were blinking like mirrors. As the coolness closed around him, Lieutenant Dunbar was suddenly overcome with a throbbing, all-encompassing fatigue. Throwing his arms out as a pillow for his head, he lay back on the smooth, sandy earth and stared up at the ceiling.

The roof of solid rock was blackened with smoke, and underneath there were distinct markings. Deep grooves had been cut in the stone, and as he studied them, Dunbar realized they had been made by human hands.

Sleep was pressing in about him, but he was fascinated by the markings. He struggled to make sense of them as a star gazer might strain to connect the outline of Taurus.

The marks immediately above suddenly fell into place. There was a buffalo, crudely drawn but bearing all the essential detail. Even the little tail was standing up.

Next to the buffalo was a hunter. He was holding a stick, a spear in all likelihood. It was pointed at the buffalo.

Sleep was unstoppable now. The idea that the spring might have been tainted occurred to him as his invisibly weighted eyes began to close.

When they were shut he could still see the buffalo and the hunter. The hunter was familiar. He wasn't an exact duplicate, but there was something of Kicking Bird in his face, something handed down over hundreds of years.

Then the hunter was him.

Then he went out.

two

The trees were bare of leaves.

Patches of snow lay on the ground.

It was very cold.

A great circle of uncounted common soldiers waited lifelessly, their rifles standing at their sides.

He went from one to another, staring into their frozen, blue faces, looking for signs of life. No one acknowledged him.

He found his father among them, the telltale doctor's bag hanging from one hand like a natural extension of his body. He saw a boyhood chum who had drowned. He saw the man who owned a stable in his old town and who beat the horses when they got out of line. He saw General Grant, still as a sphinx, a soldier's cap crowning his head. He saw a watery-eyed man with the collar of a priest. He saw a prostitute, her dead face smeared with rouge and powder. He saw his massively bosomed elementary-school teacher. He saw the sweet face of his mother, tears frozen to her cheeks.

This vast army of his life swam before his eyes as if it would never end.

There were guns, big, brass-colored cannons on wheels.

Someone was coming up to the waiting circle of soldiers.

It was Ten Bears. He walked smoothly in the brittle cold, a single blanket draped over his bony shoulders. Looking like a tourist, he came face-to-face with one of the cannons. A coppery hand snaked out of the blanket, wanting to feel the barrel.

The big gun discharged and Ten Bears was gone in a cloud of smoke. The upper half of his body was somersaulting slowly in the dead winter sky. Like water from a hose, blood was pouring out of the place where his waist had been. His face was blank. His braids were floating lazily away from his ears.

Other guns went off, and like Ten Bears, the lodges of his village took flight. They gyrated through space like heavy paper cones, and when they came back to earth, the tipis stuck into the iron-hard ground on their tips.

The army was faceless now. Like a herd of joyous bathers hustling to the seashore on a hot day, it swept down on the people who had been left uncovered beneath the lodges.

Babies and small children were flung aside first. They flew high into the air. The branches of the bare trees stabbed through their little bodies, and there the children squirmed, their blood running down the tree trunks as the army continued its work.

They opened the men and women as if they were Christmas presents: shooting into their heads and lifting off the skull tops; slitting bellies with bayonets, then parting the skin with impatient hands; severing limbs and shaking them out.

There was money inside every Indian. Silver poured from their limbs. Greenbacks spewed from their bellies. Gold sat in their skulls like candy in jars.

The great army was drawing away in wagons piled high with riches. Some of the soldiers were running next to the wagons, scooping the overflow off the ground.

Fighting broke out in the ranks of the army, and long after they had disappeared, the sound of their battling flashed on and off like lightning behind the mountains.

One soldier was left behind, walking sad and dazed through the field of corpses.

It was himself.

The hearts of the dismembered people were still beating, drumming out in unison a cadence that sounded like music.

He slipped a hand under his tunic and watched it rise and fall with the beat of his own heart. He saw his breath freezing in front of his face. Soon he would be frozen, too.

He lay down among the corpses, and as he stretched out, a long, mournful sigh escaped his lips. Instead of fading, the sigh gained strength. It circled over the slaughtering ground, rushing faster and faster past his ears, moaning a message he could not understand.

three

Lieutenant Dunbar was cold to the bone.

It was dark.

Wind was whistling through the cleft.

He jumped straight up, cracked his head against the ceiling of solid rock, and sank back to his knees. Blinking through the sting of the blow, he could see a silvery light shining through the cleft's entrance. Moonlight.

Panicked, Dunbar scrambled off in an apelike stoop, one hand held overhead to gauge the ceiling. When he could stand unimpeded he ran for the mouth of the cleft and didn't slow until he was standing in the brilliant moonlight of the clearing.

Cisco was gone.

The lieutenant whistled high and shrill.

Nothing.

He walked farther into the clearing and whistled again. He heard something move in the cottonwoods. Then he heard a low nicker, and Cisco's buckskin hide flashed like amber in the moonlight as he came out of the trees.

Dunbar was going for the bridle he left at the spring when a movement flickered in the air. He looked back in time to glimpse the tawny form of a great horned owl as it swooped past Cisco's head and went into a steep climb, finally vanishing in the branches of the tallest cottonwood.

The owl's flight was disturbingly eerie, and it must have had the same effect on Cisco, for when he reached him the little horse was trembling with fright.

four

They backtracked out of the canyon, and when they were on the open prairie again it was with the kind of relief a swimmer feels on coming to the surface after a long, deep dive.

Lieutenant Dunbar shifted his weight slightly forward and Cisco was off, carrying him over the silvery grasslands at an easy gallop.

He rode invigorated, thrilled to be awake and alive and putting distance between himself and the strange, unsettling dream. It didn't matter where the dream had come from and it didn't matter what it meant. The images were too fresh and too profound to rehash now. He spurned the hallucination in favor of other thoughts as he listened to the gentle pounding of Cisco's hooves.

A feeling of power was coming over him, increasing with each passing mile. He could feel it in the effortless movement of Cisco's canter and he could feel it in the oneness of himself: oneness with his horse and the prairie and the prospect of returning whole to the village that was now his home. In the back of his mind he knew there would be a reckoning with Stands With A Fist and that the grotesque dream would have to be assimilated somewhere down the line of his future.

For the moment, however, these things were small. They didn't threaten him in the least, for he was charged with the notion that his life as a human being was suddenly a blank and that the slate of his history had been wiped clean. The future was as open as the day he was born, and it sent his spirits soaring. He was the only man on earth, a king without subjects, rambling across the limitless territory of his life.

He was glad they were Comanches and not Kiowas, for he remembered their nickname now, heard or read somewhere in the dead past.

The Lords of the Plains, that's what they were called. And he was one of them.

In a fit of reverie he dropped the reins and crossed his arms, laying each hand flat against the breastplate that covered his chest.

"I'm Dances With Wolves," he cried out loud, "I'm Dances With Wolves."

five

Kicking Bird, Wind In His Hair, and several other men were sitting around the fire when he rode in that night.

The medicine man had been worried enough to send out a small party to scout the four directions for the white soldier. But there was no general alarm. It was done quietly. They had come back with nothing to report, and Kicking Bird put the matter out of his mind. When it came to matters beyond his sphere of influence, he always trusted to the wisdom of the Great Spirit.

He'd been more disturbed by what he saw in the face and manner of Stands With A Fist than he had been with the disappearance of Dances With Wolves. At the mention of his name he'd perceived a vague discomfort in her, as though she had something to hide.

But this, too, he decided, was beyond his control. If something important had happened between them, it would be revealed at the proper time.

He was relieved to see the buckskin horse and its rider coming up to the firelight.

The lieutenant slid off Cisco's back and greeted the men around the fire in Comanche. They returned the salutation and waited to see if he was going to say anything significant about his disappearance.

Dunbar stood before them like an uninvited guest, twisting Cisco's reins in his hands as he looked them over. Everyone could see his mind was working on something.

After a few seconds his gaze fell squarely on Kicking Bird, and the medicine man thought he had never seen the lieutenant looking so calm and assured.

Dunbar smiled then. It was a small smile, full of confidence.

In perfect Comanche he said, "I'm Dances With Wolves."

Then he turned away from the fire and led Cisco down to the river for a long drink.

CHAPTER XXIV

one

Ten Bears's first council was inconclusive, but the day after Lieutenant Dunbar's return another meeting was held, and this time a solid compromise was reached.

Instead of leaving immediately, as the young men had wanted, the war party against the Pawnee would take a week to make necessary preparations. It was also decided that experienced warriors would be included.

Wind In His Hair would lead and Kicking Bird would go along also, providing critical spiritual guidance on the practical matters of choosing campsites and times for attack as well as divining unforeseen omens, several of which were sure to appear. It was to be a small party of about twenty warriors and they would be looking for booty rather than revenge.

There was great interest in this group because several of the young men would be going out for the first time as full-fledged warriors, and the addition of such distinguished men to lead them produced enough excitement to upset the normally placid routine of Ten Bears's camp.

Lieutenant Dunbar's routine, already altered by his strange

day and night in the ancient canyon, was upset, too. With so much going on, the meetings in the brush arbor were constantly interrupted, and after two days of this, they were discontinued.

Besieged as he was, Kicking Bird was happy to turn his full attention to planning for the raid. Stands With A Fist was glad for the cooling-off period, and so was Dances With Wolves. It was plain to him that she was making an extra effort to keep her distance, and he was relieved to see the sessions end for that reason if for no other.

Preparations for the war party intrigued him, and he shadowed Kicking Bird as much as he could.

The medicine man seemed to be in touch with the entire camp, and Dances With Wolves was delighted to be included, even if it was only to observe. Though far from fluent, he was close now to the gist of what was being said and had become so proficient in sign language that Stands With A Fist was rarely called upon during the final days before the war party left.

It was a first-rate education for the former Lieutenant Dunbar. He sat in on many meetings at which responsibilities were delegated to each member of the party with remarkable care and tact. Reading between the lines, he could see that, among Kicking Bird's many outstanding qualities, none counted more than his ability to make each man feel he was a crucially important member of the coming expedition.

Dances With Wolves also got to spend time with Wind In His Hair. Because Wind In His Hair had fought the Pawnee on many occasions, his stories of these encounters were in demand. In fact, they were vital to the preparation of the party's younger men. Informal classes in warfare were conducted in and around Wind In His Hair's lodge, and as the days sped by, Dances With Wolves became infected.

The infection was low-grade at first, nothing more than idle reflections on what the warpath would be like. But eventually he was caught up with a strong desire to take the trail against the Comanches' enemies.

He waited patiently for opportune times when he could ask about going along. He had his chances, but the moments came and went without him finding his tongue. He was made shy by the fear of someone saying no.

Two days before the party's scheduled departure, a large herd of antelope was sighted near camp, and a group of warriors, including Dances With Wolves, rode out in search of meat.

Using the same surrounding technique they had employed with the buffalo, the men were able to kill a great number of the animals, about sixty head.

Fresh meat was always welcome, but more importantly, the appearance and successful hunting of the antelope was taken as a sign that the little war against the Pawnee would have a good result. The men going out would be made securer with the knowledge that their families wouldn't be hard-pressed for food, even if they were gone several weeks.

A dance of thanks was held the same evening, and everyone was in high spirits. Everyone but Dances With Wolves. As the night wore on he watched from a distance, growing more and more morose. He was thinking only of being left behind, and now he could not stand the thought.

He maneuvered himself close to Stands With A Fist, and when the dance broke up, he was at her side.

"I want to talk to Kicking Bird," he said.

Something was wrong, she thought. She read his eyes for clues but could find none.

"When?"

"Now."

two

For some reason he couldn't calm himself down. He was uncharacteristically nervous and fidgety, and as they walked to the lodge, both Stands With A Fist and Kicking Bird could see this.

His anxiety was still evident when they had seated themselves in Kicking Bird's tipi. The medicine man skated over the usual formalities and came quickly to the point.

"Make your talk," he said, speaking through Stands With A Fist.

"I want to go."

"Go where?" she asked.

Dances With Wolves shifted restlessly, working up his courage.

"Against the Pawnee."

This was relayed to Kicking Bird. Except for a slight widening of his eyes, the medicine man seemed unfazed.

"Why do you want to make war on the Pawnee?" he asked logically. "They have done nothing to you."

Dances With Wolves thought for a moment.

"They are Comanche enemies."

Kicking Bird didn't like it. There was something forced about the request. Dances With Wolves was rushing.

"Only Comanche warriors can go on this ride," he said flatly.

"I have been a warrior in the white man's army longer than some of the young men who are going have been apprentices. Some of them are making war for the first time."

"They have been taught in the Comanche way," the medicine man said gently. "You have not. The white man's way is not the Comanche way."

Dances With Wolves lost a little of his resolve then. He knew he was losing. His voice dropped.

"I cannot learn the Comanche way of war if I stay in camp," he said lowly.

It was difficult for Kicking Bird. He wished it was not happening.

His affection for Dances With Wolves was deep. The white soldier had been his responsibility, and the white soldier had shown himself to be worthy of the risks Kicking Bird had taken. He was more than worthy.

On the other hand, the medicine man had risen to a high and revered position through the dedicated gathering of wisdom. He was wise now and was able to understand the world well enough to be of great service to his people.

It was between affection for one man and service to his community that Kicking Bird was split. He knew it was no contest. All of his wisdom said it would be wrong to take Dances With Wolves.

As he struggled with the question he heard Dances With Wolves say something to Stands With A Fist.

"He asks that you talk to Ten Bears on this," she said.

Kicking Bird looked into the hopeful eyes of his protégé and hesitated.

"I will do that," he said.

three

Dances With Wolves slept poorly that night. He cursed himself for being too excited to sleep. He knew that no decision would be rendered until the next day, and tomorrow seemed too far away. He slept for ten minutes and woke for twenty all through the night. Half an hour before dawn he finally gave it up and went down to the river to bathe.

The idea of waiting around camp for word was unbearable and he jumped at the chance when Wind In His Hair asked if he wanted to go on a buffalo scout. They ranged far to the east, and it was well into the afternoon before they were back in camp.

He let Smiles A Lot take Cisco back to the pony herd and, with his heart beating wildly, stepped into Kicking Bird's lodge.

No one was there.

He was determined to wait until someone returned, but through the back wall he could hear women's voices mixed with the clatter of work, and the longer he listened, the less he could imagine what was going on. Not many minutes passed before curiosity drove him outside.

Directly behind Kicking Bird's home, a few yards from the arbor, he found Stands With A Fist and the medicine man's wives putting the final touches on a newly erected lodge.

They were stitching the last of the seams and he watched them work for a few moments before he spoke.

"Where's Kicking Bird?"

"With Ten Bears," she said.

"I will wait for him," said Dances With Wolves, turning to go.

"If you want," she said, not bothering to look up from her work, "you can wait in here."

She stopped to brush at the beads of sweat running along her temple and faced him.

"We make this for you."

four

The talk with Ten Bears didn't last long, at least the substance of it didn't.

The old man was in a good mood. His long-suffering bones loved the hot weather, and though he wasn't going, the prospects for a successful venture against the hated Pawnee delighted him. His grandchildren were round as butterballs from summer feasting, and all three of his wives had been especially cheerful of late.

Kicking Bird could not have picked a better time to see him about a delicate matter.

As the medicine man told him about Dance With Wolves's request, Ten Bears listened impassively. He repacked his pipe before replying.

"You have told me what is in his heart," the old man wheezed. "What is in yours?"

He offered Kicking Bird the pipe.

"My heart says he is too anxious. He wants too much, too soon. He is a warrior, but he is not a Comanche. He will not be a Comanche for a while."

Ten Bears smiled.

"You always speak well, Kicking Bird. And you see it well."

The old fellow lit the pipe and passed it over.

"Now tell me," he said, "what is it that you would like my advice on?"

five

It was a terrible letdown at first. The only thing he could compare it to was a reduction in rank. But it was more disappointing than that. He had never been so disappointed.

And yet he was shocked at how quickly the hurt of it passed. It was gone almost as soon as Kicking Bird and Stands With A Fist left the lodge.

He lay on the new bed in his new home and wondered about this change. It had only been minutes since he got the word, but he wasn't crushed at all now. It was a tiny disappointment now.

It's something to do with being here, he thought, being with these people. It's something to do with being unspoiled.

Kicking Bird had done everything very precisely. He came trailed by the two women carrying robes, Stands With A Fist and one of his wives. After they'd made up the new bed the wife had departed, and the three, Kicking Bird, Stands With A Fist, and Dances With Wolves, had stood facing one another in the center of the tipi.

Kicking Bird never made mention of the raid or the decision that had gone against him. He just started talking.

"It would be good if you make talk with Stands With A Fist while I'm gone. You should do this in my lodge so that my family can see. I want them to know you while I'm gone and I want you to know them. I will feel better to know that you are looking after my family while I'm away. Come to my fire and eat if you are hungry."

Once the invitation to dinner was made, the medicine man turned abruptly and left, Stands With A Fist following him.

As he watched them go, Dances With Wolves was surprised to feel his depression evaporating. In its place was a feeling of elation. He didn't feel small at all. He felt bigger.

Kicking Bird's family would be under his protection, and the idea of serving them in that role was one he looked forward to instantly. He would be with Stands With A Fist again and that, too, gave him heart.

The war party would be gone for some time, thus giving him the opportunity to learn a lot of Comanche. And in learning he knew he would be picking up more than language. If he worked very hard he would be on a whole new level by the time his mentors returned. He liked that idea.

Drums had started up in the village. The big send-off dance was beginning and he wanted to go. He loved the dancing.

Dances With Wolves rolled off the bed and looked around his lodge. It was empty, but before long it would hold the slim trappings of his life, and it was pleasant to think about having something to call his own again.

He stepped through the lodge flap and paused in the twilight outside. He had daydreamed his way past dinner, but the woodsmoke from the cooking fires was still thick in the air and the smell of it satisfied him.

A thought came to Dances With Wolves then.

I should be staying here, he said to himself, it's much the better idea.

He started off toward the sound of the drums.

When he reached the main avenue he fell in with a pair of warriors he knew. In signs they asked him if he would dance tonight. Dances With Wolves's reply was so positive that it made the men laugh.

CHAPTER XXV

one

Once the party was away, the village settled into a life of pastoral routine, a timeless rotation of dawn to day to dusk to night that made the prairie seem the only place on earth.

Dances With Wolves fell quickly into step with the cycle, moving through it in a pleasant, dreamlike way. A life of riding and hunting and scouting was physically taxing, but his body had adapted well, and once the rhythm of his days was established he found most activities effortless.

Kicking Bird's family required much of his time. The women did virtually all of the work around camp, but he felt obliged to monitor their day-to-day lives and those of the children, the result being that somehow his hands were always full.

Wind In His Hair had presented him with a good bow and a quiver of arrows at the farewell dance. He was thrilled with the gift and sought out an older warrior named Stone Calf, who taught him the finer points of its use. In the space of a week the two became fast friends, and Dances With Wolves showed up regularly at Stone Calf's lodge.

He learned how to care for and make quick repairs on

241

weapons. He learned the words to several important songs and how to sing them. He watched Stone Calf make fire from a little wooden kit and saw him make his own personal medicine.

He was a willing pupil for these lessons and quick to learn, so quick that Stone Calf gave him the nickname Fast.

He scouted a few hours each day, as did most of the other men. They went out in groups of three or four, and in a short time Dances With Wolves had a rudimentary knowledge of necessary things, like how to read the age of tracks and determine weather patterns.

The buffalo came and went in their mysterious way. Some days they would see none at all, and some days they would see so many that it became a joke.

On the two points that counted, the scouting was a success. There was fresh meat for the taking and the countryside was devoid of enemies.

After only a few days he was wondering why everyone didn't live in a lodge. When he thought of the places he had lived before, he could envision nothing but a collection of sterile rooms.

To him the lodge was a true home. It was cool on the hottest days, and no matter what sort of fuss was going on in camp, the circle of space inside seemed filled with peace.

He came to love the time he passed there by himself.

His favorite part of the day was late afternoon, and more often than not, he could be found close to the lodge flap, performing some little job like cleaning his boots while he watched the clouds change formation or listened to the light whistle of wind.

Without really trying, these late afternoons by himself shut down the machinery of his mind, letting his mind rest in a refreshing way.

two

It didn't take long, however, for one facet of his life to dominate all the others.

That was Stands With A Fist.

Their talks began again, this time under the casual but always present eyes of Kicking Bird's family.

The medicine man had left instructions to keep meeting, but without Kicking Bird to guide them, there was no clearcut direction for the lessons to take.

The first few days consisted mainly of mechanical, unexciting reviews.

In a way, it was just as well. She was still confused and embarrassed. The dryness of their first one-on-one meetings made it easier to pick up the thread of the past. It allowed her needed distance in getting used to him again.

Dances With Wolves was content to have it that way. The tedium of their exchanges was measured against his sincere desire to patch up whatever had damaged the link between them, and he waited patiently through the first few days, hoping for a thaw.

The Comanche was coming well, but it soon became apparent that sitting in the lodge all morning placed limitations on how fast he could learn it. So many things he needed to know about were outside. And family interruptions were never-ending.

But he waited on without complaint, letting Stands With A Fist skip over words she couldn't explain.

One afternoon just after the noon meal, when she couldn't find the word for grass, Stands With A Fist finally took him outside. One word led to another, and on that day they didn't return to the lodge for more than an hour. Instead, they strolled through the village, so intent on their studies that time ran out with little thought of its passage.

The pattern was repeated and reinforced in the days that followed. They became a common sight, a pair of talkers roving the village, oblivious to all but the objects comprising their work: bone, lodge flap, sun, hoof, kettle, dog, stick, sky, child, hair, robe, face, far, near, here, there, bright, dull, and on and on and on.

Every day the language took deeper root in him and soon Dances With Wolves could make more than words. Sentences were forming and he strung them together with a zeal that caused many mistakes.

"Fire grows on the prairie."

"Eating water is good for me."

"Is that man a bone?"

He was like a good runner who falls every third stride, but he kept hacking at the morass of the new language, and by sheer force of will he made remarkable progress.

No amount of failure could flag his spirits, and he scrambled over every obstacle with the kind of good humor and determination that makes a person fun.

They were in the lodge less and less. The outside was free, and a special quiet was now in place over the village. It had become unusually peaceful.

Everyone was thinking about the men who had gone out to face uncertain events in the country of the Pawnee. With each timeless day relatives and friends of the men in the war party prayed more devoutly for their safety. Overnight it seemed, prayers had become the single most obvious feature of camp life, finding their way into every meal, meeting, and job, no matter how small or fleeting.

The holiness that shrouded the camp gave Dances With Wolves and Stands With A Fist a perfect environment in which to operate. Sunk as they were in this time of waiting and prayer, other people paid little attention to the white couple. They moved around in a serene, well-protected bubble, an entity unto themselves.

They shared three or four hours each day, without touching and without talking about themselves. On the surface a careful formality was observed. They laughed at things together and they commented on ordinary phenomena like the weather. But feelings about themselves lay concealed at all times. Stands With A Fist was being careful with her feelings, and Dances With Wolves respected that.

three

A profound change took place two weeks after the party went out.

Late one afternoon, after a long scout under a brutal sun, Dances With Wolves returned to Kicking Bird's lodge, found no one there, and, thinking the family gone to the river, headed down to the water.

Kicking Bird's wives were there, scrubbing their children. Stands With A Fist was not around. He hung about long enough to get splashed by the kids and climbed back up the path to the village.

The sun was still brutal, and when he saw the arbor, the thought of its shade pulled him over.

He was halfway inside before he realized she was there. The regular session had already been held, and both of them were embarrassed.

Dances With Wolves sat down at a modest distance from her and said hello.

"It . . . it is hot," she answered, as if making an excuse for her presence.

"Yes," he agreed, "very hot."

Though he didn't have to, he swiped at his forehead. It was a silly way of making sure she could see he was here for the same reason.

But as he made the fake gesture, Dances With Wolves checked himself. A sudden urge had come over him, an urge to tell her how he felt.

He just started to talk. He told her he was confused. He

told her how good it felt to be here. He told her about the lodge and how good it was to have it. He took the breastplate in both hands and told her how he thought of it, that to him it was something great. He lifted it to his cheek and said, "I love this."

Then he said, "But I'm white . . . and I'm a soldier. Is it good for me to be here or is it a foolish thing? Am I foolish?"

He could see complete attention in her eyes.

"Is no . . . I don't know," she answered.

There was a little silence. He could see she was waiting.

"I don't know where to go," he said quietly. "I don't know where to be."

She turned her head slowly and stared out the doorway.

"I know," she said.

She was still lost in thought, staring out at the afternoon, when he said, "I want to be here."

She turned back to him. Her face looked huge. The sinking sun had given it a soft glow. Her eyes, wide with feeling, had the same glow.

"Yes," she said, understanding exactly how he felt.

She dropped her head. When she looked back up, Dances With Wolves felt swallowed, just as he had felt out on the prairie with Timmons for the first time. Her eyes were the eyes of a soulful person, filled with a beauty few men could know. They were eternal.

Dances With Wolves fell in love when he saw this.

Stands With A Fist had already fallen in love. It happened at the time he began to speak, not all at once but in slow stages until at last she could not deny it. She saw herself in him. She saw that they could be one.

They talked a little more and fell silent. For a few minutes they stared at the afternoon, each knowing what the other was feeling but not daring to speak.

The spell was broken when one of Kicking Bird's little boys happened by, looked inside, and asked what they were doing.

Stands With A Fist smiled at his innocent intrusion and told him in Comanche, "It is hot. We are sitting in the shade."

This made so much sense to the little boy that he came in and flopped onto Dances With Wolves's lap. They wrestled playfully for a few moments, but the roughhousing didn't last long.

The little boy suddenly sat up and told Stands With A Fist he was hungry.

"All right," she said in Comanche, and took him by the hand.

She looked at Dances With Wolves.

"Eat?"

"Yes, I'm hungry."

They crawled out of the arbor's doorway and started for Kicking Bird's lodge to get a cooking fire going.

four

His first order of business the next morning was to visit Stone Calf. He dropped by the warrior's lodge early and was immediately invited to sit down and have breakfast.

After they'd eaten the two men went outside to talk while Stone Calf worked on forming the willow for a new batch of arrows. Except for Stands With A Fist, it was the most sophisticated conversation he'd had with anyone.

Stone Calf was impressed that this Dances With Wolves, so new among them, was talking in Comanche already. And talking well.

The older warrior could also tell that Dances With Wolves wanted something, and when the discussion suddenly shifted to Stands With A Fist, he knew that this must be it.

Dances With Wolves tried to put it as casually as he could,

but Stone Calf was too much the old fox not to see that the question was important to his visitor.

"Is Stands With A Fist married?"

"Yes," Stone Calf replied.

The revelation hit Dances With Wolves like the worst kind of news. He was silent.

"Where is her husband?" he finally asked. "I do not see him."

"He is dead."

This was a possibility he had never considered.

"When did he die?"

Stone Calf looked up from his work.

"It is impolite to talk of the dead," he said. "But you are new so I will tell you. It was around the time of the cherry moon, in spring. She was grieving on the day you found her and brought her back."

Dances With Wolves didn't ask any more questions, but Stone Calf volunteered a few more facts. He mentioned the relatively high standing of the dead man and the absence of children in his marriage to Stands With A Fist.

Needing to digest what he had heard, Dances With Wolves thanked his informant and walked off.

Stone Calf wondered idly if there might be something going on between these people, and deciding it was none of his business, he went back to his work.

five

Dances With Wolves did the one thing he could count on to clear his head. He found Cisco in the pony herd and rode out of the village. He knew she would be waiting for him in Kicking Bird's lodge, but his mind was spinning wildly with what he'd been told and he couldn't think of facing her now.

He went downriver and, after a mile or two, decided to go

all the way to Fort Sedgewick. He hadn't been there for almost two weeks and felt an impulse to go now, as if in some strange way the place might be able to tell him something.

Even from a distance he could see that late summer storms had finished the awning. It had been torn away from most of the staves. The canvas itself was badly shredded. What was left was flapping in the breeze like the ragged mainsail of a ghost ship.

Two Socks was waiting near the bluff and he threw the old fellow the slab of jerked meat he'd brought along for nibbling. He wasn't hungry.

Field mice scattered as he peeked into the rotted supply house. They'd destroyed the only thing he'd left behind, a burlap sack filled with moldy hardtack.

In the sod hut that had been his home he lay down on the little bunk for a few minutes and stared at the crumbling walls.

He took his father's broken pocket watch off its peg, intending to slip it into his trouser pocket. But he looked at it for a few seconds and put it back.

His father had been dead six years. Or was it seven? His mother had been dead even longer. He could recall the details of his life with them, but the people . . . the people seemed like they'd been gone a hundred years.

He noticed the journal sitting on one of the camp stools and picked it up. It was odd, leafing through the entries. They, too, seemed old and gone, like something from a past life.

Sometimes he laughed at what he had written, but on the whole he was moved. His life had been made over, and pieces of the record were set down here. It was only a curiosity now and had no bearing on his future. But it was interesting to look back and see how far he had come.

When he reached the end there were some blank pages,

and he had the whimsical idea that a postscript was in order, something clever and mysterious perhaps.

But when he raised his eyes to think, against the blankness of the sod wall he only saw her. He saw the well-muscled calves flashing from under the hem of her everyday doeskin dress. He saw the long, beautiful hands extending gracefully from its sleeves. He saw the loose curve of her breasts beneath its bodice. He saw the high cheeks and the heavy, expressive brows and the eternal eyes and the mop of tangled, cherry-colored hair.

He thought of her sudden rages and of the light surrounding her face in the arbor. He thought of her modesty and dignity and of her pain.

Everything he saw and everything he thought of, he adored.

When his eyes fell back on the blank page spread on his lap, he knew what to write. He was overjoyed to see it come alive in words.

> *late summer, 1863*
>
> *I love Stands With A Fist.*
>
> *Dances With Wolves*

He closed the journal and placed it carefully on the center of the bed, thinking capriciously that he would leave it for posterity to puzzle over.

When he walked outside Dances With Wolves was relieved to see that Two Socks had disappeared. Knowing he would not see him again, he said a prayer for his grandfather the wolf, wishing him a good life for all his remaining years.

Then he vaulted onto Cisco's sturdy back, whooped a good-bye in Comanche, and galloped away at full speed.

When he looked over his shoulder at Fort Sedgewick he saw only open, rolling prairie.

six

She waited almost an hour before one of Kicking Bird's wives asked, ''Where is Dances With Wolves?''

The waiting had been very hard. Each minute had been filled with thoughts of him. When the question was asked she tried to construct her answer with a tone that shielded what she felt.

''Oh, yes . . . Dances With Wolves. No, I don't know where he is.''

She went outside then to ask around. Someone had seen him leaving early, riding to the south, and she guessed correctly that he had gone to the white man's fort.

Not wanting to know why he had gone, she threw herself into finishing the saddlebags she'd been working on, trying to blot out the distractions of the camp so that she could focus only on him.

But it wasn't enough.

She wanted to be alone with him, even if it was just in her thoughts, and after the noon meal she took the main path down to the river.

Usually there was a lull following lunch, and she was pleased to find no one at the water's edge. She took off her moccasins, walked onto a thick log that ran out like a pier, and, straddling it, dipped her feet into the cooling shallows.

There was only a hint of breeze, but it was enough to blunt the day's heat. She placed a hand on each thigh, relaxed her shoulders, and gazed at the slow-moving river with half-closed eyes.

If he came for her now. If he looked at her with those strong eyes and laughed his funny laugh and said they were going. She would go right now, the where not mattering.

Suddenly she remembered their first meeting, clear as if it were yesterday. Riding back, half-conscious, her blood all over him. She remembered the safety she had felt, his arm around her back, her face pressed against the strange-smelling fabric of his jacket.

Now she was understanding what it meant. She understood that what she felt now was what she felt then. Then it had only been a seed, buried and out of sight, and she hadn't known what it meant. But the Great Spirit knew. The Great Spirit had let the seed grow. The Great Spirit, in all its Great Mystery, had encouraged the seed to life every step of the way.

That feeling she had, that feeling of safety. She knew now that it was not the safety felt in the face of an enemy or a storm or an injury. It was not a physical thing at all. It was a safety she had felt in her heart. It had been there all along.

The rarest of all things in this life has happened, she thought. The Great Spirit has brought us together.

She was reeling with the wonder of how it had all come to pass when she heard a gentle lapping of water a few feet away.

He was squatting on a little patch of beach, splashing water on his face in a slow, unhurried way. He looked at her, and without bothering to wipe at the water dripping down his face, he smiled just like a little boy.

"Hello," he said. "I was at the fort."

He said this as if they had been together all their lives. She replied in the same way.

"I know."

"Can we make some talk?"

"Yes," she said, "I was waiting to do that."

Voices sounded in the distance, near the top of the trail.

"Where should we go?" he asked.

"I know a place."

She got quickly to her feet and, with Dances With Wolves a step or two behind, led him to the old side path she had taken the day Kicking Bird asked her to remember the white tongue.

They walked in silence, surrounded by the soft plod of

their footsteps, the rustling of willows, and the singing of the birds who infested the breaks.

Inside, their hearts were pounding with the suspicion of what was about to happen and the suspense of where and when it would take place.

The secluded clearing where she had recalled the past finally opened to them. Still silent, they sat down cross-legged in front of the big cottonwood that faced the river.

They could not speak. All other sound seemed to stop. Everything was still.

Stands With A Fist dipped her head and saw a rent in the seam of his trouser leg. His hand was resting there, halfway up his thigh.

"They are torn," she whispered, letting her fingers lightly touch the tear. Once her hand was there she could not move it. The little fingers lay together unmoving.

As if guided by some outside force, their heads came together softly. Their fingers entwined. The touching was rapturous as sex itself. Neither could have retraced the sequence of how it happened, but a moment later they were sharing a kiss.

It wasn't a big kiss, just a brushing and then a slight pressing together of their lips.

But it sealed the love between them.

They placed their cheeks together, and as each nose filled with the smell of the other, they fell into a dream. In the dream they made love and when they had finished and were lying side by side beneath the big cottonwood, Dances With Wolves looked into her eyes and saw tears.

He waited a long time, but she wouldn't speak.

"Tell me," he whispered.

"I'm happy," she said. "I'm happy the Great Spirit has let me live this long."

"I have the same feeling," he said, his eyes welling.

She pressed tightly against him then and began to cry. He

held her hard as she wept, unafraid of the joy that was running down her face.

seven

They made love all afternoon, having long talks in between. When shadows finally began to fall across the clearing, they sat up, both sensing they would be missed if they stayed much longer.

They were watching the glint on the water when he said: "I talked to Stone Calf . . . I know why you ran off that day . . . the day I asked if you were married."

She rose up then and extended her hand. He took it and she pulled him to his feet.

"I had a good life with him. He went away from me because you were coming. That is how I see it now."

She led him out of the clearing and they started back, clinging to each other as they walked. When they were within hearing of the faint voices calling from the village, they halted to listen. The main trail was just ahead.

With a squeeze of their hands the lovers slipped intuitively into the willows, and as if it would help them get through the coming night of separation, they came together again, making it fast as a hurried good-bye kiss.

A step or two more from the main path leading up to the village they stopped once more, and as they embraced, she whispered in his ear.

"I'm in mourning and our people would not approve if they knew of our love. We must guard our love carefully until the time comes for all to see it."

He nodded his understanding, they hugged briefly, and she slipped through the undergrowth.

Dances With Wolves waited in the willows for ten minutes

and then followed. He was glad to find himself alone as he shuffled up the hill to the village.

He went straight to his lodge and sat on his bed, staring through the lodge flap at what was left of the light, dreaming of their afternoon in front of the cottonwood.

When it was dark he lay back on the thick robes and realized that he was exhausted. As he rolled over he discovered the smell of her lingering on one of his hands. Hoping it would stay all through the night, he drifted off to sleep.

CHAPTER XXVI

one

The next few days were euphoric for Dances With Wolves and Stands With A Fist.

There were constant smiles about their mouths, their cheeks were flush with romance, and no matter where they went, their feet seemed not to touch the ground.

In the company of others they were discreet, being careful not to show any outward signs of affection. So geared were they for concealment that the language sessions were more businesslike than ever before. If they were alone in the lodge, they took the chance of holding hands, making love with their fingers. But that was as far as it went.

They tried to meet secretly at least once a day, usually at the river. This they couldn't help doing, but it took time to find absolute seclusion, and Stands With A Fist in particular fretted about being found out.

Marriage was in their minds from the beginning. It was something they both wanted. And the sooner the better. But her widowhood was a major stumbling block. There was no prescribed period of mourning in the Comanche life way, and release could come only from the woman's father. If she had no father, the warrior who was her primary provider would take on the responsibility. In Stands With A Fist's case, she could only look to Kicking Bird for her release. He alone would determine when she was no longer a widow. And it might take a long time.

Dances With Wolves tried to reassure his lover, telling her that things would work out and not to worry. But she did, anyway. During one fit of depression over this issue she proposed that they run away together. But he only laughed, and the idea was not brought up again.

They took chances. Twice in the four days after their coming together at the river she left Kicking Bird's lodge in the darkness of early morning and slipped unnoticed into Dances With Wolves's tipi. There they would lie together until first light, whispering their conversations as they held each other naked under the robe.

All in all they did as well as could be expected of two people who had surrendered completely to love. They were dignified and prudent and disciplined.

And they fooled almost no one.

Everyone in the camp who was old enough to know what love between a man and a woman looked like could see it in the faces of Stands With A Fist and Dances With Wolves.

Most people could not find it in their hearts to condemn love, no matter what the circumstances. Those few who might have taken offense held their tongues for lack of proof. Most important, their attraction was no threat to the band at large. Even the older, conservative elements admitted to themselves that the potential union made sense.

After all, they were both white.

two

On the fifth night after the meeting at the river, Stands With
A Fist had to see him again. She had been waiting for everyone in Kicking Bird's lodge to fall asleep. Long after the
sounds of light snoring filled the tipi, she was waiting, wanting to make sure her leaving would go unnoticed.

She had just realized that the smell of rain was strong in
the air when a sudden yapping of excited voices broke the
stillness. The voices were loud enough to wake everyone,
and seconds later they were throwing aside bedding to rush
outside.

Something had happened. The whole village was up. She
hurried down the main avenue with a throng of other people,
all of them heading for a big fire that seemed to be the center
of attention. In the chaos she looked vainly for Dances With
Wolves, but it wasn't until she had pushed close to the fire
that she could see him.

As they sifted through the crowd to one another she noticed new Indians huddled by the fire. There were half a
dozen of them. Several more men were sprawled on the
ground, some of them dead, some of them horribly injured.
They were Kiowas, longtime friends and hunting partners of
the Comanche.

The six men who were untouched were wild with fear.
They were gesticulating anxiously, talking in signs to Ten
Bears and two or three close advisers. The onlookers were
hushed and expectant as they watched the Kiowa story unfold.

She and Dances With Wolves had nearly closed the space
between them when women began to scream. A moment
later the assembly came to pieces as women and children ran
for their lodges, careening into each other in their panic.
Warriors were boiling around Ten Bears, and one word was
coming from the mouths of everyone. It was rolling through

the village in the same way that thunder had begun to tremble through the black skies overhead.

It was a word that Dances With Wolves knew well, for he had heard it many times in conversations and stories.

"Pawnee."

With Stands With A Fist at his side, he pressed closer to the warriors crowding around Ten Bears. She talked into his ear as they watched, telling him what had happened to the Kiowa.

They had started out as a small group, less than twenty men, looking for buffalo about ten miles north of the Comanche camp. There they were hit by a huge Pawnee war party, at least eighty warriors, maybe more. They'd been attacked in the afterglow of sunset and none of them would have escaped were it not for darkness and a superior knowledge of the countryside.

They'd covered the retreat as best they could, but with such a large army, it was only a matter of time before the Pawnee would locate this camp. It was possible they had moved into position even now. The Kiowas thought there would be a few hours at most to get ready. That there would be an attack, probably made at dawn, was a foregone conclusion.

Ten Bears began giving orders that neither Stands With A Fist nor Dances With Wolves could hear. It was clear from the old man's expression, however, that he was worried. Ten of the band's most distinguished warriors were out with Kicking Bird and Wind In His Hair. The men left behind were good fighters, but if there were eighty Pawnee coming, they would be dangerously outnumbered.

The meeting around the fire broke up in a curious kind of anarchy, lesser warriors marching off in different directions behind the man they felt would best lead them.

Dances With Wolves had an uneasy feeling. Everything seemed so disorganized. The thunder overhead was coming at closer intervals and rain seemed inevitable. It would help to cover the Pawnee approach.

But it was his village now, and he dashed after Stone Calf with only one thought in mind.

"I will follow you," he said when he had caught up.

Stone Calf eyed him grimly.

"This will be a hard fight," he said. "The Pawnee never come for horses. They come for blood."

Dances With Wolves nodded.

"Get your weapons and come to my lodge," the older warrior ordered.

"I'll get them," Stands With A Fist volunteered, and with her dress hitched up around her calves, she took off at a run, leaving Dances With Wolves to follow Stone Calf.

He was trying to calculate how many rounds he had for the rifle and his Navy revolver when he remembered something that stopped him in his tracks.

"Stone Calf," he shouted. "Stone Calf."

The warrior turned back to him.

"I have guns," Dances With Wolves blurted. "In the ground near the white man's fort there are many guns."

They made an immediate about-face and returned to the fire.

Ten Bears was still questioning the Kiowa hunters.

The poor men, already half-crazed at the trauma of nearly losing their lives, shrank at the sight of Dances With Wolves, and it took some quick talking to get them calmed down.

Ten Bears's face jumped when Stone Calf told him there were guns.

"What guns?" he asked anxiously.

"White soldier guns . . . rifles," answered Dances With Wolves.

It was a hard decision for Ten Bears. Though he approved of Dances With Wolves, there was something in his old Comanche blood that didn't fully trust the white man. The guns were in the ground and it would take them time to dig them up. The Pawnee might be close now and he needed every man to defend the village. There was the long ride to the white man's fort to consider. And the rain would be coming any minute.

But the fight was going to be a close one, and he knew that guns could make a big difference. Chances were the Pawnee didn't have many. Dawn was still hours away, and there was enough time to make the round trip to the hairmouth fort.

"The guns are in boxes. . . . They are covered with wood," Dances With Wolves said, interrupting his thoughts. "We will need only a few men and travois to bring them back."

The old man had to make the gamble. He told Stone Calf to take Dances With Wolves, along with two other men and six ponies, four for riding and two for carrying the guns. He told them to go quickly.

three

When he got to his lodge Cisco was bridled and standing in front. A fire was going inside and Stands With A Fist was squatting next to it, mixing something in a small bowl.

His weapons, the rifle, the big Navy, the bow, the quiver stuffed with arrows, and the long-bladed knife, were laid out neatly on the floor.

He was strapping on the Navy when she brought the bowl to him.

"Give me your face," she commanded.

He stood still as she daubed at the red substance in the bowl with one of her fingers.

"This is for you to do, but there is no time and you don't know how. I will do it for you."

With fast, sure strokes, she drew a single horizontal bar

across his forehead and two vertical ones along each cheek. Using a dot pattern, she superimposed a wolf's paw print over one of the cheek bars and stepped back to look at her work.

She nodded approval as Dances With Wolves slung the bow and quiver over his shoulder.

"You can shoot?" he asked.

"Yes," she said.

"Take this then."

He handed her the rifle.

There were no hugs or words of good-bye.

He stepped outside, jumped up on Cisco, and was gone.

four

They rode away from the river, taking the straightest line possible across the grasslands.

The sky was terrifying. It seemed as though four storms were converging at once. Lightning was flashing all around them like artillery fire.

They had to stop when one of the travois came loose from its rigging, and as it was being repaired, Dances With Wolves had a chilling thought. What if he couldn't find the guns? He hadn't seen the buffalo rib marker for a long time. Even if it was still standing where he'd driven it into the ground, it would be difficult to find. He groaned inwardly at his prospects.

Rain was beginning to fall in big, heavy drops when they reached the fort. He led them to what he thought was the spot but could see nothing in the dark. He told them what to look for, and the quartet fanned out on their ponies, searching the tall grass for a long, white piece of bone.

Rain was coming harder now, and ten minutes passed with no sign of the rib. The wind was up and lightning was flashing every few seconds. The light it threw across the ground was countered by the blinding effect it had on the searchers.

After twenty dismal minutes Dances With Wolves's heart had hit bottom. They were covering the same ground now and still there was nothing.

Then, over the wind and rain and thunder, he thought he heard a cracking sound under one of Cisco's hooves.

Dances With Wolves called to the others and leaped down. Soon all four were on their hands and knees feeling blindly through the grass.

Stone Calf suddenly jumped to his feet. He was waving a long, white piece of the rib.

Dances With Wolves stood in the spot where it was found and waited for the next bolt of lightning. When the sky flashed again, he glanced quickly at the old buildings of Fort Sedgewick and, using them as a landmark, began moving in a northerly direction, going step by step.

A few paces later the prairie went spongy under one of his boots, and he cried out to the others. The men dropped down to help him dig. The earth gave easily as they scooped and minutes later two long wooden cases of rifles were being hauled out of their muddy tomb.

five

They'd been under way only half an hour when the storm hit with full power, sending rain down in great, running sheets. It was impossible to see, and the four men shepherding the two travois across the plains had to grope their way back.

But with the importance of their mission uppermost in each man's mind, they never paused, and made the return trip in amazing time.

When at last they were in sight of the village, the storm

had died down. Above it, a few long streaks of gray had appeared in the turbulent sky, and through this first feeble light of day they could see that the village was still safe.

They had just started down the depression leading to camp when a spectacular barrage of lightning struck upriver. For two or three seconds the bolts lit the landscape with the clarity of daylight.

Dances With Wolves saw it, and so did the others.

A long line of horsemen was crossing the river no more than half a mile above the village.

The lightning struck again and they could see the enemy disappearing into the breaks. The plan was obvious. They would come from the north, using the foliage along the river to move within a hundred yards of the village. Then they would attack.

In perhaps twenty minutes the Pawnee would be in position.

six

There were twenty-four rifles in each crate. Dances With Wolves personally passed them out to the fighting men clustered around Ten Bears's lodge while the old man gave last-minute instructions.

Though he knew that the main assault would be coming from the river, it was probable that they would send a diversionary force from the open prairie, thus giving the real attackers a chance to overrun the village from behind. He designated two influential warriors and a handful of followers to fight off the suspected charge from the prairie.

Then he tapped Dances With Wolves on the shoulder, and the warriors listened as he spoke.

"If you were a white soldier," the old man said wryly, "and you had all these men with guns, what would you do?"

Dances With Wolves quickly thought this over.

"I would hide in the village . . ."

Cries of derision flew from the mouths of the warriors who had been within earshot. Ten Bears quieted them with a raising of his hand and an admonishment.

"Dances With Wolves has not finished his answer," he said sternly.

"I would hide in the village, behind the lodges. I would watch only the breaks and not those coming from the prairie. I would let the enemy show himself first. I would let the enemy think we are fighting on the other side and that taking the camp will be easy. Then I would have these men hiding behind the lodges jump out and shoot. Then I would have these men charge the enemy with knives and skull crackers. I would drive the enemy into the river and kill so many that they would never come this way again."

The old man had been listening carefully. He looked out over his warriors and lifted his voice.

"Dances With Wolves and I are of the same mind. We should kill so many that they will never come this way again. Let us go quietly."

The men moved stealthily through the village with their new rifles and took up positions behind lodges that faced the river.

Before he took his place beside them, Dances With Wolves slipped into Kicking Bird's lodge. The children had been herded under robes. Sitting in silence beside them were the women. Kicking Bird's wives were holding clubs in their laps. Stands With A Fist had his rifle. They said nothing, and neither did Dances With Wolves. He'd only wanted to see that they were ready.

He stole past the arbor and stopped behind his own lodge. It was one of the closest to the river. Stone Calf was on the other side. They nodded at each other and turned their attention to the open ground in front of them. It sloped for about a hundred yards before it met the breaks.

The rain was much lighter, but it still served to obscure their view. Clouds hung thickly overhead, and the half-light of dawn was almost no light at all. They could see little, but he felt sure they were there.

Dances With Wolves glanced up and down the line of tipis to his left and right. Comanche warriors were packed in behind each one, waiting with their rifles. Even Ten Bears was there.

The light was stronger now. The storm clouds were lifting and the rain was going with them. Suddenly the sun broke through, and a minute later steam was rising off the ground like fog.

Dances With Wolves squinted through the fog at the breaks and saw the dark shapes of men, sifting like spirits through the willows and cottonwoods.

He was starting to feel something he had not felt in a long time. It was that intangible thing that turned his eyes black, that turned on the machine that could not be shut down.

No matter how big, how many, or how powerful the men moving in the mist were, they were nothing to fear. They were the enemy and they were on his doorstep. He wanted to fight them. He couldn't wait to fight them.

Gunshots rang out behind him. The diversionary force had hit the small group of defenders on the other front.

As the noise of the fighting increased, his eyes checked the line. A few hotheads tried to break away and run to the other fight, but the older warriors did a good job of holding them in check, and no one bolted.

Again he scanned the mists clinging to the breaks.

They were coming up slowly, some on foot, some on horseback. They were inching up the incline, shadowy, roach-haired enemies dreaming of a slaughter.

The Pawnee cavalry was behind the men on foot, and Dances With Wolves wanted them at the front. He wanted the mounted men to take the brunt of the fire.

Bring up the horses, he pleaded to them silently. Bring 'em up.

He looked down the line, hoping they would wait a few more seconds, and was surprised to see many eyes riveted on him. They kept watching, as if waiting for a sign.

Dances With Wolves raised an arm over his head.

A fluttering guttural sound came up the slope. It rose higher and higher, blasting through the quiet, rainy morning, like hot air. The Pawnee were sounding the attack.

As they charged, the cavalry surged ahead of the men on foot.

Dances With Wolves dropped his arm and sprang out from behind the lodge with his rifle raised. The other Comanches followed suit.

The fire from their guns hit the horsemen at a distance of about twenty yards, and as cleanly as a sharp knife cutting skin, it wrecked the Pawnee charge. Men tumbled from their horses like toys shaken off a shelf, and those not actually hit were stunned by the blistering concussion of forty rifles.

As they fired the Comanches counterattacked, streaming down through the screen of blue smoke to pounce on the dazed enemy.

The charge was so furious that Dances With Wolves crashed square into the first Pawnee he met. As they rolled awkwardly on the ground he thrust the barrel of the Navy into the man's face and fired.

After that he shot men where he could find them in the turmoil, killing two more in rapid succession.

Something large bumped him hard from behind, nearly knocking him off his feet. It was one of the surviving Pawnee war ponies. He grabbed its bridle and swung onto its back.

The Pawnee were like chickens being set upon by wolves and already they were falling back, desperately trying to make the safety of the breaks. Dances With Wolves picked out a tall warrior running for his life and rode him down. He fired at the back of the man's head, but there was no report. Flipping the barrel around, he clubbed the fleeing warrior with the butt end of the revolver. The Pawnee went down right in front of him, and Dances With Wolves felt the pony's hooves strike the body as they passed over.

Just ahead of him another Pawnee, his head turbaned with a bright red scarf, was picking himself off the ground. He, too, was going for the breaks.

Dances With Wolves kicked viciously at the pony's flanks, and as they pulled abreast of the runaway, he threw himself at the turbaned man, taking him in a headlock as he slid from the pony's back.

Momentum sent them careening across the last of the open space and they slammed hard against a large cottonwood. Dances With Wolves had the man by both sides of his head. He was bashing his skull against the tree trunk before he realized that the warrior's eyes were dead. A broken branch low on the trunk had skewered the Pawnee like meat.

As he stepped back from this unnerving sight, the dead man slumped forward, his arms flopping pitifully against Dances With Wolves's sides as if he wanted to embrace his killer. Dances With Wolves skipped back farther and the body fell flat on its face.

In the same instant he realized that the screaming had stopped.

The fight was over.

Suddenly weak, he staggered along the edge of the breaks, picked up the main path, and trotted down to the river, side-stepping Pawnee bodies as he went.

A dozen mounted Comanches, Stone Calf among them, were chasing the dregs of the Pawnee force up the opposite bank.

Dances With Wolves watched until the skirmishers disappeared from sight. Then he walked slowly back. Coming up the incline, he could hear yelling. When he reached the slope's crest, the battlefield he'd lately occupied opened wide to him.

It looked like a hastily abandoned picnic site. Refuse was scattered everywhere. There were a great number of Pawnee corpses. Comanche warriors were moving among them excitedly.

"I killed this one," someone would call.

"This one still breathes," another would announce, prompting the arrival of whoever was close by to help finish him off.

The women and children had come out of the lodges and were scurrying down to the battlefield. Some of the bodies were being mutilated.

Dances With Wolves stood stock-still, too fatigued to retreat into the breaks, too repulsed to move forward.

One of the warriors saw him and then cried out.

"Dances With Wolves!"

Before he knew it, Comanche fighters were all around him. Like ants rolling a pebble uphill, they pushed him onto the battlefield. They were chanting his name as they went.

In a daze he allowed himself to be carried along, unable to comprehend their intense happiness. They were overjoyed at the death and destruction lying at their feet, and Dances With Wolves could not understand.

But as he stood there, hearing them shout his name, understanding came to him. He had never been in this kind of fight, but gradually he began to look at the victory in a new way.

This killing had not been done in the name of some dark political objective. This was not a battle for territory or riches or to make men free. This battle had no ego.

It had been waged to protect the homes that stood only a few feet away. And to protect the wives and children and loved ones huddled inside. It had been fought to preserve the food stores that would see them through the winter, food stores everyone had worked so hard to gather.

For every member of the band this was a great personal victory.

Suddenly he was proud to hear his name being shouted, and as his eyes focused again, he looked down and recognized one of the men he had killed.

"I shot this one," he yelled out.

Someone shouted in his ear.

"Yes, I saw you shoot him."

Before long, Dances With Wolves was marching around with them, calling out the names of fellow Comanche men as he recognized them.

Sunshine spilled across the village, and the fighters began a spontaneous dance of victory, exhorting each other with back slaps and cries of triumph as they cavorted over the field of dead Pawnee.

seven

Two of the enemy had been killed by the force defending the front of the village. On the main battlefield there were twenty-two bodies. Four more were found in the breaks, and Stone Calf's team of pursuers managed to kill three. How many had gotten away wounded, no one knew.

Seven Comanches had been wounded, only two seriously, but the real miracle was in the number of dead. Not a single Comanche fighter had been lost. Even the old men could not remember such a one-sided victory.

For two days the village reveled in its triumph. Honors were heaped on all the men, but one warrior was exalted above all others. That was Dances With Wolves.

Through all his months on the plains the native perception of him had shifted many times. And now the circle had closed. Now he was looked on in a way that was close to their original idea. No one came forward to declare him a god, but in the life of these people he was the next best thing.

All day long young men could be found hanging around

his lodge. Maidens flirted openly with him. His name was foremost in everyone's thoughts. No conversation, regardless of subject, could run its course without some mention of Dances With Wolves.

The ultimate accolade came from Ten Bears. In a gesture previously unknown, he presented the hero with a pipe from his own lodge.

Dances With Wolves liked the attention, but he did nothing to encourage it. The instant and lasting celebrity pressured the management of his days. It seemed that someone was always underfoot. Worst of all, it gave him little private time with Stands With A Fist.

Of all the people in camp, he was perhaps the most relieved to see the return of Kicking Bird and Wind In His Hair.

After several weeks on the trail they had yet to engage the enemy when sudden and unseasonable snow flurries caught them in the foothills of a mountain range.

Interpreting this as a sign of an early and savage winter, Kicking Bird had called off the expedition and they had flown home to make preparations for the big move south.

CHAPTER XXVII

one

If the party had any misgivings about returning empty-handed, they were washed away with the incredible news of the Pawnee rout.

One immediate side effect of the homecoming was that it reduced the heat of celebrity that Dances With Wolves had been subjected to. He was no less revered, but because of their traditional high standing, much attention was shifted back to Kicking Bird and Wind In His Hair, and something approximating the old routine was reestablished.

Though he made no public demonstration, Kicking Bird was astounded by Dances With Wolves's progress. His bravery and ability in repelling the Pawnee attack could not be overlooked, but it was his progress as a Comanche, particularly his mastery of the language, that moved the medicine man.

He had sought only to learn something of the white race, and it was hard, even for a man of Kicking Bird's experience, to accept the fact that this lone white soldier, who months ago had never seen an Indian, was now a Comanche.

Harder to believe was that he had become a leader of other

Comanches. But the evidence was there for all to see: in the young men who sought him out and in the way all the people talked.

Kicking Bird could not figure out why all this had happened. He finally came to the conclusion that it was just another part of the Great Mystery that surrounded the Great Spirit.

It was fortunate that he was able to accept these rapid developments. It helped pave the way for yet another surprise. His wife told him about it as they lay in bed on his first night back.

"Are you certain of this?" he asked, thoroughly confounded. "This is hard for me to believe."

"When you see them together, you will know," she whispered confidentially. "It is there for all to see."

"Does it seem a good thing?"

His wife answered this question with a giggle.

"Isn't it always a good thing?" she teased, squeezing a little closer to him.

two

First thing next morning Kicking Bird appeared at the celebrity's lodge flap, his face so clouded that Dances With Wolves was taken aback.

They exchanged greetings and sat down.

Dances With Wolves had just begun to pack his new pipe when Kicking Bird, in an unusual display of bad manners, interrupted his host.

"You are speaking well," he said.

Dances With Wolves stopped working the tobacco into the bowl.

"Thank you," he replied. "I like to speak Comanche."

''Then tell me . . . what is this between you and Stands
With A Fist?''

Dances With Wolves nearly dropped his pipe. He stammered a few unintelligible sounds before he finally got something coherent out.

''What do you mean?''

Kicking Bird's face flushed angrily as he repeated himself.

''Is there something between you and her?''

Dances With Wolves didn't like this tone. His answer was
framed like a challenge.

''I love her.''

''You want to marry her?''

''Yes.''

Kicking Bird thought on this. He would have objected to
love for its own sake, but he could find nothing to disapprove
of so long as it was housed in matrimony.

He got to his feet.

''Wait here in the lodge,'' he said sternly. Before Dances
With Wolves could reply, the medicine man was gone.

He would have said yes at any rate. Kicking Bird's brusque
manner had put the fear of God into him. He sat where he
was.

three

Kicking Bird made stops at Wind In His Hair's and Stone
Calf's lodges, staying about five minutes in each tipi.

As he walked back to his own lodge he found himself
shaking his head again. Somehow he had expected this. But
it was still baffling.

Ah, the Great Mystery, he sighed to himself. I always try
to see it coming, but I never do.

She was sitting in the lodge when he came in.

"Stands With A Fist," he snapped, bringing her to attention. "You are no longer a widow."

With that he retreated back through the lodge flap and went to find his favorite pony. He needed a long, solitary ride.

four

Dances With Wolves hadn't been waiting long when Wind In His Hair and Stone Calf appeared outside his door. He could see them peeking inside.

"What are you doing in there?" Wind In His Hair asked.

"Kicking Bird told me to wait."

Stone Calf smiled knowingly.

"You might have to wait awhile." He chuckled. "Kicking Bird rode out onto the prairie a few minutes ago. It looked like he was taking his time."

Dances With Wolves didn't know what to do or say. He noticed a smirk on Wind In His Hair's face.

"Can we come in?" the big warrior asked slyly.

"Yes, please . . . please, sit down."

The two visitors took seats in front of Dances With Wolves. They were smug as schoolboys.

"I'm waiting for Kicking Bird," he said curtly. "What do you want?"

Wind In His Hair leaned forward a little. He was still smirking.

"There is talk that you want to get married."

Dances With Wolves's face began to change color. In the span of a few seconds it went from a light rosy hue to the deepest, richest red.

Both his guests laughed out loud.

"To whom?" he croaked feebly.

The warriors shared expressions of doubt.

"To Stands With A Fist," Wind In His Hair said. "That's what we heard. Isn't that the one?"

"She is in mourning," he blubbered. "She is a—"

"Not today," Stone Calf interrupted. "Today she has been released. Kicking Bird did it."

Dances With Wolves swallowed the frog in his throat.

"He did?"

Both men nodded, more serious now, and Dances With Wolves realized that there was a legitimate move afoot to go forward with this marriage. His marriage.

"What must I do?"

His visitors glanced around the nearly empty lodge with dour expressions. They ended their brief inspection with a pair of sad head shakes.

"You are pretty poor, my friend," said Wind In His Hair. "I don't know if you can get married. You must give some things up, and I don't see much in here."

Dances With Wolves looked around, too, his expression growing sadder by the second.

"No, I don't have much," he admitted.

There was a brief silence.

"Can you help me?" he asked.

The two men played out the scene for all it was worth. Stone Calf's mouth twitched noncommittally. Wind In His Hair dropped his head and stroked his brow.

After a silence that was long and agonizing for Dances With Wolves, Stone Calf sighed deeply and looked him square in the eye.

"It might be possible," he said.

five

Wind In His Hair and Stone Calf had a good day. They joked a lot about Dances With Wolves, especially the funny expressions on his face, as they walked through the village making deals for horses.

Weddings were normally quiet occasions, but the uniqueness of the bride and groom, uniting so close to the great victory over the Pawnee, had everyone bubbling over with goodwill and anticipation.

The people were eager to participate in the novelty of taking up a collection for Dances With Wolves. In fact, the whole village wanted to be part of it.

Those with plenty of horses were happy to make a contribution. Even the poorer families wanted to give up animals they could not afford. It was hard to turn these people down, but they did.

As part of a prearranged plan, contributors from all over camp began bringing horses at twilight, and by the time the evening star had appeared, more than twenty good ponies were standing in front of Dances With Wolves's lodge.

With Stone Calf and Wind In His Hair acting as tutors, the groom-to-be took the string of ponies to Kicking Bird's lodge and tied them outside.

The outpouring from his fellow villagers was deeply flattering. But wanting to give something dear of his own, he unstrapped the big Navy revolver and left it outside the door.

Then he returned to his own home, sent his tutors on their way, and passed a fitful night of waiting.

At dawn he slipped outside for a look at Kicking Bird's lodge. Wind In His Hair had said that if the proposal had been accepted, the horses would be gone. If not, they would still be standing outside the lodge.

The horses were gone.

For the next hour he made himself presentable. He shaved

carefully, polished his boots, cleaned the breastplate, and oiled his hair.

He had just finished these preparations when he heard Kicking Bird's voice call from outside.

"Dances With Wolves."

Wishing he were not quite so alone, the groom bent through the doorway of his home and stepped out.

Kicking Bird was waiting there, looking extraordinarily handsome in his finery. A few paces behind him was Stands With A Fist. Behind them the whole village had assembled and was watching solemnly.

He exchanged formal greetings with the medicine man and listened attentively as Kicking Bird launched into a speech about what was expected of a Comanche husband.

Dances With Wolves could not take his eyes off the tiny figure of his bride. She stood unmoving, her head bowed slightly. She was wearing the good doeskin dress with the elk teeth on the bodice. The special moccasins were on her feet again, and around her neck was the little pipe-bone choker.

Once, as Kicking Bird spoke, she looked up, and when he saw the whole of her striking face, Dances With Wolves was reassured. He would never tire of looking at her.

It seemed that Kicking Bird would never stop talking, but at last he did.

"Have you heard all that I have said?" questioned the medicine man.

"Yes."

"Good," Kicking Bird mumbled. He turned to Stands With A Fist and called her forward.

She came with her head still bowed, and Kicking Bird took her hand. He passed it to Dances With Wolves and told him to take her inside.

The marriage was made as they passed through the doorway. After it was done the villagers broke up quietly and drifted back to their homes.

All afternoon the people of Ten Bears's camp came in little groups to lay presents on the newlyweds' doorstep, staying only long enough to drop off the gifts. By sunset an impressive array of offerings was piled outside the lodge.

It was like a white man's Christmas.

For the time being, this beautiful community gesture went unnoticed by the new couple. On the day of their wedding they saw neither people nor their offerings. On the day of their wedding they stayed home. And the lodge flap stayed closed.

CHAPTER XXVIII

one

Two days after the wedding a high council was held. The recent heavy rains, coming late in the season, had renewed the withering grass, and it was decided to delay the winter move in favor of the pony herd. By staying a little longer the horses would be able to put on a few extra pounds, which might prove crucial in getting through the winter. The band would dally another two weeks in their summer camp.

No one was more pleased with this development than Dances With Wolves and Stands With A Fist. They were floating carelessly through the first days of their marriage and didn't want that special rhythm interrupted. Leaving the bed was hard enough. Packing up and marching hundreds of miles in a long, noisy column was, at the moment, unthinkable.

They had decided to try to make her pregnant, and people passing by rarely saw the lodge flap open.

When Dances With Wolves did emerge, he was relentlessly ribbed by his peers. Wind In His Hair was particularly merciless in this teasing. If Dances With Wolves dropped by for a smoke, he would invariably be greeted with some salutation inquiring about the health of his manhood or with mock shock at seeing him out of bed. Wind In His Hair even tried to saddle him with the nickname One Bee, an allusion to his never-ending pollination of a single flower, but fortunately for the new husband, the name didn't stick.

Dances With Wolves let the kidding slide off his back. Having the woman he wanted made him feel invincible, and nothing could harm him.

What there was of life outside the lodge was deeply satisfying. He went hunting every day, almost always with Wind In His Hair and Stone Calf. The three had become great pals, and it was rare to see one going out without the others.

The talks with Kicking Bird continued. They were fluent now and the subjects unlimited. Dances With Wolves's appetite for learning far exceeded that of Kicking Bird's, and the medicine man discoursed widely, on everything from tribal history to herbal healing. He was greatly encouraged by the keen interest his pupil showed for spiritualism, and indulged that appetite gladly.

The Comanche religion was simple, based as it was on the natural environment of the animals and elements that surrounded them. The practice of the religion was complex, however. It was rife with ritual and taboo, and covering this subject alone kept the men busy.

His new life was richer than ever, and it showed in the way Dances With Wolves carried himself. Without dramatics he was losing his naïveté but not surrendering his charm. He was becoming more manly without abandoning his spark, and he was settling smoothly into his role as a cog without losing the stamp of his distinct personality.

Kicking Bird, always attuned to the soul of things, was immensely proud of his protégé, and one evening, at the end of an after-dinner stroll, he placed a hand on Dances With Wolves's shoulder and said:

"There are many trails in this life, but the one that matters most, few men are able to walk . . . even Comanche men.

It is the trail of a true human being. I think you are on this trail. It is a good thing for me to see. It is good for my heart.''

Dances With Wolves memorized these words as they were said and treasured them always. But he told no one, not even Stands With A Fist. He made them part of his private medicine.

two

They were only a few days away from the big move when Kicking Bird came by one morning and said he was going to take a ride to a special place. The round trip would take all day and perhaps part of the night, but if Dances With Wolves wanted to go, he would be welcome.

They cut through the heart of the prairie, riding in a southeasterly direction for several hours. The enormity of the space they'd invaded was humbling, and neither man did much talking.

Close to midday they turned due south, and in an hour's time the ponies were standing at the top of a long slope which fell away for a mile until it reached the river.

They could see the color and shape of the water far to the east and west. But in front of them the river had disappeared.

It was screened by a mammoth forest.

Dances With Wolves blinked several times, as if trying to solve a mirage. From this distance it was hard to judge exact heights, but he knew that the trees were high. Some of them must be sixty or seventy feet.

The grove extended downriver for the better part of a mile, the hugeness of it contrasting wildly with the flat, empty country on all sides. It was like the fanciful creation of some mysterious spirit.

"Is this place real?" he said, half joking.

Kicking Bird smiled.

"Perhaps not. It is a sacred place to us . . . even to some of our enemies. It is said that from here the game renews itself. The trees shelter every animal the Great Spirit has made. It is said they hatched here when life began and constantly return to the place of their birth. I have not been here for a long time. We will water the horses and have a look."

As they came closer, the specter of the woods became more powerful, and on starting into the forest, Dances With Wolves felt small. He thought of the Garden of Eden.

But as the trees closed around them both men sensed that something was wrong.

There was no sound.

"It's quiet," Dances With Wolves observed.

Kicking Bird didn't reply. He was listening and watching with the single-mindedness of a cat.

The silence was suffocating as they pressed deeper into the woods, and Dances With Wolves realized with a shiver that only one thing could make this vacuum of sound. He was smelling its aroma. The taste of it was on the tip of his tongue.

Death was in the air.

Kicking Bird pulled up suddenly. The path had widened, and as Dances With Wolves looked over his mentor's shoulder, he was staggered by the beauty of what he saw.

There was open ground ahead of them. The trees were spaced at intervals, allowing enough room between to house all the lodges and people and horses of Ten Bears's camp. Sunlight poured onto the forest's floor in great, warming splotches.

He could envision a fantastic utopia, peopled with a holy race leading tranquil lives in concert with all living things.

The hand of man could make nothing to rival the scope and beauty of this open-air cathedral.

The hand of man, however, could destroy it. The proof was already here.

The place had been horribly desecrated.

Trees of all sizes lay where they had been felled, some of

them lying one over the other, like toothpicks scattered upon a tabletop. Most of them had not been shorn of their branches, and he could not imagine for what purpose they had been cut.

They started their ponies forward, and as they did, Dances With Wolves was aware of an eerie buzzing sound.

At first, thinking that bees or wasps were swarming, he scanned the branches overhead, trying to locate the insects' nest.

But as they moved toward the center of the cathedral he realized the noise was not coming from above. It was coming from below. And it was being made by the wing beats of uncounted thousands of feasting flies.

Everywhere he looked the ground held bodies, or pieces of bodies. There were small animals, badgers and skunks and squirrels. Most of these were intact. Some were missing their tails. They lay rotting where they had been shot, for no apparent reason other than target practice.

The primary objects of the genocide were deer that sprawled all around him. A few of the bodies were whole, minus only the prime cuts. Most were mutilated.

Dull, dead eyes stared up at him from the exquisite heads that had been chopped off raggedly at the neck. Some of them sat singly on the floor of the forest. Others had been tossed together haphazardly in piles as big as half a dozen.

In one spot the severed heads had been arranged nose to nose, as if they were having a conversation. It was supposed to be humorous.

The legs were even more grotesque. They, too, had been chopped clear of the bodies they once transported. Slow to decay, they looked bright and beautiful, as if they were still in good working order.

But it was sad: the delicate, cloven hooves and the graceful, fur-coated legs . . . leading to nowhere. The limbs were stacked in little bunches, like firewood, and if he had bothered, the count would have exceeded one hundred.

The men were tired from the long ride, but neither made any move to get off his horse. They continued to ride.

A low spot in the great clearing revealed four decrepit shanties sitting side by side, four ugly sores festering on the forest floor.

The men who had cut down so many trees had apparently seen their ambition as builders run out. But even if they had applied themselves, the result would likely have been the same. The dwellings they'd managed to put up were squalid even in their conception.

By any standard it was not a fit place to live.

Whiskey bottles, dropped as they were drained, lay in profusion around the awful huts. There was a multitude of other useless items, a broken cup, a half-repaired belt, the shattered stock of a rifle, all left where they were dropped.

A brace of wild turkeys, tied together at the feet but otherwise untouched, were discovered on the ground between two huts.

Behind the buildings they found a wide pit, filled to overflowing with the putrid torsos of slaughtered deer, skinless, legless, and headless.

The buzzing of flies was so loud that Dances With Wolves had to shout to be heard.

"We wait for these men?"

Kicking Bird didn't want to shout. He sidled his pony next to Dances With Wolves.

"They have been gone a week, maybe more. We will water the horses and go home."

three

For the first hour of the return trip neither man uttered a word. Kicking Bird stared ahead sorrowfully while Dances With Wolves watched the ground, shamed for the white race to which he belonged and thinking hard about the dream he'd had in the ancient canyon.

He'd told no one about it, but now he felt he had to. Now it didn't seem so much a dream after all. It might be a vision.

When they stopped to give the horses a blow, he told Kicking Bird of the dream that was still fresh in his mind, sparing none of the details.

The medicine man listened to Dances With Wolves's long recounting without interruption. When it was finished he stared somberly at his feet.

"All of us were dead?"

"Everyone that was present," Dances With Wolves said, "but I didn't see everyone. I didn't see you."

"Ten Bears should hear the dream," Kicking Bird said.

They jumped back on the horses and made quick time across the prairie, arriving back in camp shortly after sunset.

four

The two men made their report on the desecration of the sacred grove, a deed that could only have been the work of a large, white hunting party. The dead animals in the forest were undoubtedly a sideline. The hunters were probably after buffalo and would be decimating them on a much bigger scale.

Ten Bears nodded a few times as the report was made. But he asked no questions.

Then Dances With Wolves recited his grisly dream a second time.

The old man still said nothing, his expression inscrutable as ever. When Dances With Wolves had finished, he made no comment. Instead he picked up his pipe and said, "Let us have a smoke on this."

Dances With Wolves had the notion that Ten Bears was

thinking all of it through, but as they passed the pipe around, he became impatient, anxious to get something off his chest.

At last he said, "I would speak some more."

The old man nodded.

"When Kicking Bird and I first began to talk," Dances With Wolves started, "a question was asked of me for which I had no answer. Kicking Bird would ask, 'How many white people are coming?' and I would say, 'I don't know.' That is true. I do not know how many will come. But I can tell you this. I believe there will be a lot.

"The white people are many, more than any of us could ever count. If they want to make war on you, they will do it with thousands of hair-mouth soldiers. The soldiers will have big war guns that can shoot into a camp like ours and destroy everything in it.

"It makes me afraid. I'm even afraid of my dream because I know it could come true. I cannot say what must be done. But I come from the white race and I know them. I know them now in ways I did not know them before. I'm afraid for all the Comanches."

Ten Bears had been nodding through the speech, but Dances With Wolves couldn't tell how the old man was taking it.

The headman tottered to his feet and took a few steps across the lodge, stopping next to his bed. He reached into the rigging above it, pulled down a melon-sized bundle, and retraced his steps to the fire.

He sat down with a grunt.

"I think you are right," he said to Dances With Wolves. "It is hard to know what to do. I'm an old man of many winters, and even I'm unsure of what to do when it comes to the question of the white people and their hair-mouth soldiers. But let me show you something."

His gnarled fingers tugged at the bundle's rawhide draw-string, and in a moment it was undone. He pushed down the sides of the sack, gradually revealing a hunk of rusted metal about the size of a man's head.

Kicking Bird had never seen the object before and had no idea what it could be.

Dances With Wolves hadn't seen it either. But he knew what it was. He had seen a drawing of something similar in a text on military history. It was the helmet of a Spanish conquistador.

"These people were the first to come into our country. They came on horses . . . we didn't have horses then . . . and shot at us with big thunder guns that we had never seen. They were looking for shiny metal and we were afraid of them. This was in the time of my grandfather's grandfather.

"Eventually we drove these people out."

The old man sucked long and hard on his pipe, taking several puffs.

"Then the Mexicans began to come. We had to make war on them and we have been successful. They fear us greatly and do not come here.

"In my own time white people began to come. The Texans. They have been like all the other people who find something to want in our country. They take it without asking. They get angry when they see us sitting in our own country, and when we do not do as they want, they try to kill us. They kill women and children as if they were warriors.

"When I was a young man I fought the Texans. We killed many of them and stole some of their women and children. One of these children is Dances With Wolves's wife.

"After a time there was talk of peace. We met the Texans and made agreements with them. These agreements always get broken. As soon as the white people wanted something new from us, the words on the paper were no more. It has always been like that.

"I got tired of this and many years ago I brought the people of our band out here, far away from the whites. We have lived in peace here for a long time.

"But this is the last of our country. We have no place else to go. When I think of white people coming into our country now, it is as I said. It is hard to know what to do.

"I have always been a peaceful man, happy to be in my own country and wanting nothing from the white people. Nothing at all. But I think you are right. I think they will keep on coming.

"When I think of that I look at this bundle, knowing what's inside, and I'm certain we will fight to keep our country and all that it contains. Our country is all that we have. It is all that we want.

"We will fight to keep it.

"But I do not think we will have to fight this winter, and after all that you have told me, I think the time to go is now.

"Tomorrow morning we will strike the village and go to the winter camp."

CHAPTER XXIX

one

As he fell asleep that night Dances With Wolves realized that something had begun to gnaw at the back of his mind. When he woke the next morning it was still there, and though he knew it had something to do with the presence of white hunters a half-day's ride from camp and with his dream and with Ten Bears's talk, he could not put his finger on it.

An hour after dawn, when the camp was being dismantled, he started thinking about how relieved he was to be going. The winter camp would be even more remote a place than this. Stands With A Fist thought she was pregnant and he was looking forward to the protection a faraway camp would give his new family.

No one would be able to reach them there. They would be anonymous. He himself would no longer exist, except in the eyes of his adopted people.

Then it hit him, hit him hard enough to set his heart into a sudden, crazy fluttering.

He did exist.

And he had stupidly left the proof behind. The full record of Lieutenant John J. Dunbar was written down for everyone to see. It was lying on the bunk in the sod hut, secure between the pages of his journal.

Since they had little to do, Stands With A Fist had gone off to help some of the other families. It would take a while to find her in the confusion of the move, and he didn't want to lose time with explanations. Every minute of the journal's existence was now a threat.

He ran for the pony herd, unable to think of anything but retrieving the telltale record.

He and Cisco were just coming into camp when he ran into Kicking Bird.

The medicine man balked at what Dances With Wolves told him. They wanted to be under way by noon and would not be able to wait if the long round trip to the white soldier's fort took longer than expected.

But Dances With Wolves was adamant, and reluctantly Kicking Bird told him to go ahead. Their trail would be easy enough to follow if he was delayed, but the medicine man urged him to make haste. He didn't like this kind of last-minute surprise.

two

The little buckskin was happy to be racing across the prairie. During the last few days the air had turned crisp, and this morning the breeze was up. Cisco loved having the wind in his face, and they breezed over the miles to the fort.

The last familiar rise loomed ahead of them, and Dances With Wolves flattened down on his horse's back, asking him to take the last half mile at a full run.

They blew over the rise and shot down the slope to the old post.

Dances With Wolves saw everything in one stupendous flash.

Fort Sedgewick was alive with soldiers.

They covered another hundred yards before he could pull
Cisco up. The buckskin pitched and whirled madly, and
Dances With Wolves was hard-pressed to calm him. He was
struggling himself, trying to comprehend the unreal sight of
a bustling army camp.

A score of canvas tents had been thrown up around the old
supply house and the sod hut. Two Hotchkiss cannons,
mounted on caissons, were parked next to his old quarters.
The tumbledown corral was jammed with horses. And the
whole place was seething with men in uniform. They were
walking and talking and working.

A wagon was sitting fifty yards in front of him, and in its
bed, staring at him with startled faces, were four common
soldiers.

The outlines of their faces were not clear enough for him
to see that they were boys.

The teenage soldiers had never seen a wild Indian, but in
the few weeks of training following their recruitment they
had been reminded repeatedly that soon they would be fighting a deceptive, cunning, and bloodthirsty foe. Now they
were actually staring at a vision of the enemy.

They panicked.

Dances With Wolves saw the rise of their rifles just as
Cisco reared. There was nothing he could do. The volley
was poorly aimed and Dances With Wolves was thrown clear
as they fired, landing on the ground unhurt.

But one of the bullets caught Cisco square in the chest,
and the slug tore through the center of his heart. He was dead
before he hit the ground.

Oblivious to the shouting soldiers rushing toward him,
Dances With Wolves scrambled back to his downed horse.
He grabbed at Cisco's head and lifted his muzzle. But there
was no life in it.

Outrage took him over. It formed a sentence in his mind.

Look what you've done. He turned to the sound of rushing feet, ready to shout out the words.

As his face came around, the stock of a rifle slammed into it. Everything went black.

three

He could smell dirt. His face was pressed against an earthen floor. He could hear the sound of muffled voices, and a set of words came to him distinctly.

"Sergeant Murphy . . . he's coming to."

Dances With Wolves turned his face and grimaced in pain as his broken cheekbone made contact with the hard-packed floor.

He touched his injured face with a finger and recoiled again as the hurt shot along the side of his head.

He tried to open his eyes but could only manage one. The other was swollen shut. When the good eye cleared he recognized where he was. He was in the old supply house.

Someone kicked him in the side.

"Here, you, sit up."

The toe of a boot rolled him onto his back, and Dances With Wolves scooted away from the contact. The rear wall of the supply house stopped him.

There he sat staring with his good eye, first at the face of the bearded sergeant standing over him, then at the curious faces of white soldiers clustered around the door.

Someone behind them suddenly shouted, "Make way for Major Hatch, you men," and the faces in the doorway fell away.

Two officers entered the supply house, a young, clean-shaven lieutenant and a much older man wearing long, gray side whiskers and an ill-fitting uniform. The older man's eyes were small. The gold bars on his shoulders carried the oak leaf insignia of major.

Both officers were looking at him with expressions of repulsion.

"What is he, Sergeant?" asked the major, his tone stiff and cautious.

"Don't know yet, sir."

"Does he speak English?"

"Don't know that either, sir. . . . Hey, you . . . you speak English?"

Dances With Wolves blinked his good eye.

"Talk?" the sergeant queried again, putting his fingers to his lips. "Talk?"

He kicked lightly at one of the captive's black riding boots, and Dances With Wolves sat up straighter. It wasn't a threatening move, but as he made it, he saw both officers jerk back.

They were afraid of him.

"You talk?" the sergeant asked once more.

"I speak English," Dances With Wolves said wearily. "It hurts to talk. . . . One of your boys broke my cheek."

The soldiers were shocked to hear the words come out so perfectly, and for the moment they faced him in dumb silence.

Dances With Wolves looked white and he looked Indian. It had been impossible to tell which half was real. Now at least they knew he was white.

During the silence other soldiers had again crowded around the doorway, and Dances With Wolves spoke at them.

"One of those stupid idiots shot my horse."

The major ignored this comment.

"Who are you?"

"I'm First Lieutenant John J. Dunbar, United States Army."

"Why are you dressed like an Indian?"

Even if he'd wanted to, Dances With Wolves couldn't have begun to answer the question. But he didn't want to.

"This is my post," he said. "I came out from Fort Hays in April, but there was no one here."

The major and the lieutenant held a brief conversation, whispering into one another's ear.

"You have proof of that?" questioned the lieutenant.

"Under the bed in that other hut there's a folded sheet of paper with my orders on it. On top of the bed is my journal. It will tell you all you need to know."

It was all over for Dances With Wolves. He dropped the good side of his head into a hand. His heart was breaking. The band would leave him behind for sure. By the time he got clear of this mess, if he ever did, it would be too late to find them. Cisco was lying out there dead. He wanted to cry. But he didn't dare. He just hung his head.

People left the room, but he didn't look up to see who it was. A few seconds ticked off and then he heard the sergeant whisper coarsely: "You turned Injin, didn'cha?"

Dances With Wolves lifted his head. The sergeant was bending over him with a leer.

"Didn'cha?"

Dances With Wolves didn't answer. He let his head fall back into his hand, refusing to look up until the major and lieutenant had appeared again.

This time the lieutenant did the talking.

"What is your name?"

"Dunbar . . . D-u-n-b-a-r . . . John, J."

"Are these your orders?"

He was holding up a yellowed sheet of paper. Dances With Wolves had to squint to make it out.

"Yes."

"The name here is Rumbar," the lieutenant said grimly. "The date is entered in pencil, but the rest is in ink. The signature of the issuing officer is smeared. It's not legible. What do you have to say about that?"

Dances With Wolves heard the suspicion in the lieutenant's voice. It began to sink in that these people did not believe him.

"Those are the orders I was given at Fort Hays," he said flatly.

The lieutenant's face twisted. He looked dissatisfied.

"Read the journal," said Dances With Wolves.

"There is no journal," the young officer replied.

Dances With Wolves watched him carefully, sure he was lying.

But the lieutenant was telling the truth.

A member of the advance party, the first to reach Fort Sedgewick, had found the journal. He was an illiterate private named Sheets and he had slipped the book into his tunic, thinking it would make good toilet paper. Sheets heard now that a certain journal was missing, one that the wild white man said was his. Maybe he ought to turn it in. He might be rewarded. But on second thought Sheets worried that he might be reprimanded. Or worse. He'd done time in more than one guardhouse for petty theft. So the journal stayed hidden under his uniform coat.

"We want you to tell us the meaning of your appearance," the lieutenant continued. He sounded like an interrogator now. "If you are who you say you are, why are you out of uniform?"

Dances With Wolves shifted against the supply house wall.

"What is the army doing out here?"

The major and the lieutenant whispered to one another again. And again the lieutenant spoke up.

"We are charged with recovering stolen property, including white captives taken in hostile raiding."

"There has been no raiding and there are no white captives," Dances With Wolves lied.

"We will ascertain that for ourselves," the lieutenant countered.

The officers again fell to whispering, and this time the

conversation went on a while before the lieutenant cleared his throat.

"We will give you a chance to prove your loyalty to your country. If you guide us to the hostile camps and serve as interpreter, your conduct will be reevaluated."

"What conduct?"

"Your treasonable conduct."

Dances With Wolves smiled.

"You think I'm a traitor?" he said.

The lieutenant's voice rose angrily.

"Are you willing to cooperate or not?"

"There is nothing for you to do out here. That's all I have to say."

"Then we have no choice but to place you under arrest. You can sit here and think your situation over. If you decide to cooperate, tell Sergeant Murphy, and we will have a talk."

With that the major and the lieutenant left the supply house. Sergeant Wilcox detailed two men to stand guard at the door, and Dances With Wolves was left alone.

four

Kicking Bird stalled for as long as he could, but by early afternoon Ten Bears's camp had started the long march, heading southwest across the plains.

Stands With A Fist insisted on waiting for her husband and became hysterical when they forced her to go. Kicking Bird's wives had to get rough with her before she finally composed herself.

But Stands With A Fist wasn't the only worried Comanche. Everyone was worried. A last-minute council was convened just before they pulled out, and three young men on fast ponies were sent to scout the white man's fort for Dances With Wolves.

five

He'd been sitting for three hours, fighting back the pain in his battered face, when Dances With Wolves told the guard he needed to relieve himself.

As he walked toward the bluff, sandwiched between two soldiers, he found himself repulsed by these men and their camp. He didn't like the way they smelled. The sound of their voices seemed rough to his ears. Even the way they moved seemed crude and ungainly.

He peed over the edge of the bluff, and the two soldiers started him back. He was thinking about escape when a wagon loaded with wood and three soldiers rumbled into camp and skidded to a stop close by.

One of the men in the wagon bed called lightheartedly to a friend who had stayed in camp, and Dances With Wolves saw a tall soldier amble over to the wagon. The men in the bed were smiling at one another as the tall man came near.

He heard one of them say, "Look what we brung ya, Burns."

The men in the wagon took hold of something and heaved it over the side. The tall man standing below them leaped back frightfully as Two Socks's body landed at his feet with a thump.

The men in the wagon leaped out. They taunted the tall man as he backed away from the dead wolf.

One of the woodcutters cackled, "He's a big 'un, ain't he, Burns."

Two of the woodcutters lifted Two Socks off the ground, one taking his head, the other his back feet. Then, accompanied by the laughter of all the soldiers, they started to chase the tall man around the yard.

Dances With Wolves covered the ground so quickly that no one moved until he'd slammed into the soldiers carrying Two Socks. In short, chopping strokes he pounded one of them senseless with his fist.

He sprang after the second man, knocking his feet out from under him as he tried to run. Then his hands were around the man's throat. His face was turning purple and Dances With Wolves saw his eyes begin to glaze when something struck him in the back of the head and a dark curtain dropped over him again.

It was twilight when he regained consciousness. His head was throbbing so hard that he didn't notice at first. At first he only heard a light rattle when he moved. Then he felt the cold metal. His hands were chained together. He moved his feet. They were chained, too.

When the major and lieutenant came back with more questions, he answered them with a killing glare and spat out a long string of Comanche insults. Each time they asked him something, he answered in Comanche. Finally they tired of this and left him.

Later in the evening the big sergeant placed a bowl of gruel before him.

Dances With Wolves kicked it over with his manacled feet.

six

Kicking Bird's scouts brought the dreadful news in around midnight.

They had counted more than sixty heavily armed soldiers at the white man's fort. They had seen the buckskin horse lying dead on the slope. And just before dark they had seen Dances With Wolves being led to the bluff by the river, his feet and hands in chains.

The band went into evasive action immediately. They packed up their things and marched out at night, little groups of a dozen or less, heading in all different directions. They would rendezvous days later in the winter camp.

Ten Bears knew he would never hold them back, so he didn't try. A force of twenty warriors, Kicking Bird and Stone Calf and Wind In His Hair among them, left within the hour, promising not to engage the enemy unless they could be sure of success.

seven

Major Hatch made his decision late the same night. He didn't want to be bothered with the thorny problem of a savage, half-Indian white man sitting under his nose. The major was not a visionary thinker, and from the first he'd been baffled and afraid of his exotic prisoner.

It didn't occur to the shortsighted officer that he could have used Dances With Wolves to great advantage as a bargaining tool. He wanted only to get rid of him. His presence had already unsettled the command.

Shipping him back to Fort Hays seemed a brilliant idea. As a prisoner he would be worth much more to the major back there than out here. The capture of a turncoat would stand him in very good stead with the top brass. The army would talk about this prisoner, and if they talked about the prisoner, the name of the man who caught him was bound to come up just as often.

The major blew out his lamp and pulled up his covers with a self-satisfied yawn. Everything was going to work out nicely, he thought. The campaign couldn't have asked for a better beginning.

eight

They came for the prisoner early the next morning.

Sergeant Murphy had two men pull Dances With Wolves to his feet and asked the major, "Should we put him in uniform, sir, spruce him up some?"

"Of course not," the major said sharply. "Now, get him in the wagon."

Six men were detailed for the trip back: two on horseback up front, two on horseback in the rear, one to drive, and one to guard the prisoner in the wagon bed.

They went due east, across the rolling prairie he loved so much. But on this bright morning in October there was no love in Dances With Wolves's heart. He said nothing to his captors, preferring to bump along in the back of the wagon, listening to the steady clank of his chains as his mind considered the possibilities.

There was no way to overpower the escort. He might be able to kill one, or perhaps even two. But they would kill him after that. He thought of trying it anyway. To die fighting these men would not be so bad. It would be better than landing in some dismal jail.

Every time he thought of her his heart would begin to crack. When her face would start to form as a picture in his head he forced himself to think of something else. He had to do this every few minutes. It was the worst kind of agony.

He doubted that anyone would be coming after him. He knew they would want to, but he could not imagine that Ten Bears would compromise the safety of all his people for the sake of a single man. Dances With Wolves himself would not do that.

On the other hand, he felt certain they had sent out scouts and that they knew by now of his desperate situation. If they'd hung around long enough to see him leave in the wagon, with only six men to guard him, there might be a chance.

As the morning dragged on Dances With Wolves clung to

this idea as his only hope. Each time the wagon slowed to gain a rise or lurched down into a draw he held himself breathless, wishing for the swish of an arrow or the crack of a rifle.

By midday he had heard nothing.

They'd been away from the river for a long time, but it was coming up again. Searching for a place to ford, they followed it for a quarter mile before the soldiers up front found a well-traveled buffalo crossing.

The water wasn't wide, but the breaks around the river were exceptionally thick, thick enough for an ambush. As the wagon creaked down the incline, Dances With Wolves kept his eyes and ears open.

The sergeant in charge called for the driver to stop before they entered the stream, and they waited as the sergeant and another man crossed over. For a long minute or two they probed the breaks. Then the sergeant cupped his hands and called for the wagon to come along.

Dances With Wolves clenched his fists and shifted to a squatting position. He could see nothing and he could hear nothing.

But he knew they were there.

He was moving at the sound of the first arrow, far faster than the guard in the wagon, who was still fumbling with his rifle as Dances With Wolves looped the hand chain around the man's neck.

Rifle fire exploded behind him and he yanked the chain taut, feeling the flesh beneath it give as the soldier's throat caved in.

From the corner of his eye he saw the sergeant tumble forward off his horse, an arrow deep in the small of his back. The wagon driver had jumped over the side. He was knee-deep in water, firing wildly with a pistol.

Dances With Wolves landed on top of him and they grappled briefly in the water before he could work himself free. Using the chain like a two-handed whip, he lashed at the driver's head and the soldier turned limp, rolling slowly in the shallow water. Dances With Wolves gave him more vicious whacks, stopping only when he saw the water turning red.

There was yelling downstream. Dances With Wolves looked up in time to see the last of the troopers trying to escape. He must have been wounded because he was flopping loosely in the saddle.

Wind In His Hair was right behind the doomed soldier. As their horses came together Dances With Wolves heard the dull thud of Wind In His Hair's skull cracker as it crushed the man's head.

Behind him it was quiet, and when he turned he saw the men of the rear guard sprawled dead in the water.

Several warriors were jabbing lances into the bodies, and he was overjoyed to see that one of them was Stone Calf.

A hand grabbed his shoulder and Dances With Wolves spun into the beaming face of Kicking Bird.

"What a great fight," the medicine man crowed. "We got them all so easy and no one's hurt."

"I got two," Dances With Wolves yelled back. He lifted his chained hands into the air and cried out, "With these."

The rescue party didn't waste any time. After a frantic search they found the keys to Dances With Wolves's chains on the body of the dead sergeant.

Then they jumped on their ponies and galloped away, taking a course that swung many miles to the south and west of Fort Sedgewick.

CHAPTER XXX

one

An inch of early snow fell fortuitously on Ten Bears's fleeing people, covering their tracks all the way to the winter camp.

Everyone made excellent time, and six days later the splinter groups had reunited on the bottom of the mammoth canyon that would be their home for several months.

The place was steeped in Comanche history and was aptly named The Great Spirit Steps Here. The canyon was miles long, a mile wide in most places, and some of its sheer walls ran half a mile from top to bottom. They had spent the winter here for as long as most people could remember, and it was a perfect spot, providing forage and plenty of water for the people and ponies and ample protection from the blizzards that raged overhead all winter. It was also far from the reach of their enemies.

Other bands passed the winter here, too, and there was great rejoicing as old friends and relatives saw each other again for the first time since spring.

Once they had reassembled, however, Ten Bears's village settled in to wait, unable to rest easy until the fate of the rescue party was known.

At midmorning on the day after their return a scout thundered into camp with the news that the party was coming down the trail. He said that Dances With Wolves was with them.

Stands With A Fist sprinted up the trail ahead of everyone. She was crying as she ran, and when she caught sight of the horsemen, riding single file high on the trail above, she called his name.

She didn't stop calling it until she had reached him.

two

The early snow was the prelude for a fearsome blizzard that struck that afternoon.

People stayed close to their lodges for the next two days.

Dances With Wolves and Stands With A Fist saw almost no one.

Kicking Bird did the best he could for Dances With Wolves's face, taking down the swelling and trying to speed its recovery with healing herbs. There was nothing to be done with the fragile, shattered cheekbone, however, and it was left to mend on its own.

Dances With Wolves wasn't concerned with his injury at all. A heavier matter was hard upon him, and in struggling with it, he was not inclined to see anyone.

He talked only to Stands With A Fist, but not much was said. Most of the time he lay in the lodge like a sick man. She lay with him, wondering what was wrong but waiting for him to tell her, as she knew he eventually would.

The blizzard had begun its third day when Dances With Wolves went for a long, solitary walk. When he returned he sat her down and told her of his irreversible decision.

She turned away from him then and sat for almost an hour, her head bowed in silent contemplation.

Finally she said, "This is the way it must be?" Her eyes were glistening with sadness.

Dances With Wolves was sad, too.

"Yes," he said quietly.

She sighed mournfully, fighting back her tears.

"Then it will be."

three

Dances With Wolves asked for a council. He wanted to speak with Ten Bears. He also asked for Kicking Bird, Wind In His Hair, Stone Calf, and anyone else Ten Bears thought should attend.

They met the next night. The blizzard was tailing off and everyone was in good spirits. They ate and smoked their way through a lively set of preliminaries, telling animated stories about the fight at the river and the rescue of Dances With Wolves.

He waited through all this with good humor. He was happy to be with his friends.

But when the conversation finally started to wane he took the first silence and filled it.

"I want to tell you what is on my mind," he said, and the council officially began.

The men knew that something important was coming and they were at their most attentive. Ten Bears turned his best ear toward the speaker, not wanting to miss a single word.

"I have not been among you for very long, but I feel in my heart that it has been all my life. I'm proud to be a Co-manche. I will always be proud to be a Comanche. I love the Comanche way and I love each of you as if we were of the same blood. In my heart and spirit I will always be with you. So you must know that it is hard for me to say that I must leave you."

The lodge erupted with startled exclamations, each man furious with disbelief. Wind In His Hair jumped to his feet and stomped back and forth, waving his hands in scorn for this foolish idea.

Dances With Wolves sat still through the uproar.

He stared into the fire, his hands folded quietly in his lap.

Ten Bears held up a hand and told the men to stop talking. The lodge became silent again.

Wind In His Hair was still prowling about, however, and Ten Bears barked at him.

"Come and sit down, Wind In His Hair. Our brother is not finished."

Grudgingly Wind In His Hair complied, and when he was seated, Dances With Wolves continued.

"Killing those soldiers at the river was a good thing. It made me free and my heart was filled with joy to see my brothers coming to help me.

"I did not mind killing those men at all. I was glad to do it.

"But you do not know the white mind as I do. The soldiers think I'm one of them who has gone bad. They think I have betrayed them. In their eyes I'm a traitor because I have chosen to live among you. I do not care if they are right or wrong, but I tell you truly that this is what they believe.

"White men will hunt a traitor long after they have given up on other men. To them a traitor is the worst thing a soldier can be. So they will hunt me until they find me. They will not give up.

"When they find me they will find you. They will want to hang me and they will want the same kind of punishment for you. Maybe they will punish you even if I'm gone. I don't know.

"If it was just ourselves, I might stay, but it is more than just us men. It is your wives and your children and those of your friends. It is all the people who will be hurt.

"They cannot find me among you. That is all. That is why

I must go. I have told Stands With A Fist about this and we will go together.''

No one stirred for many seconds. They all knew he was right, but no one knew what to say.

"Where will you go?" Kicking Bird finally asked.

"I don't know. Far away. Far from this country."

Again there was silence. It was at its most unbearable when Ten Bears coughed lightly.

"You have spoken well, Dances With Wolves. Your name will be alive in the hearts of our people for as long as there are Comanches. We will see that it is kept alive. When will you go?"

"When the snow breaks," Dances With Wolves said softly.

"The snow will break tomorrow," Ten Bears said. "We should go to sleep now."

four

Ten Bears was an extraordinary man.

He had beaten the odds against longevity on the plains, and with each succeeding season of his life the old man had built a remarkable store of knowledge. This knowledge had grown until at last it collapsed inward upon itself, and in the dusk of his life Ten Bears had reached a pinnacle. . . . He had become a man of wisdom.

The old eyes were failing, but in the dimness they saw with a clarity that no one, not even Kicking Bird, could match. His hearing was muted, but somehow the sounds that mattered never failed to reach his ears. And lately, a most extraordinary thing had begun to happen. Without relying on the senses that were now beginning to play out, Ten Bears had actually begun to *feel* the life of his people. From boyhood he had been vested with a special shrewdness, but this was much more. This was seeing with his whole self, and instead of feeling old and used up, Ten Bears was invigorated by the strange and mysterious power that had come to him.

But the power that was so long in coming and seemed so infallible had broken. For two full days after the council with Dances With Wolves the headman sat in his lodge and smoked, wondering what had gone wrong.

"The snow will break tomorrow."

The words had not been measured. They had come to him without forethought, appearing on his tongue as if placed there by the Great Spirit Himself.

But the snow had not stopped. The storm had gained strength. At the end of two days the drifts were high against the hide walls of all the tepees. They were getting higher by the hour. Ten Bears could feel them inching up the walls of his own lodge.

His appetite vanished and the old man ignored everything but his pipe and fire. He spent every waking minute staring into the flames that waved in the center of his home. He beseeched the Great Spirit to take pity on an old man and grant one last bit of understanding, but it was all to no avail.

At last Ten Bears began to think of his miscalculation as a sign. He began to think it was a call to end his life. It was only when he was fully resigned to the idea and had begun to rehearse his death song that something fantastic happened.

The old woman who had been his wife all through the years saw him rise suddenly from the fire, drape himself with a robe, and start out of the lodge. She asked where he was going, but Ten Bears made no reply.

In fact, he had not heard her. He was listening to a voice that had come into his head. The voice uttered a single sentence and Ten Bears was obeying its command.

The voice said, "Go to the lodge of Dances With Wolves."

Oblivious to his effort, Ten Bears struggled through the

drifting snow. When he reached the lodge at the edge of camp he hesitated before knocking.

There was no one about. The snow was falling in large flakes, wet and heavy. As he waited Ten Bears thought he could hear the snow, thought he could hear each flake as it fell to earth. The sound was heavenly, and standing in the chill, Ten Bears felt his head begin to spin. For a few moments he thought he had passed into the beyond.

A hawk screamed, and when he looked for the bird, he saw lively smoke curling out of the hole in Dances With Wolves's lodge. He blinked the snow from his eyes and scratched at the flap.

When it opened, a great wall of warmth rushed to meet him. It wrapped itself around the old man, sucked him past Dances With Wolves, and ushered him into the lodge like a living being. He stood in the center of the home and felt his head begin to spin again. Now it was spinning with relief, for in the time it took to go from the outside to the inside, Ten Bears had solved the mystery of his mistake.

The mistake was not his. It had been made by another and had slipped past without his seeing it. Ten Bears had merely compounded the mistake when he said, ''The snow will break tomorrow.''

The snow was right. He should have listened to the snow in the first place. Ten Bears smiled and gave his head a toss. How simple it was. How could he have missed it? I still have some things to learn, he thought.

The man who made the error was standing next to him now, but Ten Bears felt no anger toward Dances With Wolves. He only smiled at the puzzlement he saw on the young man's face.

Dances With Wolves found enough of his tongue to say, ''Please . . . sit at my fire.''

When Ten Bears settled himself he gave the lodge a brief inspection, and it confirmed what his spinning head had told him. It was a happy, well-ordered home. He spread his robe, letting more of the fire's heat inside.

"This is a nice fire," he said genially. "At my age a good fire is better than anything."

Stands With A Fist placed a bowl of food next to each man, then retreated to her bedside at the back of the lodge. There she picked up some sewing. But she kept an ear turned to the conversation that was sure to come.

The men ate in silence for a few minutes, Ten Bears chewing his food carefully. Finally he pushed his bowl to one side and coughed lightly.

"I've been thinking since you spoke at my lodge. I wondered how your bad heart was doing and thought I would see for myself."

He scanned the lodge. Then he looked squarely at Dances With Wolves.

"This place doesn't seem so bad-hearted."

"Uhhh, no," Dances With Wolves stammered. "Yes, we are happy here."

Ten Bears smiled and nodded his head. "That's how I thought it would be."

A silence came between the men. Ten Bears stared into the flames, his eyes closing gradually. Dances With Wolves waited politely, not knowing what to do. Perhaps he should ask if the old man wanted to lie down. He had been walking in the snow. But now it looked too late to say that. His important guest seemed to be dozing already.

Ten Bears shifted and spoke, saying the words in a way that made it seem like he was talking in his sleep.

"I have been thinking about what you said . . . what you said about your reasons for going away."

Suddenly his eyes flew open and Dances With Wolves was startled by their brightness. They were glittering like stars.

"You can go away from us anytime you like . . . but not for those reasons. Those reasons are wrong. All the hair-mouth soldiers in the world could search our camp and none would find the person they are looking for, the one like them who calls himself Loo Ten Nant.''

Ten Bears spread his hands slightly and his voice shook with glee. ''The one called Loo Ten Nant is not here. In this lodge they will only find a Comanche warrior, a good Comanche warrior and his wife.''

Dances With Wolves let the words sink in. He peeked over his shoulder at Stands With A Fist. He could see a smile on her face, but she was not looking his way. There was nothing he could say.

When he looked back he found Ten Bears staring down at a nearly finished pipe that was poking out of its case. The old man pointed a bony finger at the object of his interest.

''You are making a pipe, Dances With Wolves?''

''Yes.''

Ten Bears held out his hands and Dances With Wolves placed the pipe in them. The old man brought it close to his face, running his eyes up and down its length.

''This might be a pretty good pipe. . . . How does it smoke?''

''I don't know,'' Dances With Wolves replied. ''I haven't tried it yet.''

''Let's smoke it a while,'' Ten Bears said, handing the pipe back. ''It's good to pass the time this way.''

CHAPTER XXXI

It was a winter for staying under the robes. Except for an occasional hunting party the Comanches rarely ventured out of their lodges. The people spent so much time around their fires that the season came to be known as the Winter of Many Smokes.

By spring everyone was anxious to move, and at the first breaking of the ice they were on the trail again.

A new camp was set up that year, far from the old one near Fort Sedgewick. It was a good spot with plenty of water and grass for the ponies. The buffalo came again by the thousands and the hunting was good, with very few men getting hurt. Late that summer many babies were born, more than most people could remember.

They stayed far from the traveled trails, seeing no white men and only a few Mexican traders. It made the people happy to have so little bother.

But a human tide, one that they could neither see nor hear, was rising in the east. It would be upon them soon. The good times of that summer were the last they would have. Their time was running out and would soon be gone forever.

About the Author

Michael Blake has worked in pill factories, newspaper offices, Christmas tree lots, radio stations, dishwashing rooms, and many other places. DANCES WITH WOLVES is his first novel.

The author lives in California with two dogs (Bear and Pal) and two horses (Project and Quanah). He is currently at work on his next novel.